Trent impulsively decided he would keep his secrets and take his chances.

If nothing else, he would have a few more days with Anna and the family. Precious days he could shelter in his heart in the years to come.

The longing in her beautiful gray eyes made his heart ache. He slid his fingers into her hair, cupping the back of her head, and drew her closer. "Would a kiss make you happy?"

"I don't know." She rested her hands on his shoulders, leaning toward him. "But I'd like to find out," she whispered.

"So would I." He touched her lips with reverence, wanting to show her how deeply he treasured her. But he was the one who felt treasured. A silken thread of tenderness entwined through the chains that bound him to the past, softening a link here, forging a crack there. For that brief moment, the hurt faded away.

Trent searched her eyes for regret but found only a soft glow.

Dear Reader,

If you've never read a Harlequin Historical, you're in for a treat. We offer compelling, richly developed stories that let you escape to the past—by some of the best writers in the field!

Sharon Harlow is making her Harlequin debut with *For Love of Anna,* but this talented and versatile writer is no stranger to publishing. She's a bestselling author of inspirational romances for Multnomah and Palisades, and has written historical romances for Berkley. This sweet, heartwarming Western is about Trent Malloy, a handsome cowboy "outlaw" who is stranded in a blizzard and finds shelter—and love—at the ranch of a young widow with children.

Elizabeth Mayne returns with *The Highlander's Maiden,* a Scottish Medieval tale about a fearless female mountain guide and the handsome mapmaker from an enemy clan she's ordered to help. And in *Hawken's Wife* by Rae Muir, book three of THE WEDDING TRAIL series, a beautiful tomboy falls for an amnesiac mountain man whose past threatens their future.

Rounding out the month is *A Rose at Midnight* by rising talent Jacqueline Navin. In this dark and passionate Regency tale, a powerful earl who thinks he's dying marries a penniless countess to have his child. Amid secrets and betrayal, a profound love emerges. Don't miss it!

Whatever your tastes in reading, you'll be sure to find a romantic journey back to the past between the covers of a Harlequin Historical® novel.

Sincerely,
Tracy Farrell, Senior Editor

Please address questions and book requests to:
Harlequin Reader Service
U.S.: 3010 Walden Ave., P.O. Box 1325, Buffalo, NY 14269
Canadian: P.O. Box 609, Fort Erie, Ont. L2A 5X3

SHARON HARLOW

FOR LOVE OF ANNA

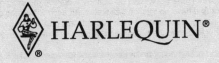

HARLEQUIN®

TORONTO • NEW YORK • LONDON
AMSTERDAM • PARIS • SYDNEY • HAMBURG
STOCKHOLM • ATHENS • TOKYO • MILAN • MADRID
PRAGUE • WARSAW • BUDAPEST • AUCKLAND

ISBN 0-373-29048-9

FOR LOVE OF ANNA

SHARON HARLOW

lives near Seattle with her husband of thirty years, their son who is a college student and a spoiled sixty-pound lapdog, a black Lab-kelpie mix. Her husband shares her love of history and often goes along to browse through antique stores and antiquarian bookstores.

Sharon has published eleven romances, including four written for the inspirational market as Sharon Gillenwater. She enjoys writing about West Texas in the late 1800s as well as England and Scotland in the Regency time period. All of her contemporaries have been set in a fictional area of West Texas suspiciously resembling her hometown.

To my wonderful editors—
Karen Kosztolnyik,
thank you for your guidance, understanding and
encouragement through far too many delays,
and
Patience Smith,
thank you for being such a joy to work with and for
making revisions painless.

Prologue

West Texas, March 20, 1890

Trent Malloy figured he might die young, but he had expected something more exciting—a bad fall from a mean-tempered bronc, a bullet over some piddling disagreement or maybe even dangling from the end of a rope. He never thought he'd wind up a block of ice.

Keeping his back to the pelting sleet and piercing north wind, he urged his horse forward, staying near the barbed wire fence that ran beside the snow- and ice-covered dirt road. Whether the fence would be his salvation or his doom was yet to be determined. If he could get past it, he might find protection along a creek bank or in a gully; but the odds weighed heavily against stumbling across either one. The boundary was well maintained. No post had been conveniently knocked down by an ornery longhorn, and cutting another man's wire was a penitentiary offense.

Trent preferred death to prison.

He followed the fence line, hoping to find some kind of shelter. Leaning low over his horse's back, he murmured encouragement to his tired friend. "It's up to you, Polecat. Find us a nice warm bed."

Although his oiled yellow slicker kept out the moisture, the coat seemed to trap the cold, layering it against his body like a mantle of ice. He had wrapped a thin blue blanket over his hat and around his face and upper body when he first mounted. The wool offered protection for a while, until it became wet and frozen. Sleep drew closer, and Trent knew he couldn't fight it much longer.

He thought he felt his horse turn, but when he opened his eye—the one that wasn't puffy and black—all he could see through the veil of snow was the ghostly stretch of barbed wire. Twilight had fallen, but he didn't know if the encroaching blackness signaled the end of day or the end of consciousness.

Trent's thoughts rambled, drifting back over his life. He had done plenty of things he regretted and little of which he was proud. An image of his mother rose from the tattered pages of his memory—a woman worn by illness and hardship, yet she had believed in him. He was glad she couldn't see what he had become.

As the darkness settled over him, he was once again a little boy sitting on his mother's fragile knee. He heard her sweet, loving voice prompting him to say his prayers. Trent obeyed. His appeal was not lengthy, nor was it eloquent, but it came straight from his heart.

Please, God, give me another chance.

Chapter One

Wiping the steam from the pane, Anna Caldwell peered out at the storm, fear for her cattle growing with each window-rattling gust. She had held on to her faith far longer than most of her neighbors, firmly believing they could outlast the drought and harsh winters. Now as the temperature plummeted, she clung to hope by a gossamer thread. "Please, Lord, give those poor animals more wisdom than they come by naturally. Lead them to shelter," she whispered. "Please let them survive."

A tug on her skirt and a small child's frightened voice brought her out of her reverie. "Who you talkin' to?"

"I'm talking to God, Mitch." Anna smiled and slid her arm around her son's shoulders, gently pressing him against her side. "I'm worried about the cattle, and I was askin' the Lord to take care of them."

"You 'fraid they're gonna blow away?"

"No, but I am worried about the snow and the cold." Anna bent down and picked up the five-year-old, something she wouldn't be able to do much longer. He put his arms around her neck and snuggled close. "It's been so warm these past few weeks that they've already shed their heavy winter coats. They'll have a hard time staying warm."

He leaned back so he could see her face. "Will they get sick?"

"Some of them might."

"Will they die?"

"Maybe. If they get too cold, they might freeze to death."

Mitch was silent and very still for a moment, staring out the window at the blowing snow. "Are we gonna die, Mama?" he whispered.

Anna's heart constricted at the pain and fear in his voice. "We'll all die someday, sweetheart, and then we'll go to heaven just like Papa, but it sure won't be because we froze to death. We're snug as a bug in a rug in this ol' ranch house." She could see he wasn't quite convinced. Grinning, she ruffled his soft, light brown hair, so like her own. "Warm as a turtle on a mesquite stump."

Mitch giggled and played with a wispy curl on her forehead that had escaped her long, single braid. "Turtles can't climb up stumps."

"Oh, I don't know. Maybe they can. How about—warm as a turtle on a rock?" she asked. He nodded and Anna kissed his cheek, giving it a big smack. When she looked up, she met her stepson Duncan's twinkling gaze.

"Only if it's a warm, sunny day in January," said Duncan.

"Why?" asked Mitch.

"Well, if it's cloudy, the rock would be cold and the turtle wouldn't get warm."

"But why January? Why not summer?"

Duncan winked at Anna, and she smiled in understanding. Although Mitch's constant questions could be trying at times, they were happy he asked them. He had hardly spoken for three months after his father died. She wondered sometimes if he thought he was to blame for Edwin's death. *Not you, Mitch. Me.*

"For the same reason we don't sit on a rock in the summer, little britches. It's too hot." Duncan leaned forward and wiped the moisture from the other side of the windowpane. "Sure can't see much. I'm glad we got the horses into the corrals before it turned this bad."

Anna glanced out the window and shook her head. "We never would have found them all." Having the animals protected beneath the three-sided sheds in the corrals gave her some consolation. The covered area was small for thirty horses, but being crowded would only help keep them warm. The Double Deuce Ranch was known across West Texas for the quality of their cow ponies. Even if she lost the remainder of the cattle, she could still feed her family as long as she had horses to sell. But holding on to all of their land might be a challenge.

"I broke the ice in the trough, but the water was already startin' to freeze around the edges when I came in," said Duncan. "Do you want me to go chop it up?"

"You can do it in the morning. I don't want you outside any more tonight." She wished his father could see how hard he worked, could watch him becoming a man. Duncan had greatly changed in the two years since her husband's death. At fifteen, his voice was deep, with a rich quality many grown men envied, and women, both young and old, admired. The women liked his blond hair and blue eyes, too.

Duncan needs you, Edwin. So do I. A deep ache filled her heart, a pain that refused to heal. Anna handed Mitch to Duncan and turned aside so he wouldn't see her unhappiness. She adjusted the flame on the coal oil lamp she had hung up earlier on a hook in front of the window.

Mitch watched her, glancing at another lantern hanging

by the other front window. "How come you put them up there?"

"So a traveler can see the light and know he's found shelter from the storm," said Anna.

The child frowned. "Hardly nobody goes by here 'cept the neighbors, and they know we live here."

"Yes, but even a neighbor might be unsure of the way on a stormy night. Hanging the lamps in the windows may not help, but it's all we can do." That seemed to satisfy the little boy. She met Duncan's gaze once more. "You did a good job today. Just like every day."

Duncan grinned. "Yeah? So, when you gonna start payin' me what I'm worth?"

Anna laughed. He wasn't paid a regular salary. She knew he didn't really expect one—not yet, at least—but there would soon come a time when he would need more than pocket money. She hoped she could provide it. "When we start makin' money, I promise you'll get your share."

"Good enough." He guided her away from the window. "Maybe it would help the little boys if I read them a story."

"And take my mind off the storm, too?"

He grinned again. "It'll have to be some story."

Ten minutes later, Anna sat in her walnut rocking chair with the orange-flowered cushions, listening as Duncan enthralled the family with the adventures of Denver Dan and His Band of Dead Shots. The story from The Wide-Awake Library was one of the many dime novels in his collection. He loved to read out loud and did it so well that she sometimes wondered if he secretly wanted to be an actor.

Holding Mitch in her lap, Anna slowly looked around the room, watching the faces of her family. Only Mitch was hers by birth, but she claimed them all just the same, binding them to her and to each other by the love in her heart.

Duncan's older sister Rachel sat across from him in the old dark brown upholstered arm chair. Sweet-tempered and caring, the lovely blue-eyed blonde was a budding woman of seventeen. Anna knew men would start calling on her stepdaughter any day, and she dreaded it. When Rachel married and moved to a home of her own, she would leave a void none of the boys could fill.

Duncan sat on one end of the dark gold tapestry sofa, with nine-year-old Davy beside him. Red-haired and freckle-faced, he listened intently to the story and lightly rubbed the heel of his shoe across the top of his dog's head. The black-and-gray long-haired mutt, aptly named Dig, was spoiled rotten and loved everyone, greeting strangers as well as neighbors with tail-wagging joy.

It had been four years since the sheriff found Davy sitting on the steps of his office. When he brought him out to the ranch, the boy was frightened and underfed, but he bore no signs of physical abuse. A scrawled note pinned to his shirt said it all. ''Too many kids. He's the runt.''

No one knew who he was, and all Davy could—or would—tell them was his first name. He never mentioned his family, and on the few occasions when Anna asked about any relatives, he merely shrugged away her inquiry.

Resting her cheek against the top of Mitch's head, Anna cherished the moment. Her worries faded, eased by deep contentment and peace. She knew that after the children were in bed, her fears would return tenfold. Without their laughter, the wind's moans would once again skitter down her spine. Without the brightness of their happy, loving faces, the darkness of her empty bedroom would be deep and lonely. But for now, she could relax.

She closed her eyes but opened them a few minutes later

when Dig barked softly. The dog jumped to his feet, his ears peaked attentively. Cocking his head to one side, he walked slowly toward the door, moving as if he weren't quite sure what he was supposed to do. Suddenly, the hair on the back of his neck bristled, and he lunged at the door with sharp, urgent barks. Anna tensed and listened anxiously, even as Duncan ordered the dog to be quiet.

"It's just the wind, mutt." But the animal ignored Duncan and continued barking furiously.

"Hush, Dig!" Davy jumped up from the sofa and raced toward the window. The dog quit barking but stood his ground and growled softly. Davy swiped a circle on the glass with his hand and, stretching up on tiptoe, peered out. Gasping, he turned back to the others, his eyes wide and frightened. "It's a ghost rider!"

"There's no such thing," said Duncan, closing the dime novel and tossing it on the sofa as he stood.

"Is, too! It says so in one of them books." Davy rested his fists on his hips and glared at the older boy.

"It was only a story, squirt. A yarn." Duncan stepped up beside Davy, ruffling his hair. He cleaned a spot higher on the window and shielded his eyes against the lamplight. A second later, he moved toward the coatrack by the back door, glancing at Anna as she shifted Mitch off her lap and stood. "It's a rider, all right. And he looks bad."

Anna rushed to his side. Putting on a heavy navy blue wool coat, she gave instructions to Rachel. "We'll need about five quilts. There should be enough in the trunk in my room. Make a pallet with two, but don't put it close to the stove. It's harmful to warm him too quickly." She fastened the last button on her coat and grabbed a long, black woolen scarf, draping it over her head and wrapping the ends around her neck. Pulling on her brown leather gloves, she glanced at Duncan, satisfied that he was also dressed warmly. "Hang on to Dig. We don't need him underfoot." Davy obeyed, kneeling and circling the dog's neck with his arms.

Duncan opened the front door and snow swirled into the room. When he stepped onto the porch, Anna was right behind him. She closed the door, and he took hold of her arm. "Careful, it's slick."

As they turned toward the rider, he toppled from his horse, lying motionless in the snow. They walked gingerly down the icy steps, desperate to hurry but knowing that they didn't dare. Once on the ground, the going was a little easier although still slippery. When they reached the cowboy, Anna knelt beside him. "We'll get you inside," she said, raising her voice against the wind. There was no response. She looked up at Duncan. "He's unconscious."

Uncoiling the reins from around the rider's stiff hand, Duncan nudged the horse out of the way. They pulled the man to a sitting position and slung his arms across their shoulders. Standing, they hoisted him upright and dragged him to the porch, the toes of his boots digging twin furrows in the snow.

Duncan's foot slipped as they stepped onto the porch, but he grabbed the post in time to save a fall. Seconds before they reached the door, Rachel flung it open, slamming it shut again the instant they passed through.

Anna stopped a few feet inside the room. "Put him down here so we can take off his wet clothes." They carefully lowered him to the floor and knelt beside him. She jerked off her gloves and tossed them aside, then quickly shed her scarf, dropping it on the floor nearby. Duncan removed his gloves, but didn't bother with his hat.

He lifted the cowboy's head and shoulders as Anna unwound an ice-coated blue blanket from his head and face, revealing a black eye, split lip and dark bruise on his jaw.

Although she noted his injuries, she was more concerned by the pallor of his skin, starkly visible through the black stubble of a day-old beard, and the swelling of his face, which she feared was due to his low body temperature.

"Is that frostbite?" Duncan pointed to the cowboy's left cheek.

Anna glanced at the white, oblong patch of skin and nodded. "Looks like it. That part of his face must not have been covered well. At least his nose and ears look all right."

"Why is he so pale? I thought the cold would make his face red. Always does mine."

"He's beyond that," Anna said grimly. "Doc Meadows says when a body is close to freezing, most of the blood stays deep inside to keep the organs warm. Very little blood goes to the skin, so it is pale. And because the circulation is poor, the hands and feet, even the face, puff up."

She threw the blanket and his worn gray Stetson hat by the door. Pulling gently, she eased the partially frozen, dark brown leather gloves from his hands. His fingers were stiff and swollen, but the pale skin did not look as bad as the place on his cheek.

"He was all bent over when he rode up," said Duncan. "That probably protected his hands some." She unbuttoned his slicker and gray, heavy cotton vest. Duncan helped her slip them off, leaving them on the floor beneath the man.

"I'll hold him still while you pull off his boots," said Anna, with a troubled frown. "Go easy. I'm afraid his feet didn't fare as well as his hands. Those boots look awfully old." She laid him flat on the floor and put her hands beneath his arms to steady him. Duncan tugged off the scuffed black boots, worn thin from hard use, and set them beside the icy blanket. She scooted down to his feet and very gently peeled off one tan cotton sock, absently noting that it was practically brand-new. When she examined his foot, her heart sank. "Oh, dear."

"What's wrong, Mama?" asked Davy.

She looked up to see the two younger boys huddled by her rocking chair, staring at the cowboy's foot. Dig leaned against Davy, intently watching the stranger. Behind them, Rachel was making a pot of coffee, but she glanced over her shoulder, meeting Anna's gaze with a worried frown.

"How come the ends of his toes got them funny lookin' white spots?" asked Mitch, tightly clutching Davy's hand.

"They got too cold, honey. It's called frostbite." She gently touched the cowboy's toes. "They're stiff but the skin isn't hard. That's a good sign," she said softly to Duncan.

"Will he be all right?" asked Davy.

"I hope so." She frowned as she slipped the sock from his right foot. The tell-tale white of frostbitten skin covered a large portion of his toes. As she had expected, this foot was worse. His right side would have been exposed to the brunt of the wind and snow as he rode up to their house. She carefully touched his toes.

"Bad?" whispered Duncan, his expression filled with concern.

"The little toe and the one next to it are hard as a rock. The other places aren't as bad."

"How you gonna make 'em better?" asked Mitch.

"To start, we'll warm them up." *And pray.* She turned back to the cowboy and unbuttoned the waistband of his faded blue denim pants, trying to ignore the discomfort of doing something so intimate for a stranger. There was no time for modesty.

Duncan rested his hand on her shoulder. "I'll take care of it, Anna."

Relieved, she nodded her thanks and moved aside.

"Are you going to take off everything?" asked Rachel.

Anna looked up at her stepdaughter's shocked expression. "Down to his underwear. The bottom of his pant legs are soaked and frozen." They were ragged, too. "The slicker kept most of his clothes from getting wet, but they're ice-cold. The less he has between him and the quilts, the easier it will be for him to get warm."

Duncan pulled off the pants, and Anna turned her attention to the man's well-worn green plaid shirt. She unfastened the five buttons between the collar and the bottom of the front opening at mid-chest, as well as the buttons on the frayed sleeve cuffs. As she tugged the shirttail up toward his chest, her fingers skimmed over the sharp ridges of his ribs. He was far too thin to simply be called slim. Both his pants and shirt were fairly clean, but, unlike his new socks, they were almost threadbare in places. Although his pants fit, the shirt seemed a size too large.

Duncan moved across from her and lifted the man's head and shoulders off the floor. She pulled the bottom of the shirt up as far as she could, then slipped the sleeves from his arms. As she slid her hand across his back to help hold him, she felt several long diagonal welts beneath the lightweight wool of his gray, long-sleeved undershirt. Bracing him against her arm, she whispered to Duncan as he pulled the shirt free over the man's head, "Unbutton his undershirt a little. I want to look at his back."

Duncan sent her a questioning look but complied, peering over the cowboy's shoulder as he pulled down the top edge of the undershirt.

"Lord have mercy." Anna stared at the long, thick scars crisscrossing his back and his shoulders. A smaller one, barely visible, snaked up the side of his neck. "He's been whipped."

"Looks like it happened a long time ago." His expression troubled, Duncan met her gaze as she lowered the cowboy to the floor. "What do you reckon he did to make somebody take a bullwhip to him?"

"There's no telling. Some men are just plain mean enough to whip a man for no reason."

"Sometimes, but usually there's a cause."

"That's his business. We have no right to pry. Let's move him over to the pallet. You take his shoulders. I'll get his legs."

"I'll help," said Rachel. In spite of her obvious embarrassment at seeing a stranger in nothing but his underwear, she bent over, curling her hands around the calf of one leg.

"Thanks." Anna picked up the other leg as Duncan slid his hands beneath the man's arms and lifted him off the floor. They carried him the short distance to the pallet and laid him down carefully, resting his head on a pillow.

Anna straightened, taking a deep breath as she looked at Duncan. "You'd better see to his horse. Try to put him in the corral and up in the shed with the other horses. If they raise a ruckus, put him in the barn. Rachel and I can finish up here."

Duncan nodded and pulled on his gloves. "I'll be back as soon as I can."

"Be careful."

Rachel and Anna spread three homemade patchwork quilts over the unconscious man. "Rachel, work on his arms and hands. We have to get his blood moving. Rub briskly, but not hard." Anna tended to his feet, following her own advice but avoiding his toes. All the directions she had read or heard about frostbite indicated that the area had to be warmed slowly or the damage would be worse. They worked over him for several minutes.

"That's probably all the good we're going to do." Anna pulled the cover down to his waist. "Lay his hands on his chest." Rachel did as she instructed, then helped her draw the quilts up and tuck them around his chin.

Mitch stepped up and handed Anna the crib blanket she had purchased from a mail order catalog before he was born. "This will make his feet feel better, Mama," he said solemnly.

"Thank you, honey." A twinge of regret mingled with a swell of pride as she took the tattered cloth from her son. Her little boy had just broken his last tie to babyhood. He had never shared his blanket with anyone. She carefully wrapped the stranger's feet in the soft wool and pulled the quilts loosely over them.

It had only been minutes since they brought the man inside, but it seemed like hours. Anna shrugged out of her coat and picked up her hat and gloves, placing them on the coatrack before crossing the room to the black, cast-iron cookstove. She held out her hands to the warmth and watched as Rachel draped the cowboy's clothes and blanket on a wooden rack nearby. She perched his hat on one corner of the rack and set his boots on the floor farther away from the stove so the leather wouldn't dry out too fast.

"Is there anything else we can do?" Rachel anxiously watched the stranger. "He's so still. I'd think he was dead if that thread by his chin didn't move every time he breathed."

"All we can do now is try to warm him up. As soon as he comes to, we'll give him some sweetened coffee to get his blood stirring a bit. Later he can have broth."

"I'll warm up the soup from supper." Rachel hurried to the stove, clearly thankful for something more to do.

"How can we help?" asked Davy, studying the cowboy and shaking his head. "He don't look too good."

"No, he doesn't, but we need to have faith that he'll

make it. Why don't you boys sit over on the sofa and sing?''

"Sing?" Davy stared at her as if she had gone daft.

"Yes, something cheerful and fun. Don't get too loud, but a little noise might help him wake up quicker."

"Yes, ma'am." Davy and Mitch silently climbed up onto one end of the sofa, sitting close together. Seconds later, they began a whispered rendition of "Oh, Susanna."

Anna chuckled at their serious expressions. "You don't have to be that quiet."

The boys sang softly at first, but soon their exuberance overcame their hesitation and the words and tune rang out loud and clear.

Anna settled down on the floor beside the cowboy. Brushing a long lock of straight, black hair off his forehead, she noted that he was badly in need of a haircut. She placed her warm hand gently over the ice-cold, frostbitten spot on his face. The skin along his cheekbone felt smooth beneath her rough fingertips, and the dark stubble on his jaw barely tickled the work-hardened palm of her hand. *I wish my hands were soft and smooth.* The thought surprised her, and she told herself she only wanted to keep from irritating his skin. In her heart, Anna knew differently.

Judging from his mistreated face and day-old whiskey breath, he was probably like many of the cowboys she had known over the years. They worked hard and played hard, often spending a whole month's wages in one rousing weekend of liquor, women and gambling. They were a breed all their own—loyal to the brand, yet wild and free, with wandering in their blood and elusive dreams in their hearts—the kind of men smart women avoided.

But it didn't seem to matter. Something about this rugged, battered cowboy stirred a feeling deep inside, a whisper of womanly yearning she thought had died with her husband.

Chapter Two

Trent fought the dark, overwhelming fear. He was too cold to be in hell, but hurt too much to be in heaven. Was there somewhere in between? One moment, a black empty space thundering with the hoofbeats of a million slaughtered buffalo and haunted for eternity by the war cries of the Comanche; the next, a deep, narrow pit shrouded by impenetrable walls of stone, holding him forever in a reeking, gray mist, never to see the sun or smell a flower or feel the wind upon his face.

He struggled to rise above the suffocating haze, fleeing the terror of days long past and days just lived, desperately seeking that place of light and laughter, where children sang off-key and a soft, gentle voice drew him away from torment. Suddenly he broke free. The Comanche's screams of hatred became a child's shrill squeal of joy, and the thundering of the ghostly buffalo was nothing more than the frantic pounding of his own heart.

Relief surged through him, calming him, and chasing some of the confusion from his mind. He'd seldom been around youngsters and had vaguely considered them a bit of a nuisance when they were underfoot. Now, as they sang, ''Jimmy crack corn and I don't care,'' he knew he had heard only one sweeter sound—the voice of the woman who saved him from his darkest fears.

He breathed deeply, savoring the scent of hot food, relishing even more the clean, faintly soapy fragrance of the woman sitting beside him. Her hand rested on his cheek, bringing both pain and comfort—pain as her warmth thawed his frozen flesh, comfort in the gentleness of her touch.

Opening his eyes, he blinked against the light and turned his head toward the voice. It took a moment for his vision to focus. At first glance, Trent felt a tiny twinge of disappointment. In a way, he'd been hoping to see an angel. After all, heaven would have been nice—a land of peace and eternal happiness where sins and failures were forgiven and forgotten.

The woman wasn't plain, but she wasn't a beautiful, ethereal spirit capable of working miracles, either. Then she smiled. He looked into her tender gray eyes and knew he was wrong. She might be flesh and blood, but she had an angel's heart. The light that had guided him to her door had not been merely a lamp hanging in a window, but her kindness reaching out to soothe his weary soul.

Anna knew she was staring, but she couldn't seem to help it. She had never seen a man with such beautiful amber eyes—at least the one that hadn't gotten too friendly with another man's fist was beautiful. Almost golden in the lamplight, they contrasted dramatically with his black hair. The black-and-purple bruise covering his left eye and down to his cheekbone lessened the impact, but she could easily imagine how he would look when the swelling and discoloration disappeared. She moved her hand, resting it on her lap. "Hello, cowboy."

Because she sat so close, Trent easily heard her in spite

of the children's rambunctious tune. "Evenin', ma'am."
He barely recognized the raspy voice as his own.

"Would you like some coffee?" she asked quietly, her
expression gentle.

"Please," he whispered. He didn't know how he would
manage to hold the cup. He was as weak as a day-old pup,
and his arms and hands felt as stiff as a new rawhide rope.

"It's been sitting for a little while so it shouldn't be too
hot." She slid her arm beneath his shoulders and helped
him raise up. "I'll hold it. Go easy."

He moved his head toward the rim of the cup. Even
sweet, the warm liquid soothed his parched throat like rain-
water in the desert.

Although she wasn't very big, she had no trouble holding
his weight plus a pile of quilts. Her strength was cushioned
in feminine softness, the kind that reminded even a half-
dead wretch he was a man. Self-disgust shot through him.
Hadn't he learned his lesson? He glanced around the room.
Instead of an irate husband, three young, beaming faces
stared back. He breathed a sigh of relief.

"Reckon our singin' woke you up," said the oldest boy
with a broad grin. "Mama said it might help."

"It did. Thanks." Trent searched the room again, wondering where her man was, wishing his mind would work
a little faster. *Polecat.* He tried to sit up, but she stopped
him.

"You're too weak so just stay put. After you rest a bit,
Rachel will dish up some soup for you. Maybe then I'll let
you sit up." A tiny smile touched her lips, as if she found
it amusing to order him around.

Defeated, he sank back against the pillow. "My horse?"

"Duncan led him down to the corral. He'll take good
care of him." She glanced at the others. "We should introduce ourselves. I'm Anna Caldwell. These are my chil-

dren, Rachel, Davy and Mitch. Welcome to the Double Deuce Ranch.''

They smiled and greeted him in turn as she said their names. He knew Rachel couldn't be her child. They were too close in age, so she must be a stepdaughter. The two boys were young enough to be hers, though they didn't look anything alike. He'd heard of the Double Deuce. Even ridden some of their horses in years past.

''Trent Malloy.'' He tensed, waiting for recognition to dawn in her eyes. To his surprise and relief, his name didn't appear to mean anything to her. ''Pleased to meet you, ma'am.''

''I suppose you are,'' she said, her eyes twinkling. ''And we're mighty glad you found us, Mr. Malloy.'' She placed her hand on his cheek again and smiled, her face filled with warmth and caring.

A sudden swell of emotion caught him off guard, tightening his chest. He closed his eyes against the ache, thinking how a man foolishly took things for granted, not realizing their value until he lost them. The simple sweetness of a woman's touch. The beauty of a smile. Respect and trust. Freedom.

She lifted her hand. ''I'm sorry. Did I hurt you?''

He opened his eyes. A frown wrinkled her brow. ''No...well, yes, a little. But I reckon it'll have to hurt some before it gets better.'' Trent wasn't thinking only of his cheek. He clung desperately to the hope that in time people would forgive, maybe even forget. All he wanted was the opportunity to prove himself, but so far he hadn't run across anyone willing to give it.

''How are your hands?'' She glanced at where they rested beneath the quilt, her frown deepening in concern.

''Stinging, swollen. Can't bend my fingers.''

''How about your feet?''

"Left one feels like I've been dancin' barefoot with a porcupine."

She shook her head. "You won't be dancing with anybody for a while. What about the right one?"

"Most of it burns, but there's only a dull ache in my toes." His eyes drifted shut, and he rested a few seconds before opening them again. "Don't reckon that's good."

"You have a lot of frostbite on that foot. Especially the little toe and the one next to it. The skin was hard last time I checked. We'll watch it. If it looks like infection is setting in, we'll take you into Antelope Springs to the doctor."

Trent grimaced, which made his face hurt worse. "I wouldn't be too welcome in town, ma'am."

She studied his face, her gaze going from his black eye to his split lip. To his surprise, her expression held no censure, only thoughtfulness and a hint of sympathy. She glanced at the boys. They were hanging on to every word. The sympathy vanished. "I don't hold with fighting, Mr. Malloy," she said sternly. "Disagreements should be settled with talk, not action. If discussion won't clear the air, then you should walk away from the situation."

"Yes, ma'am." He cast a furtive glance at the boys and almost smiled at their disappointment. Trouble was, he knew she was right. It was a lesson he should have learned long ago. Anger and resentment screamed in protest. Some wrongs couldn't be ignored; some deeds demanded retaliation. He met her gaze. "Sometimes a man reacts before he thinks things through."

"Or if he's been drinking, he can't think."

Trent realized his breath was probably rank enough to knock down a mule. Embarrassed, he turned his head. Several foul words ran through his mind, but he managed to hold his tongue. That in itself was a minor miracle, but not one he could brag about. He glanced in her direction, seeing a tiny sparkle of amusement in her eyes. She knew what he was thinking. He silently cussed again. A woman like Anna wasn't supposed to know such words.

"I think I've made my point, Mr. Malloy," she said softly, tipping her head slightly toward the boys. "Can you sit up a bit?"

"I think so."

As she helped him raise up, Rachel hurried over to stuff more pillows behind him. The room whirled, and he was grateful to lean back against the mound of pillows instead of trying to sit up straight.

"That will do for now. Are you warming up?"

He shook his head drowsily. "Got ice chunks in my veins. Hear 'em clinkin' together."

"I don't think you should go to sleep yet. Rachel, will you bring Mr. Malloy some soup?"

"Of course." Rachel smiled shyly at Trent.

He smiled back, as much as his sore lip would allow, and tried not to breathe on her. She was one of the prettiest young women he had ever seen, with golden blond hair and pale blue eyes. She was too shy to have had many gentlemen callers, but they would soon be knocking down the door. This little lady would have her choice of men from fifty, maybe a hundred miles around. He watched her walk gracefully across the room.

"She's lovely, isn't she?" said Anna.

"Yes, she is. She have a beau?"

"No. She's barely seventeen."

He thought he heard a faint note of alarm in Anna's voice. "Don't worry. I'm not askin' for myself. I was just thinkin' that her daddy has his work cut out for him."

Sadness settled over her face, her eyes haunted and filled with pain. Through sheer determination, Trent pulled his arm from beneath the quilts and carefully laid his hand over hers. He couldn't bend his fingers to clasp it, but some kind of touch was better than nothing. "Ma'am, are you all right?"

She swallowed hard, blinking quickly. "My husband died of a heart attack two years ago."

"I'm sorry." Trent didn't have to guess how much she loved her husband, but the ease with which he offered her comfort surprised him. Although his compassion once would have come as naturally as breathing, he hadn't reached out to anyone in a very long time. The dim spark of hope in his heart burned a little brighter. Maybe there was some goodness left in him after all. "He must have been a fine man."

"He was. I've never met anyone who could hold a candle to him."

The sudden stomping of heavy boots on the back porch caught Trent's attention. Seconds later, the kitchen door flew open and a young man hurried inside. Turning, he put his shoulder against the door and shoved it closed. "Lord-a-mercy, that wind's gettin' higher by the minute."

The lad dropped Trent's saddlebags on the floor and placed his gun belt and pistol on the shelf above the coat-rack. He pulled off his Stetson and brushed the snow from the brim and crown before setting it upside down on the shelf by the gun. He tugged off his gloves and tossed them on a table near the stove, then shrugged out of his coat. Scooping a bit of snow from one shoulder of the coat, he flicked it at the younger boys with a grin. They dodged and giggled in delight, then pounced on him, easily wrestling away the coat.

As the boys tried to scrape up enough snow for a tiny snowball each, the newcomer picked up the saddlebags and walked over to Trent and Anna. Squatting down beside him, he set the saddlebags nearby. "Glad you've come around. I was worried about you." He looked at Trent's hand, which still covered Anna's, and his smile faded. A challenging glint lit his eyes as he met Trent's gaze, but he spoke quietly. "I'm Duncan Caldwell. I'd appreciate it, sir, if you'd let go of my mama's hand."

Trent slowly moved his hand, sliding it back beneath the quilts. He didn't particularly like taking orders from a kid, but he understood the boy's need to protect Anna. She had to be his stepmother, but it was clear he respected and cared for her. "You've roped the wrong steer, Duncan. I wasn't takin' liberties with your mama."

Duncan looked at Anna for confirmation.

"I was telling him about Edwin." She shrugged and glanced at Trent. "He was only offering comfort."

Duncan slid his gaze back to him. "Sorry, mister..."

"Trent Malloy. No apology needed. You did what was right."

Duncan accepted his words with a nod. "Your name sounds familiar. Where you workin'?"

"No place right now. Been pretty much all over at one time or another, but haven't had anything regular for a while." At least not the kind of work the boy meant.

"Yeah, it's been rough for too long. Hope you don't mind me puttin' your gun up on the shelf. Keeps it away from the little boys."

And me. Trent respected the boy's caution and didn't figure he'd have a need for his pistol right away. Besides, he couldn't even hold the thing. "I understand. Thanks for bringing in my gear and for takin' care of my horse. How is he?"

"Cold and tired. I gave him some water and a bag of oats. Brushed the ice out of his coat. He's cozy in the middle of the herd in the corral shed. Had perked up some by the time I left." He smiled. "The way they were all nick-

erin' and such, you'd think he was telling them all about
his adventure.'' Duncan looked up and grinned at Rachel
as she stepped up beside him, carrying a bowl of soup. "No
thanks, Sis, I've already eaten.''

"This isn't for you. It's for Mr. Malloy. Now move so
I can feed it to him.''

Duncan stood and stepped out of Rachel's way. "You'd
better watch these women, Mr. Malloy. They'll drive you
crazy with their pamperin'.''

"I think I can stand it for a while.'' Starved as he was
for the gentle side of human contact, Trent didn't think he
would mind if they fussed over him for a week.

"I'll bring you some more coffee when you've finished
eating.'' Anna rose and took the soup bowl from Rachel.
After the younger woman had settled on the floor, she
handed it back to her.

"Can you hold the spoon, Mr. Malloy, or do you want
me to feed you?'' asked Rachel.

"I'm afraid you'll have to help me, ma'am. My fingers
won't bend.''

"I don't mind. I'll try not to spill it on you. It's mostly
broth.'' She lifted the spoon to his mouth.

Trent took his time swallowing that first sip. He hadn't
eaten anything since breakfast the day before. Though the
soup was mostly chicken broth, it was fit for a king.
"That's mighty tasty, Miss Rachel.''

Rachel smiled. "Thank you. I let it simmer all afternoon.''

"You made this?''

"I do most of the cooking. Anna has all she can handle
running the ranch. Duncan helps, of course. He's fifteen
but already does a man's job,'' she said with pride. "But
it takes both of them working from sunup to sundown to

get things done. I take care of the house and keep an eye on the younger boys.''

She continued to spoon-feed him the soup until the bowl was empty. To his surprise, it satisfied his hunger. He couldn't remember a meal he had appreciated more.

His gaze strayed to Anna. Her gray-blue wool dress buttoned down the front and was made in a loose style that he thought was called a Mother Hubbard. She wore a belt of the same material tied comfortably at the waist. She had a nice figure.

Somehow he had trouble thinking of her as Mrs. Caldwell or even Miss Anna, which would have been considered polite. He wanted to get to know her well enough to dispense with formalities. He told himself he didn't want anything more than friendship and didn't expect he'd get that. She sat in the rocking chair, talking to the boys. She teased them, yet at the same time, kept a watchful eye on him and Rachel. *She can't be more than twenty-seven or twenty-eight,* he thought. *Too young to be such a mother hen.*

Duncan and Rachel were definitely brother and sister, with almost identical golden blond hair and pale blue eyes, although Rachel's features were much more delicate than her brother's. The youngest boy had Anna's light brown hair and gray eyes, but otherwise, he bore a striking resemblance to Duncan and Rachel. The middle boy didn't appear to be kin to any of them. The youngster had red hair, green eyes and about a million freckles.

''Do you want anything else to eat, Mr. Malloy?'' asked Rachel.

Trent looked back at her. ''No, thank you, ma'am. I'm full up. But that was fine eatin'.''

''Thanks.'' She beamed him a smile, then rose lithely to her feet. ''Do you want more coffee?''

"No, thank you." He smiled again, as much at his good manners as at her. In spite of little use, some teachings weren't ever forgotten. It just took a couple of pretty ladies to remind a man they were needed.

"Boys, do you want me to finish the story?" asked Duncan, picking up a book from the sofa before he sat down.

"Yeah."

"Yep."

The answers melded together in a jumbled affirmative, accompanied by scurrying and shoving as the boys raced to sit beside him.

Trent closed his eyes, weary through and through.

"Mr. Malloy, will it bother you if I read awhile?" asked Duncan. "We were just gettin' to the good part. Dan and his Dead Shots are about to capture the desperados."

Trent felt a jab of panic. *Calm down, stupid. It's only a story.* He cleared his throat and looked at Duncan. "Go ahead. Hope you don't mind if I fall asleep."

"I don't mind. But you'll miss how they rescue Miss Sue from the bank robbers."

When Duncan grinned and wiggled his eyebrows, Trent could practically hear him adding "and from a fate worse than death" to his description of Miss Sue's rescue. His tension eased slightly. He remembered being fifteen and having a vivid imagination, although he suspected he had been more experienced at that age than Duncan was.

Trent's eyelids drifted closed. In a few minutes, Duncan finished the story, and the youngsters cheered. Trent opened his eyes and found Anna watching him. Did she guess? Was he so transparent that she could see his shame, sense his fear?

She walked over and knelt beside him. Folding the quilts back over his knees, she carefully unwrapped the soft baby blanket from his feet. "You've been honored," she said with a smile. "Mitch wanted you to feel better so he loaned you his blanket. He usually throws a fit if anyone goes near it. I have to sneak it away to get it in the wash."

Trent was deeply touched by the little boy's gift. "I'll be sure and thank him. It does help." He watched as she cradled his right foot in her hands and gently examined it. Most of the foot was red and swollen, but he knew the main concern was his little toe, which had begun to throb painfully.

"It looks like a burn," she said quietly.

"Feels like one."

"I have laudanum if you need something for pain."

"I think I can do without it. That stuff gives me nightmares." He had enough of those already. He hated to think what his mind would conjure up with a tincture of opium.

She covered his feet and scooted up to inspect the frostbite on his face. "The white is gone from your cheek. No, don't touch it." When he reached up, she grabbed his hand, frowning when he winced. "I'm sorry. It's red, like a burn, too. I have some ointment we can put on it. Does it hurt badly?"

"Everything hurts. But having you takin' care of me makes it easier," he added softly.

A hint of pink touched her cheeks, but instead of releasing his hand, she examined it, turning it first one way and then another. She laid it carefully on the multicolored log cabin quilt and picked up the other one. "At least they aren't still pale. Your circulation must be improving."

He turned his hand over and unsuccessfully tried to curl his stiff fingers around hers. Without thinking, he ran his thumb lightly across her inner wrist. A jolt shot through him, and her gaze flew to his. Awareness and confusion flickered across her face. He figured he looked just as spooked. "I do appreciate all you're doing for me."

"I would have done the same for anyone." She eased her hand away from his.

"I know." *But would you look at another man the way you're looking at me? Would he see the loneliness in your eyes? The yearning?* Even though he knew it was wishful thinking, he hoped not.

Mitch stepped up and dropped his arm across Anna's shoulders, leaning comfortably against her. "Mama, is Mr. Malloy gonna sleep with you?"

"What?" Anna gasped, staring at her son. A hot flush spread across her cheeks. "Of course not."

"But you're the only one that gots any room." He gave her a little hug. "You're gonna be awful cold in that big bed by yourself. You ain't got nobody to snuggle up with. And he ain't got no place to sleep."

The thought of snuggling up with Anna did more to warm Trent's blood than all the quilts. He was tempted to point out the logic in the little boy's reasoning, but when her face and throat turned completely scarlet, he didn't have the heart. "Men and women aren't supposed to sleep together unless they're married, half-pint," he said. As if drawn by the huskiness of his voice, Anna looked at him.

"How come?" asked Mitch.

"Just one of the rules of living." Trent met Anna's gaze briefly, then glanced away, afraid she would read too many of his thoughts.

"Sounds kinda dumb to me."

"Seems kinda dumb to me sometimes, too. But there are good reasons for it. Gets complicated. I can sleep just fine right here. And your mama can always put another quilt on the bed."

"I guess so." For a moment, Mitch appeared unconvinced, then his expression cleared. "Davy said you probably got that shiner in a saloon brawl. Is he right?"

Trent blinked at the sudden change in conversation. "Yes."

"Were you fightin' over some whore?"

Trent almost choked and shook his head.

"Mitchell Gregory Caldwell! Where did you learn that word? Or even hear of such a thing?" Anna cast a scathing glance at the other boys.

Davy shook his head, appearing as innocent as the day he was born. Duncan struggled to keep from laughing. When Anna pinned him with her angry stare, his countenance sobered instantly. "Not from me, Anna."

"Was, too," piped up Davy.

"I don't use that word," Duncan said indignantly. "Pa said to call a woman like that a dance hall gal, even if she doesn't just dance."

"Tim O'Brien called 'er a—"

Anna clamped her hand over Mitch's mouth.

"We heard you and him talkin' last time we were in town," said Davy. "He was tellin' you how he got his nose broke. Remember, it was all swolled up and purple? And he said he got it busted in a fight with another cowboy over a, uh, dance hall gal. Only that wasn't what he called her. Him and that other cowboy both wanted to take her upstairs. And he was all mad, 'cause he won the fight but couldn't go have fun because his nose hurt too bad."

Trent managed to pull the quilt up to his eyes, hoping to hide his amusement. Anna stared at the boys in astonishment. Poor Duncan tried to fade into the sofa. Rachel's eyes were wide, but he sensed she was soaking up every word.

Anna let her hand slip from Mitch's mouth. He barely had time to take a breath before he chimed in again. "And Tim said his soiled duck went off with another feller, sash-swayin' up the stairs, tauntin'—"

Anna clamped her hand over Mitch's mouth again. "Enough!"

Trent covered his head with the quilt and slumped down, burying his face in the pillow, shaking with silent laughter. The movement jarred his aching body and hurt his lip, but even the additional pain couldn't dampen his mirth. It felt too good to laugh.

"I will not have that kind of talk in this family," Anna said firmly. "Do you all understand?"

From beneath the quilt, Trent heard three male voices in varying octaves answer in the affirmative. It struck him that each response was polite and respectful, even Duncan's. Trent had never been given such an edict by his grandmother. She had never been too concerned with what came out of her mouth or anyone else's. She'd taught him a few basic manners, but most of what he knew he'd learned from other cowboys—men who grew up with mothers like Anna Caldwell.

"Now, go to bed."

Trent kept his head beneath the quilt until he thought he could come out with a straight face. He heard the clatter of boots and shoes on the wooden floor as they all scampered to do Anna's bidding. When it grew quiet, he peeked out from beneath the cover, pushing it down until his hands and arms were free. Anna sat beside him, hunched over with her face in her hands. Her body shook, and she sniffed loudly.

Trent's first impulse was to hold her, but he quickly decided that wasn't a good idea even if he had the strength to do it. "Anna, don't cry."

She shook her head and mumbled something he couldn't understand.

"Even a stranger like me can see that they're good boys, especially Duncan. But he's growing up. He's bound to talk to his friends. He's goin' to learn about all kinds of things you might not approve of. Maybe even do some of them.''

''He'd better not!'' Pulling a white handkerchief from her skirt pocket, she dabbed at her eyes. ''I'll have to ask Shane to talk to him.''

''Shane?'' Trent hoped he was her brother or something.

Anna finally looked up, and Trent's heart sank. From the glow on her face and the smile in her eyes, she wasn't talking about any brother. He reminded himself that it didn't matter. He was a drifter. Always had been. Always would be.

''Shane Parker. He owns a ranch down the road. He was Edwin's best friend and is mine, too. He'll know the right things to tell Duncan.''

She surprised Trent by leaning closer. Her eyes sparkled, and her lips curved up with merriment. ''I thought I was going to bust when Davy told that story about Duncan's friend,'' she whispered.

''I thought you were horrified,'' he whispered back, trying to ignore what her closeness did to his senses. He was relieved but also felt a little foolish for offering sympathy when she had been laughing instead of crying.

''Well, I was surprised, and I'm not pleased that the younger boys heard such a tale. Thank goodness they don't understand what they were talkin' about. But to hear them tell it with such wide-eyed innocence. Poor Duncan. Did you see how he squirmed?''

Trent nodded. A smile began in his heart and spread to his face.

''You didn't help one bit, Trent Malloy.''

He shrugged. ''Sorry.''

''If you hadn't covered up your head, I would have done it for you,'' she said with a grin. ''I was having a terrible time keeping a straight face and trying to sound stern.''

"You did an admirable job. I wasn't doin' too bad until Mitch called her a soiled duck."

She giggled and tears of glee welled up in her eyes. "Who sash-swayed instead of sashayed."

For a man who had been almost dead only an hour or so before, Trent felt amazingly alive. "Yeah, and here I thought ducks waddled."

She let out a whoop and covered her mouth with her hand, shaking with laughter. Trent laughed with her, trying to do so quietly. A few seconds later, she gasped for breath. Tears rolled down her cheeks. "Do you think she quacks?" She whooped again and buried her face against his quilt-covered chest to muffle her giggles.

Trent's laughter died as her boldness caught him by surprise. *Not again.* In disbelief and fear, he scanned the room. *No bullwhip.* But a couple of shotguns hung on the wall. What would Duncan do if he stepped into the room? Would he note that Trent's arms were at his side, that he wasn't holding her? Or would he only see what he wanted to see, believe what he wanted to believe? And would Anna lie, proclaiming her innocence and his guilt?

Trent held his breath, ordering himself to settle down and quit overreacting. The situation wasn't the same as it had been five years ago. Anna wasn't like Rosie Williams. She couldn't be a loose woman out to make trouble, and she didn't have a jealous husband.

Anna suddenly went still. She slowly raised up and glanced at him with stricken eyes, her face crimson. "Please forgive me," she whispered. "I don't know what came over me."

She jumped to her feet and hurried across to the stove, adding more wood on the fire. A few minutes later, she poured a glass of water from the bucket on the dry sink

and brought it to him. ''Do you need another quilt or anything?'' she asked, without meeting his gaze.

''No, thank you.'' He tried to keep his expression and
tone even.

She softly told him good-night, again without looking at
him, and fled to her bedroom.

Trent sighed as she disappeared behind the closed door.
He should have said something to ease her guilt, but he
couldn't find the words. He was just too tired. His mind
didn't seem to work anymore.

The house grew quiet and dark shortly thereafter, and
Trent settled down for some much needed sleep. He'd
never been a praying man, but it seemed right to thank God
for sparing his life. ''I'll do a better job this time around.
Won't make the same mistakes,'' he promised sleepily.

He thought of Anna and the sweetness of her head resting against his chest, even through the quilts. Lingering on
the fringes of sleep, he wondered if he had just made a
promise he couldn't keep.

Chapter Three

By the next afternoon, Anna wasn't sure any of them would survive the storm if it continued another day. They had enough food and wood to last a couple of weeks but being shut up with two little boys used to running free was enough to drive anyone loco. She tried to put the hours of confinement to good use, spending more time on their school lessons than they had in months, but the boys soon rebelled, chasing each other around the room.

She read to them, played games with them and even tried to teach them how to make biscuits. They wound up having a shoot-out with the dough. Dig joined in, barking and jumping from one boy to the other, trying to nab a bite. She started to stop them, but when she saw Trent smile for the first time that day, she let the "bullets" fly. His amusement vanished in a roar when a big wad of gooey dough smacked him in the face. Davy said it was only a ricocheted bullet, and Mr. Malloy should have kept his head down, and he was a sissy for making such a fuss.

In a voice that would have done a hog caller proud, Trent informed her brash son that since his bullet was the size of a cannonball, it couldn't have ricocheted off anything. He further pointed out that Davy couldn't hit the broad side of a barn if he was standing two feet in front of it.

Davy wailed.

Trent scowled.

And Anna lost her temper with them all. She slammed the rolling pin down on the table, rattling the tin biscuit pans. "Davy, stop bawling, or I'll put you to bed this minute."

The little boy choked down a sob and glared at Trent.

He glared back.

"Please do not yell at my children, Mr. Malloy."

"Then control the little hellions."

"They are not hellions." Tempted to grab the rolling pin and give him a lump on his head to go with the black eye, Anna moved away from the table. "I apologize for their unruly behavior. They aren't used to being cooped up in the house." Even though she meant it, the apology didn't sound completely sincere. Trent shifted in the chair, grimacing as he moved his foot on the needlepoint-covered cushion of the footstool, making Anna instantly ashamed.

"I think perhaps you're the one who should go to bed, Mr. Malloy," she said quietly, stopping beside his chair. She had not been as attentive to her patient as she should have been. Keeping the children occupied had only been part of it. Embarrassment over her actions the night before was the greater cause of her neglect.

Trent glanced at the pallet on the floor. When he'd tried to rest earlier, Mitch had tripped over him during a game of tag. "And get trampled? No thanks."

"I didn't mean in here. Why don't you go lie down in my bed for a while? It's colder in there, but it won't be as noisy or as dangerous. I'm afraid the boys can't sit still for long. Keeping them quiet for more than ten minutes seems to be an impossibility today."

Trent was so tired he didn't think he could hold his head up much longer. He had more sore places than he could count. Some were from the brawl. They would heal. He wasn't so sure about the frostbite. His hands were still red and swollen; the skin cracked open in places. They itched and burned despite the ointment Anna had gently rubbed on them. His feet were pretty much in the same condition, but a couple of toes on the right one had him worried. Blisters covered his little toe. The one next to it also had a small blister, and they both throbbed with pain. Anna had applied some of Mr. Chesebrough's ointment to his feet and wrapped them in soft, clean cloths, but it did little to ease the pain.

"I am worn-out. Maybe if I rested I'd quit bellerin'."

"We're all suffering from cabin fever." Anna looked at Davy's sullen face. "Davy, could you come here, please? Be careful you don't trip on your bottom lip." Pouting and looking at the floor, the little boy shuffled over and stopped in front of Trent's chair. "Do you have something to say to Mr. Malloy?"

Davy slanted her a glance, his unhappy silence clearly asking if he had to. When she nodded, he looked down at the floor again, rubbing the toe of his shoe on the wood. "Sorry I hit you with the biscuit dough."

"It's all right, Davy. I know you didn't mean to." Trent felt as if he should apologize to the boy for yelling at him, but he wasn't sure he was supposed to. He'd been yelled at plenty when he was a kid, and no one had ever apologized to him. He glanced up at Anna, silently asking what he should do. Her expression softened, and she gave him a tiny nod and an encouraging smile.

"I'm sorry I yelled at you, Davy. I reckon you usually can hit a barn or anything else you're aiming at."

"I'm sorry I called you a sissy. I know you ain't one."

"Right now, I might argue with you on that, pardner."

"Davy, go help your brother scrape up the dough. I don't want to find a speck of it anywhere." Anna ruffled the boy's bright red hair as he started to leave. "And don't let Dig eat it all. It will make him sick."

Davy glanced back over his shoulder with a wide grin. "Then you'd better scrape Mr. Malloy's face before Dig decides to wash it for him."

Trent watched the dog help the boys by devouring everything in sight. "He wouldn't dare."

Anna laughed. "Oh, I don't know, Mr. Malloy. You're a pretty tempting morsel."

Trent's first impulse was to tease her back, then he thought of how he must look. He didn't figure any woman would be tempted by a man with a black eye and a face that was frostbitten, bruised and covered with thick black stubble dotted with gobs of white stuff. Besides, he'd sworn off women. Too bad he couldn't seem to remember it around this one.

He glanced up, noting her pink cheeks, and kept his tone light. "Maybe to a hollow-legged dog." He brushed his fingers over his beard and winced. The whiskers grated against his irritated skin. The dough, already dry in places, stuck to him like flour-and-water paste. "It's gonna take water."

"I'll get some." Anna fled just as she had done the night before.

He sensed she wasn't intentionally flirting with him. It just seemed to bubble out of her, which made it all the sweeter to him and probably that much harder for her. Her actions obviously surprised and troubled her, loading her down with guilt if the look in her eyes was any indication.

Her interest in him was real. Trent saw it in her eyes every time she looked at him, felt it every time she touched him, sensed it when she was near. The attraction was mutual, but it could never lead to anything. She wasn't the kind of woman to take a lover, and he wasn't husband material, even when healthy.

He chanced a look at Duncan, anticipating the frown on his face. The young man wasn't full-grown, but he was close enough to see what was happening. Trent glanced at Anna as she wrung the water out of a washcloth over a basin in the dry sink. He met Duncan's gaze and gave a tiny nod in her direction.

Surprise flickered across the lad's face, but he followed Trent's unspoken suggestion by intercepting her. "I'll take care of Mr. Malloy, Anna. Could you mix up some more biscuits? I was lookin' forward to them."

"I'd be glad to. Would you help him into bed?"

Duncan nodded and brought the washcloth over to Trent. "Tip your head up."

Trent obeyed, half expecting the boy to be rough, but he wasn't. *Warm water.* Trent sighed softly in pleasure. "Thanks. That feels better."

"You ready to lie down?"

"I'm past ready."

Duncan had helped Trent put on his pants and shirt that morning, but he still felt the loss of warmth when he pushed the quilt off his legs. He wasn't sure he would ever be completely warm again. The young man moved to the right of the chair, taking hold of his arm. Trent stood, gasping as pain shot through his feet.

Duncan slid his arm around Trent's waist. "Lean on me."

He draped his arm around the boy's shoulders, clenched his teeth, and let him help support his weight. They made their way across the room, one agonizing step at a time. Rachel ran ahead of them and turned down the covers, stuffing a pillow beneath them near the foot of the bed to keep the heavy quilts off his feet. Trembling and panting, Trent collapsed on the side of the bed. He was as hot as a branding iron fresh from the fire. A drop of sweat trickled down the side of his face and dripped onto his collar. He could have sworn the china washbasin and pitcher flew past his head, and the ornate walnut dresser and wardrobe traded sides of the room before settling back into their proper places.

"Lift up his feet." Anna seemed to appear out of nowhere, sliding her arm across his upper back as Duncan lifted his feet and swiveled him around on the bed. She eased him down on the mattress and covered him with a thick layer of quilts.

He tried to push them off. "Burning up."

She firmly held them in place. "And you'll take a chill if you throw off those covers in this cold room."

Out of the corner of his eye, Trent noticed Rachel push her scowling brother through the doorway. The washbasin whizzed past again. "Anna, I'm roastin'."

She wiped the moisture from his face with the edge of her apron. When his skin immediately grew damp again, she relented and drew back two of the quilts. She let him pull his arms free from the covers, then sat down on the edge of the bed, trapping the remaining quilt in place when he tried to push it aside. "Relax, Trent," she said quietly, unfastening the top two buttons on his shirt, loosening the collar. She gently patted his face with the soft, pink calico apron. "Breathe slowly. That's it, cowboy. Close your eyes and sleep awhile."

His eyelids weighed a ton, but when he let them rest, the bed whirled around like a top. He opened his eyes and grabbed her forearm to steady himself, ignoring the pain in his hand. "The room keeps movin'. Unless I look at you."

"Hogwash." She smiled and shifted slightly, settling more fully onto the bed. He reluctantly released her arm, and she put her hands in her lap.

"Truth." He kept his gaze locked on her face and forced himself to breathe slower.

"It's a terrible feeling, isn't it? I got drunk once, and I'll never forget how the stars spun."

"Somebody spike the punch at a dance?"

"No. I was awfully unhappy where I worked. Old Lady Ledbetter was a mean old biddy. No matter how hard I tried, I couldn't seem to do anything to suit her. I wanted to go somewhere else, but it was my first real job. I was terrified no one else would hire me if I quit. One day she got so angry I thought sure she would fire me, but she assured me I wouldn't get off so easy. It was her duty to teach me how to be a good domestic servant, to show me my place in the world."

How could anyone be mean to this sweet, gentle woman?
"I would have taken her to the Comancheros. 'Course I'd probably have to pay them to keep her."

She chuckled. "Well, I solved my problem. I'd heard about people drowning their sorrows so I stole a bottle of whiskey from the liquor cabinet. It didn't take much before I got sick all over her favorite imported Oriental rug."

"Uh-oh."

"That's not the best part. She happened to be wearing her favorite evening gown and sitting in her favorite chair—"

"In the middle of the Oriental rug," he said with a small smile.

"Yep." She grinned. "It was worth being thrown out into the street just to see the look on her face. I laid there in the alley with no place to go and watched the stars swirl around me. I was sick as a dog, but happier than I'd been in months. When I still felt miserable the next morning, I wasn't quite so happy. I never had another drop of the stuff."

"Smart lady." His eyelids drooped a bit, but he kept them open. The room had stopped spinning, but he liked looking at her.

She shook her head. "Smart girl. I was only twelve. Being that sick made quite an impression."

It had been easy for Trent to walk away from his grandfather's farm at age fifteen, but he wasn't sure he could have done it at twelve. "Were you on your own?"

"My parents died when I was five, and I was sent to live with mother's maiden great-aunt. As best we could figure, she was my only relative. After she died, our neighbor got me the job at Ledbetter's."

"Your neighbor have something against you?"

Anna smiled. "No. It was the only job available. Aunt Gerti was practically penniless when she died, and I had promised her that I wouldn't let her be buried in Pauper's Row. I talked the county and the undertaker into letting me put down as much as I could for the funeral and burial plot and pay the rest on time."

Trent liked hearing her talk and learning about her. He also liked the way her hip and thigh lightly touched his side through the quilt, pleasant yet comfortable. "So when you left Ledbetter's you didn't have any money."

She nodded. "I had made the final payment the week before, and I was broke. Fortunately, a preacher found me wandering the streets and took me home to live with his family. They couldn't pay me anything for helping out around the house, but it didn't matter. They had a large and loving family, and they gave me a home. I stayed with them three years."

He tried to hold back a yawn but failed.

She brushed a lock of hair to the side of his forehead and touched his cool, dry skin. "You don't look quite so much like a ghost now. Are you feeling better?"

"Yes." He yawned again. "And you're gettin' cold. Better go." He slid his arms beneath the cover. When she stood and drew the other quilts over him, he sleepily thanked her. "Don't close the door. Can't stand to be closed in."

"Spoken like a true cowboy." A gust of wind rattled the window. "And it would be too cold if I shut the door. Sleep well."

"Will." A soft mattress. Clean sheets. A warm bed. It had been so long. No one hacking and coughing in the bunk above him. No moans of pain or cries of fear in the darkness. No hollow footsteps echoing down the long, empty stone corridor.

Trent turned on his side, breathing in the fresh sunshine smell of the sheets and the whisper of lavender clinging to the pillowcase. Her scent. Light and flowery. Sweet, like her. Thoughts of Anna blocked out the grim memories, bringing peace and rest.

He awoke to darkness. For one terrifying moment, he thought it had all been a dream, that Anna and the children were only a figment of his tortured mind, and freedom was only a fantasy. Then he felt the pain in his foot and the clean softness of the sheets.

Trent shoved the covers back and sat up on the side of the bed. His stomach rumbled, and he thought about the biscuits Anna had planned to make for supper. Bracing one hand on the small oak lamp table by the bed, he stood carefully, wincing at the pain in his feet but thankful it wasn't as intense as it had been earlier. He inched his way along the wall to the bureau washstand, using it to guide him to the window.

Sliding the yellow gingham curtains aside, he rubbed the frost from the windowpane. Pale moonlight sparkled off the pristine whiteness, and stars twinkled in the sky as the clouds drifted apart. The snow appeared to be a foot deep in the flat stretches and maybe three or four feet in some of the drifts—heavy for that part of West Texas. Beautiful but deadly for anyone caught out in it unprepared. Trent shivered and turned away from the window.

Leaving the curtains open for light, he walked back to the bed and pulled off a quilt, wrapping it around him. He slowly and painfully made his way into the main room, using whatever was handy for support—bed, dresser, door, chair, sofa back. Bathed in soft moonlight, Anna slept soundly on his pallet near the stove. She lay on her side with her knees drawn up and the cover up to her chin, her long, light brown hair flowing in gentle waves across the quilts.

Trembling and weak, he eased down on the sofa, tucking the quilt around his feet, and watched her sleep. So peaceful and serene, as if she didn't have a care in the world. He knew otherwise. Running a ranch and raising a family were heavy responsibilities for a woman alone.

There were probably half a dozen men vying for her hand. Even a ready-made family wouldn't stop many men from going after a pretty young widow, especially if she owned a reputable ranch like the Double Deuce. It wasn't as large as many in Texas, but some of the cow ponies at other spreads where he had worked originally wore the side-by-side double two brand. The Caldwells had a reputation for good stock before the hard times hit. He wondered what the situation was now.

Anna wiggled and murmured something unintelligible. Afraid she would awaken and find him staring at her, Trent quickly leaned his head against the back of the sofa and closed his eyes. When she didn't say anything, he peeked at her. She had turned over, freeing one arm from the covers, wrapping it around the pillow. She shifted again, and the quilt slid off her shoulder, revealing a prim and proper high-necked, pink striped flannel nightgown.

Trent's mouth went dry. Seeking a distraction to corral his wild thoughts, he threw the quilt aside and stood cautiously. He walked over to the stove and lifted the coffeepot, gently sloshing the liquid inside. Filling a nearby cup, he took a sip. Hot, black and thick as molasses from sitting on the stove all night. Remembering a few of the hundreds of times he had ridden into camp after a shift as night guard and drank coffee that tasted the same brought a bittersweet pain to his heart.

The long trail drives had pretty much ended, due to the settling up of the country and common use of barbed wire and the railroads. Sometimes herds were still driven to fresh range land not connected to the main ranch, distances far enough to require several nights on the trail, but he wouldn't be doing that kind of work. The drives and roundups requiring night guards were mainly on the big ranches. Trent's chance of hiring onto one of those outfits was about as good as seeing a catfish walk across the desert.

He set the cup down and added wood to the fire. Lifting a thick towel from a tin pan on the warming rack above the stove, he found four biscuits left from supper. He picked up the pan and cup of coffee, hobbling back to the sofa. Placing his meal on a small round table, he moved the footstool so he could use it and wrapped up in the quilt. Finally settled down, he plucked a biscuit from the pan. It had dried out a bit, but he didn't care. A beggar was thankful for any food that came his way.

Trent's gaze drifted to Anna. Even the noise he made adding wood to the stove didn't disturb her. He sipped his coffee, wondering if she was slow to wake up in the mornings. Did she stay in bed as long as she could, then stumble out into the kitchen to stoke the fire in her nightgown and bare feet, her hair mussed from sleep and hanging down to her waist? Was she grumpy until she had a cup of coffee, or soft and cuddly?

He gave himself a mental shake. He had no business thinking about her that way. It would only lead to grief. Flat broke, he had nothing to offer a woman, and probably never would. Eating another biscuit, Trent looked around the room and considered his options—all two of them.

He could ride out as soon as he was able and try to live off the land until he found work. The idea held some appeal. He could barely tolerate sleeping indoors and liked his horse's company. Polecat didn't judge him and seldom talked back. Unfortunately, there was little open land left, and he might be shot for trespassing before he could bag his first meal.

Nor was it likely he would find anyone willing to give him the kind of job he wanted. Not that he was too picky. He'd settle for just about any kind of ranch work, even clearing brush or cleaning stalls, but he didn't want to sweep out any more saloons or wash another dish for a meal.

The other alternative was to try to convince Anna to hire him. Trent wasn't afraid of hard work and was well acquainted with longhorns. It would take awhile to get his roping rhythm back, and if she had any shorthorns, he'd have to learn about them.

Once upon a time, he'd been known for his horse sense and had been one of the best bronc busters around. He had developed his own method—one much less painful on horse and rider than the traditional way. He didn't figure that was something a man forgot, even after a five-year absence. Trouble was, that time had aged him ten years in body and fifty in soul. He might remember how to break a horse, but he didn't know if he had the will to keep trying.

His gaze settled on Anna once again, and he knew what he had to do. The best chance he had of rebuilding his life was right here. He needed to be around decent folk so he could remember how to act, but he needed time alone, too. Rachel had told him the ranch wasn't big enough for a bunkhouse, but there was a room in the barn for a hired hand. She hinted that they could use the help. Between working out on the range and having a place to himself, he'd have the peace and quiet he craved, but he could also be around people when he wanted to.

Trent sighed and leaned his head against the back of the sofa, weary in heart, body and soul. It would never happen. He couldn't gain anyone's trust by telling lies, and if he told her the truth, she'd run him off faster than Dig could chase a rabbit. Not even kindhearted Anna Caldwell would hire a horse thief, especially if he had spent the last five years in prison for the crime.

Chapter Four

That afternoon Trent sat alone in the empty house, watching out the front window as Rachel battled Mitch and Davy in a furious snowball fight. Dig bounded back and forth between them, barking happily, then raced through the deep snow in great leaps.

Anna and Duncan had helped them build a snowman and two snow forts before riding out around one o'clock to check on the herd. Knowing she did much of the work around the ranch, he'd expected Anna to wear denim pants. He'd even anticipated the pleasure of seeing her in them. Instead, she wore something he'd never seen before—a skirt of heavy brown cotton, divided up the middle like wide trousers. It was practical for working and riding, yet she still looked feminine and modest.

Trent glanced at the large clock on the shelf in the kitchen and frowned. They'd only been gone a couple of hours, but it seemed like twice as long. "Enjoy the peace and quiet, Malloy," he muttered. He had—for about fifteen minutes, then, to his surprise, he discovered he missed the kids' noise and activity. That was when he dragged the rocking chair and footstool over by the window so he could see them play.

Mitch hit Rachel smack-dab in the stomach with a snow-ball. Jumping up and down in excitement, his feet slipped, and the little boy fell backward in the snow, his high-pitched giggles making Trent grin. Laughing, Rachel continued the war, taking a few more hits in the process.

"She throws pretty good for a girl." Trent yawned and looked at the clock again, worrying about Anna and Duncan. "Wish I could have gone with them." Though some of the snow had melted, it was still plenty deep. He knew they planned to stay together, but searching for the cattle could be dangerous.

Trent shifted his feet and grimaced with pain. He was as useless as a milk bucket under a bull. "You've done some stupid things, Malloy, and this one rates right up there. Not at the top but close."

Weary, he closed his eyes, trying to ignore his throbbing feet and burning hands by thinking about Anna. Her smile. Her touch. The way her eyes warmed when she glanced his way and met his gaze. He pulled the quilt up around his shoulders. "You're being an idiot again." Knowing it was one thing. Doing something about it was another.

Trent dozed off but awakened half an hour later as the boys and Rachel stopped on the porch to stomp the snow off their boots. The door flew open, and Davy raced into the room with Dig and Mitch right behind him.

"Too bad you can't come outside, Mr. Malloy," Davy said breathlessly. "I ain't never had so much fun."

"Don't use *ain't*," said Rachel with a smile, pulling off her gloves and cap. "Boys, after you warm your hands, you'd better get into some dry clothes. Mr. Malloy, do you need anything before I change?"

"No, ma'am. I'm fine." He smiled at her, then at Davy. "Who won?"

"It was a draw. We weren't really keepin' score or nothin'."

"I hitted her good," said Mitch, grinning as Rachel unbuttoned his coat.

"I saw that," said Trent. "You ducked good afterward, too."

Mitch giggled. "I wasn't duckin'. I fell down, but it was fun." He gave Rachel a pretty-please look. "Can we have some hot cider?"

"Yes. Soon as we put on dry clothes."

"Come on, squirt," said Davy. "We'll hurry."

They all disappeared into their bedrooms. The boys emerged a few minutes later, complaining because it took Rachel so long to change.

"Womenfolk have more layers to work through," said Trent.

"She's probably fussin' with her hair," said Davy, rolling his eyes. "We don't care what it looks like."

"I'm not too particular right now, either," said Rachel, walking into the room, her long blond hair pulled back and tied with a pale green ribbon at the nape of her neck. She'd changed into a green calico shirtwaist tucked into a dark green wool skirt. "But I did have to take the rest of the pins out." She grinned at Trent. "They knocked my cap off."

"Twice," crowed Davy. "Mitch and I both sent it flyin'."

"Don't brag, or I won't give you any cookies to go with the cider."

"She's just teasin'," Mitch confided, leaning against the side of the rocker and Trent's arm. "She always gives us somethin' good to eat in the afternoon, even if it's biscuits and jelly."

The boy's innocent acceptance and unconditional affection tugged at Trent's heart. Mitch would learn to be more selective with his trust. Trent expected he would play a major role in that lesson, and it saddened him.

"Don't pester Mr. Malloy," Rachel said quietly.

"I ain't pesterin' him." Mitch looked up at Trent, a tiny doubt lurking in his eyes.

"He's not bothering me," Trent said with a wink at Mitch. "He was just telling me what a nice sister he has."

She laughed, lifting the jug of cider from a shelf in the corner. "Only when I give him good food."

When Mitch leaned closer, Trent lowered his head so the boy could speak softly in his ear. "She's all right most of the time. Takes a lot to make her mad."

"Like what?" asked Trent.

An impish twinkle lit the child's eyes. "She got kinda riled when we tied the legs of all her drawers in knots."

Trent chuckled. "I suppose that would be a mite irritating."

"But the time she real got mad was when we trapped her in the outhouse." Mitch grinned. "Davy propped a board against the door so she couldn't open it."

Trent tried hard not to smile, but he wasn't quite successful. "How long did you leave her in there?"

"Not long. Just until we finished off the cake. She sure did holler and carry on." His forehead wrinkled in a frown. "Mama gave us a whippin'." He pondered the situation for a minute, then looked up at Trent with another grin. "But it sure was good cake. I had this much." He measured about a foot of air with his hands.

Trent almost laughed out loud. "That must have been a mighty big cake. If I had a sister who cooked like Miss Rachel, I think I'd try as hard as I could to stay on her good side."

Mitch nodded. "Yeah, she didn't bake nothin' except hard biscuits for two whole weeks after that."

"Lesson learned?"

"Yep. Want some cider?"

"Sure." Trent rested his head against the back of the chair as Mitch went off to tell Rachel to fill another cup when the cider was warm. The clock struck a quarter past four. He noticed Davy go to the back window and search the countryside. "See any sign of them?"

"No." The boy turned away from the window, looking at Trent. "I thought they'd be back by now."

"I did, too." Trent threw the quilt aside, letting it hang over the chair arms, and stood carefully. Holding on to the back of the sofa and chairs, he walked slowly across the room on his heels and peered out the window. "How far do you expect they went?"

"Around to the other side of those hills, if they could get there. That's where she was hoping the cattle are. It's rough country—mostly hills, ravines and canyons—but part of it is good shelter. Maybe I should go try to find them," Davy said reluctantly.

Trent caught Rachel's worried glance. "You'd better let me go this time." He draped an arm casually over the boy's shoulders. "I'm an old hand at riding in the snow."

"Mr. Malloy, with the condition of your hands and feet, you can't ride anywhere," said Rachel, joining them at the window.

"You help me put on my boots and gloves, get me on a horse, and I can ride."

She watched Davy carry Trent's boots across the room. Turning back toward the window, she said quietly, "He won't let me leave without him, though he's never ridden under these conditions. He's scared, and I don't blame him. I don't see how you can ride, but I'd be very grateful if you could go with me. I've never been out in this kind of snow before, either.''

''You're staying here. It will be dark in another hour or so, and I can move faster on my own. I'll need some blankets, a lantern, some dry wood and matches.''

''I'll gather them up. I'll get Daddy's heavy coat for you, too. I don't think I should let you go alone.'' Rachel looked down at Trent's swollen feet, wrapped in strips of an old, clean sheet. ''Daddy's boots may be bigger than yours. Do you want to try them?''

''Might help.'' The ones he had were snug to begin with. Trent made his way back to the rocker and sat down. Walking was sheer misery, but he figured once he was in the saddle, it wouldn't be so bad.

Rachel returned, carrying a pair of dark brown boots and a heavy, sheepskin-lined leather coat. She laid the coat on one end of the sofa and placed the boots in front of him. ''Are you sure you want to try?''

Trent studied the boots. They were practical, without too much fancy stitching. Though well broken in, they were considerably better than his and were slightly longer and wider. He nodded and picked one up, holding it by the top with both hands. Fiery pain shot through his fingers, but he gingerly eased the toes and ball of his left foot into the opening. *Anna, I don't think I'd do this for anybody but you.* He set the boot on the floor and pushed his foot farther into it. Sweat broke out on his forehead and upper lip. ''Help me pull it on.''

He clenched his teeth, barely stifling a cry when Rachel tugged the boot up as he shoved his foot all the way into it. Leaning back in the chair, he closed his eyes and breathed deeply, fighting the pain.

Rachel stood, shaking her head. ''Mr. Malloy, this is crazy.''

"It'll settle down in a minute." *It has to.*

"Mama, you're back!" cried Davy. "Mr. Malloy was gonna go look for you."

Trent opened his eyes, meeting Anna's startled gaze as she came through the back door.

"We was worried," chimed in Mitch. He and Davy raced across the room to meet her and Duncan.

"And Rachel told him he couldn't ride 'cause of his hands and feet, but he said all we had to do was get him on a horse," said Davy.

Anna glanced down at Trent's feet with a frown. He thought moisture shimmered in her eyes, but when she glared at him, he decided he imagined it.

"She gots him Daddy's boots to wear 'cause they're bigger," said Mitch.

Anna blinked rapidly, and Trent was certain he saw a tear on her lashes. Maybe Rachel was right; maybe he was loco. Or was she upset because of the boots?

"Rachel was thinking about goin' with him," said Davy.

Duncan shook his head, frowning thoughtfully at his sister and Trent, but he didn't say anything.

Neither did Anna. She turned away, taking off her hat and gloves, throwing them on a shelf. Duncan put his away, too, glancing at her a couple of times, waiting for her response.

Anna hung her coat on the peg and swung around to face them. "I'm sorry we worried you. We took the long way home since the snow wasn't quite as deep in the south pasture. Then we met Shane coming over to check on us. We visited with him for a few minutes."

She walked across the room and put her arm around Davy's shoulders. "I appreciate your concern, but you know not to go off on a wild-goose chase in this kind of weather." She lowered her arm, frowning at Rachel. "So do you. I thought you had better sense," she said angrily.

Rachel's face turned scarlet. "You were gone too long. We were afraid you'd been hurt."

"We went together so if something happened to one of us, the other one would be there to help. Or didn't you think of that? Your job is to stay here with the boys and take care of them. I depend on you to do that, Rachel. I can't worry about you taking a notion to ride off after us. We might have been anywhere on the ranch. Where would you have looked?"

Trent frowned, wondering why Anna was being so hard on the girl. "I figured I'd follow your tracks in the snow," he said quietly.

Anna marched across the room and stopped in front of him, her eyes blazing. "And how did you plan to do that? I saw your face when you put on that boot. You went white as a sheet, and the other foot is a lot worse. What if you had managed to ride out after us? What would Rachel have done when you passed out from the pain?"

"She wasn't going with me." He studied her face. The cold might have made her nose rosy, but he doubted it had made her eyes puffy and red.

"So, you would have just lain there in the snow and frozen to death." She shook her head. "I was wrong about you. You're a fool, Trent Malloy. I can take care of my family and my ranch, but I don't need to worry about you, too." She spun around, heading for her bedroom, and slammed the door behind her.

No one said a word. Trent looked at the younger boys. Davy and Mitch stared at Anna's closed door, their eyes wide and frightened. Mitch's lips began to tremble, and Davy swallowed hard, fighting tears.

Rachel sniffed, drawing Trent's gaze. Wiping her eyes

with the side of her hand, she moved toward the stove. Duncan stopped her halfway there, giving her a quick hug. He looked at Trent with sorrowful, apologetic eyes.

"How many head did you lose?" Trent asked quietly.

"Five calves and ten cows." Duncan cleared his throat. "We had to put four down."

"What does that mean?" asked Davy.

Rachel walked over to the boys and knelt in front of them, reaching for Mitch's and Davy's hands. "It means they had to kill them," she said softly. "The cows were dying and in great pain. So Anna—" she glanced at Duncan, and he nodded. "Your mama shot them so they wouldn't suffer anymore. It made her very sad. That's why she's so upset."

Mitch's lips trembled even more, and a tear slid down his cheek. Then another. "She's not mad at Mr. Malloy?"

"No, not really."

Trent didn't agree, but he kept his mouth shut.

Rachel held Mitch for a few minutes, rubbing his back until he quit crying. When he straightened, she gently wiped his cheeks. "Better?"

He sniffed one last time and nodded solemnly. "I'm hungry. Can I have a cookie?"

"We'd better wait until after supper. I'll warm up the beans and corn bread. It will only take a few minutes. Still want some cider?" When he nodded, she picked him up and carried him over to the table.

Duncan knelt in front of Trent, eyeing the boot. "Need some help taking that off?"

Trent nodded. "I hate to admit it, but it hurts like the devil."

"I won't mention it to Anna." Duncan smiled in understanding and tugged the boot. His promise was worthless unless Anna had suddenly gone deaf. Trent figured his yell stampeded half the cows in the county.

Trent woke up with a start, sensing someone nearby in the darkness. His mind cloudy with sleep, he reached for his pistol. It wasn't there. Heart pounding, he slid his hand around, looking for a rock—and felt the thick layers of quilts lying on the smooth wooden floor. Realizing he was in Anna's kitchen, he breathed a sigh of relief and rolled over. Anna sat on the sofa, just visible in the moonlight, hugging a red-and-white quilt wrapped around her, with her feet curled up on the cushion beside her.

"Can't sleep?" he asked softly, raising up on his elbows.

"Every time I close my eyes, I see those poor cattle." She ran her fingers through her hair, shoving it back from her forehead. "I hate this part of ranching."

He pushed the cover aside and scooted closer to the kitchen table, taking one of the quilts with him.

"Do you need some help?"

"I can make it." Using the table, he pulled up to stand, silently cursing his pride, thankful his back was to her so she wouldn't see his grimace. He wrapped the quilt around his shoulders, holding it closed at the waist with one hand to hide his drawers. Hobbling over to the sofa, he sat down, making sure his lower half was well covered. His aim was a bit off, and he wound up closer to her than he should have been.

Anna didn't tell him to move over. Instead, she looked down at her lap, her long, soft hair hiding her face. "I'm sorry for what I said this afternoon," she whispered.

"You were upset."

"But I shouldn't have taken it out on you. I'm so used to watching out for myself and the family that it never occurred to me you might have worried. When I saw you putting on the boot, I knew what you were about to do, even before Davy said anything. It terrified me. You're in no shape to be out in that bitter cold. You could have died trying to help me.'' She looked up at him, her eyes ghostly pale in the shadowy room, her face filled with anguish. ''I couldn't bear that, Trent. Not again.''

His breath caught. She blamed herself for someone's death—but whose? ''What do you mean, not again?'' he asked gently.

She looked away, absently adjusting her quilt with a trembling hand. ''Edwin died because of me.''

Trent frowned in confusion. ''I thought you said he had a heart attack.''

''He did, but I caused it. I took Mitch down to the corrals to see some horses we had brought in the day before. We looked at them for a few minutes, peeking through the fence, then went over to the other pen to see Edwin work with a little mare. Mitch was only three, and I was afraid for him to climb up on the rail, even if I was up there with him. So we stayed on the ground and watched. I thought he was right beside me, but when I looked down, he was gone.''

''Kids are quick.'' Though she wasn't looking right at him, he could see her despair.

''Yes, they are, which is all the more reason I should have paid closer attention to him.'' She paused, taking a deep breath. ''I found him in the corral with the other horses. He had crawled through the fence and was walking toward them, chatting away. The horses milled around in one corner, but he didn't understand the danger. I yelled for Edwin and went in after Mitch. The horses started running around the edge of the corral, bunched up together. I grabbed Mitch and raced toward the fence. Edwin came running and arrived as I reached it. I had just enough time to throw Mitch over the railing to him and scramble out of the way, back to the middle of the corral.

"The horses panicked and scattered, running in every direction. Edwin jumped into the corral to help me." Her voice broke, and Trent laid his hand on her shoulder. She took a deep, shuddering breath, waiting almost a full minute before she could continue. "He hollered and waved his hat in the air, keeping them away so I could make it over the fence.

"He'd had pains in his chest three times before. Doc said it was his heart and told him to take it easy, get plenty of rest and avoid excitement. Edwin made it over the fence, practically leaping over the top, and stumbled to his knees." She stopped again, closing her eyes.

Trent put his arm around her shoulders. He wanted to tell her not to finish the story, but he sensed she needed to talk about it. He knew the price of keeping painful secrets, and he suspected she had hidden this wound from just about everyone.

"He was in agony," she whispered, misery etched on her face. "I could see it on his face. Poor Mitch was scared and crying at the top of his lungs. I screamed at him to be quiet and knelt in front of Edwin. He knew he was dying—knew he'd never see Rachel marry, Duncan become a man, Mitch and Davy grow up. I helped him lie down and held him close. He told me to be strong and that he loved me.

"Edwin held on until the other children reached us. He told them he loved them and to mind their mama, that I'd teach them what is right. Teach them what is right?" she asked, her voice breaking. "He died because of my stupidity. If I'd watched Mitch better, none of it would have happened, and Edwin would still be alive."

When she choked back her tears and heartache, Trent drew her into his arms, cradling her head against his shoulder. "Anna, don't torture yourself. You didn't cause his death. Hearts just give out sometimes. He could have died walking to the house."

She shook her head, her hair brushing against the side of his neck. "Sometimes at night, I see his face in the darkness, hear his whispered words. The sorrow in his eyes haunts me."

"He wouldn't want you to feel that way, but he probably knew you would. I expect that's one reason he was so sad. Sure, he regretted the things he would miss, but he treasured the time he had with you and the kids." Trent longed to rest his cheek against her hair but didn't. "That's what a man thinks about when he's dying, the good memories." *If he has any.* She straightened slowly, and he moved his arms, resting one on his lap and the other along the back of the sofa instead of across her shoulders.

She wiped her eyes on the sleeve of her heavy, dark green robe. "What did you think about when you were in the blizzard?"

A giant knot instantly formed in his stomach. His mind raced, searching for an acceptable answer. "My mama." It wasn't the most truthful response, but he reasoned it was the appropriate one. Smiling ruefully, he said, "I also spent a right smart bit of time thinking up new names for the sheriff."

She smiled and leaned her head against the back of the sofa. "And probably none of them complimentary."

"Not a one."

Anna laughed softly. "He's a good man, but he doesn't tolerate mischief."

"If you call a saloon brawl mischief, then no, ma'am, he doesn't."

She looked at him, silently studying his face for so long

it made him nervous. "Thanks for letting me talk," she said finally.

He shrugged. "I'm good at listening."

"Yes, you are. I didn't mean what I said this afternoon. I don't think you're a fool." Her expression softened even more as tenderness filled her eyes.

Yes, I am. And I'm gonna be a bigger one if you don't quit looking at me like that. He forced his gaze away from hers. "I'm glad." He could name plenty of people who would disagree with her.

"Given your health, going after us wouldn't have been the smartest thing to do, but it shows you're a brave man. A good man."

A good man. How long had he waited to hear someone say those words? They watered his soul and gave him the courage to ask for the chance to prove them true. "You could use some help around here."

"Ever break horses?"

"Not in several years. Used to quite a bit on the Snider Ranch down in South Texas. Did some training, too, but I expect you could teach me a lot about both. I've ridden some Double Deuce horses in the past. Heard you have a special way of working with them. It showed." He took a deep breath and met her gaze. "I sure could use a job if you're lookin' for somebody. All my cow experience is with longhorns, but I don't reckon working with Durhams would be that much different."

"They're easier to handle. You don't have to spend so much time dodging horns. Duncan and I have about worn ourselves out trying to keep this place up. I couldn't give you much more than room and board to start."

"The way Miss Rachel cooks, I'd be plenty grateful for that."

"If the grass holds up, I could increase your wages in a month or two, bring it up to the standard pay."

He grinned. "That's even better." *Tell her.* His smile faded as he tried to find the words that would make him an honest man.

He couldn't.

Chapter Five

The warm weather returned quickly, melting the snow. Over the following three weeks, rain showers ended the drought and brought an abundance of grass and wildflowers. Anna had never seen anyone work harder than Trent. He seemed driven to prove that he could do the job better and more diligently than any other man. It didn't matter if he was looking for a wayward calf, working with the horses, or cleaning out the barn, he appeared to enjoy it.

Most evenings, he stayed at the house after supper, playing dominoes with the boys or listening to Duncan read a story. Occasionally, he told a tale of his own—about going on his first trail drive when he was sixteen, seeing one of the last herds of buffalo on the range, or trying to impress a girl with some fancy riding and winding up facedown in a mud puddle.

In her opinion, he started to work too quickly given his injuries. His hands didn't bother him much as long as he wore gloves, but he should have stayed off his feet for at least another week. Even though she had given him Edwin's boots, he still limped, sometimes badly by nightfall.

At first, more often than not, he dozed off in the big brown chair after supper, too weary to keep his eyes open.

Sometimes he would sleep until bedtime, rousing groggily when she shook his shoulder or Mitch and Davy hugged his neck and told him good-night.

She often spotted Trent beside the barn at dawn, rolling up his bedroll. His room was modest but not cramped. Why he chose to sleep outside puzzled her. When she asked him if it was too small, he said it was larger than what he was used to. She asked if the bed was uncomfortable, but he smiled and said it was fine. He just enjoyed looking at the stars as he fell asleep.

One afternoon Anna and Duncan rode out to the northwest corner of the ranch to round up several cows that would soon calve. As a precaution, they would move them to a pasture closer to the house. Since Trent was mending fence nearby and hadn't come in for dinner, they decided to stop and see if he needed anything.

They spotted him in a wide valley, working on the fence that formed the northern boundary of her property and separated it from the Kingsley spread. Robert Kingsley wasn't a bad neighbor, but he had a quick temper. When Edwin was alive, the other rancher raised a ruckus if any Double Deuce cattle wandered onto his land to sample the grass. She had to admit, however, that he had been much more sympathetic since her husband's death.

Topping a small rise, she reined in her horse. Duncan did likewise, glancing at her. "Let's wait here a minute and see if he knows what he's doing," she said quietly.

"Anna, we've already passed three stretches of fence he's fixed, and they were fine." He frowned at her. "You just want to look at him."

Her cheeks grew hot. "I want to see how he works."

"In a pig's eye."

Surprised by Duncan's angry retort, Anna glanced away in confusion. She did like looking at Trent Malloy, far more than she should. His split lip had healed the first week. All the swelling and bruises around his eye had disappeared, and the redness from the frostbite on his cheek faded a little more each day. He was a very handsome man. Sometimes when he glanced at her, the contrast of his black hair and amber eyes, especially if they were twinkling or held a certain warmth, almost took her breath away.

He'd gained weight since they dragged him out of the blizzard. His shirt no longer appeared a size too large but fit him nicely. If she ran her fingertips over his ribs now, she'd feel hard muscle instead of sharp ridges. The thought made her flush even more.

"We don't know anything about him," warned Duncan.

Anna watched as Trent hammered a staple into the cedar post to hold a taut strand of barbed wire in place. Straightening, he pushed up the front brim of his hat, wiped his forehead on his sleeve, and stood still for a minute, looking out across the countryside. He walked to the wagon and laid the pouch of staples and the combination hammer and nippers in the back. Pulling off his gloves, he tossed them on the seat.

Instead of climbing onto the wagon, Trent picked up his canteen and limped halfway up the side of a small hill to a patch of wildflowers. Anna frowned, noting that his limp was much more pronounced than usual. He sat down, took a long drink of water, then picked a flower and lifted it to his nose. After a minute or two, he took off his gray hat and placed it on the grass nearby. Still holding the flower, he laid back on the grass and looked up at the sky.

Anna looked up, spying a hawk circling high overhead. She couldn't remember when she had taken time to enjoy the fragrance of a flower or appreciate the beauty of the magnificent birds gliding through the sky. Trent seemed to appreciate everything around him, even treasure it. "Maybe we know the things that count," she said quietly.

Duncan practically snorted. "What? That he gets you all hot and bothered?"

"Duncan! You've been spending too much time with Tim O'Brien."

"And Malloy is spending too much time with our family. We don't need him here, Anna."

"You know we need help on the ranch."

"We can manage fine without him."

Anna stared at her stepson. He couldn't possibly believe what he just said. "Duncan, I couldn't have kept the ranch going without you. You've done a man's work ever since your father died. But we've worn ourselves to a frazzle. There is more than enough work for three people."

Duncan scowled and fumed for a minute. "I agree we need a hired hand."

"But?"

"He ought to act more like one. Go to the barn after supper instead of staying at the house like he belongs there. The boys hang on to his every word, as if what he says is gospel."

"Have you heard him say anything in front of them that he shouldn't?"

"Not yet," he admitted grudgingly.

"Duncan, I don't think you realize how much you guide Davy and Mitch, or how much they look up to you. You're helping me teach them the way your father would have."

"How long do you think that will last?" Worry wrinkled his brow, and hurt hovered in the depths of his eyes. "They already halfway treat Trent like a father, especially Mitch. Pretty soon, they won't remember Daddy at all."

"I won't ever let them forget Edwin," she promised earnestly.

Duncan's jaw tightened. "How are you going to do that? Seems to me you've forgotten him already."

Anna flinched, feeling as if she'd been slapped. "I'll always love your father."

"Will you? Or is Trent taking his place?"

"No one can take his place in my heart." She wouldn't lie to him. "But I'm awfully lonely, Duncan."

"You've got us." He sighed heavily. "But I know that's not nearly the same. It's not fair for me to want you to live the rest of your life alone. But don't expect me to treat him like a father." Duncan glared at Trent. "I won't."

"You act like I'm going to marry him tomorrow," Anna said in a teasing tone, trying to ease the tension between them.

"It's obvious that you're interested. And I see the way he looks at you, especially when you're busy doing something else and won't notice."

"The way he looks at me?" She couldn't quite keep the eagerness out of her voice.

Duncan rolled his eyes and shook his head. "Like he can barely keep his hands off you." When Anna blushed, he glanced away, then looked back at her, his expression apologetic. "I'm sorry. I don't like what's happening between you two, but that's no excuse for being disrespectful." He toyed with the end of the reins. "I don't think he'd force himself on you or anything. I reckon he cares about you, but you could still get hurt. We all could."

"I know," she said quietly. Duncan had his father's gentle spirit, Edwin's caring ways. He looked after those he loved and tried to protect them. He had been man of the house for two years. Without one word of complaint, he had shouldered responsibilities many grown men would have shirked. "You're very much like your father. He would be proud of you. I don't tell you that often enough."

He smiled sadly. "I hope to be as good a man as he was."

"You will be." Anna leaned forward, patting her horse on the neck.

"I hope so." Duncan glanced at Trent, then turned his horse toward the other pasture. "I'll head on over there. See you in a few minutes."

Trent sat up, looking around. When he spotted Anna, he waved and stayed right where he was.

She rode to the base of the hill and dismounted, leaving her horse to graze while she talked to Trent. Even in his usual jeans and a worn blue-striped shirt, he was handsome. As she walked up the hill, she wondered how he thought she looked. Her rose pink chambray shirtwaist fell into the category of work clothes, but she knew the color flattered her complexion and eyes. It also went well with her dark gray cotton riding skirt.

"Caught me wastin' daylight," he said with a smile when she walked up in front of him.

"Yep. I don't know about you. You spend your time looking for sundown, shade and payday." Grinning because the saying about a lazy worker was so inappropriate, she pulled off her gloves and sat down beside him. She removed her beige felt Stetson, laying it next to the gloves. Plucking the purple verbena from between his fingers, she lifted it to her nose and inhaled the sweet fragrance. "I'd forgotten how wonderful these smell."

Anna let her gaze travel slowly over the valley and sighed in contentment. Great masses of purple, lavender and yellow adorned the lush green grass. Some of the low-lying hills beyond it appeared to be covered with snow, others with gold. "I'd also forgotten how beautiful spring can be when we have rain. There were times when I wondered if we would ever see green grass or flowers again."

"A person appreciates the beauty more if he hasn't seen it for a while. You've done better than many ranchers. I've lost count of the outfits that went broke these last few years. You must be a real good manager."

Anna glanced at him, pleased at his praise. "We would have gone under, too, if it hadn't been for the horses. Though if we'd had another bad year, they wouldn't have made a difference. I can't sell them unless there are ranchers left who need them. I still don't anticipate many buyers anytime soon."

"They'll be around quicker than you might think. I expect the ones who have land left are trying to figure out how to stock it."

"I used most of my reserve funds buying extra hay last fall, so I'll sell some of my cattle as soon as they've fattened up a little. Not more than ten or twelve head, though. If one of the other ranchers isn't interested, the cattle buyer in Antelope Springs will take them and ship them off to who knows where."

"Having that hay paid off." Admiration shone in his smile. "I expect most of the ranchers thought you were loco to spend the money."

"Yes, they did, though I only fed the cattle when things were desperate." She handed him the flower with a soft smile. "Thanks."

He nodded, a hint of a smile playing across his mouth. "Anytime."

They sat in comfortable silence for a few minutes, enjoying the quiet beauty around them. When Anna chanced a peek in his direction, she found him watching her.

"You should do this more often," he said.

Anna grinned. "Sit out on the prairie with you?"

He shrugged and twirled the stem of the flower between his fingers. "I meant relax."

"I know." She smiled gently, meeting his gaze. "And I do enjoy your company. But you should go on back to the house. Your foot is troubling you."

His mouth tightened. "Not any more than usual."

"Yes, it is. I can tell by the way you walk." She glanced at his foot as he moved it. "And you keep shifting it while we're sitting here. Climbing up and down out of the wagon probably hasn't helped it a bit."

"I don't have much fence left to check. I'll finish up first."

"You'll head back now. You won't do yourself or me any good if you can't walk at all tomorrow."

"I'll be fine tomorrow," he said irritably. "I earn my pay."

"You've more than earned your pay ever since you started working. I've never seen anyone work as hard as you. Know when to quit, Malloy."

"I'll quit when the job is done."

Anna frowned at his stubbornness. "And ruin that foot in the process? I'm giving you an order, cowboy. You'll finish this job when I tell you to."

He opened his mouth to protest again, but Anna laid her hand gently on his arm, stopping him. "Let it go, Trent. You've proven yourself. You don't have to keep trying so hard. Don't run the risk of permanently damaging your foot."

Trent met her gaze and saw caring in her eyes—not only compassion but a woman beginning to have deep feelings for a man. He longed for her love, dreamed of it, ached for it, but he didn't deserve her and never would. Her gaze dipped to his lips, then back up again as she slowly leaned toward him. His throat constricted as he forced himself to remain still. "Anna, don't," he whispered.

Hurt clouded her eyes, and her face turned red as she

began to pull away. He hated to cause her pain, yet better to do it now than later when it would be much greater. Cupping her face gently with his hand, he halted her movement. "I want to kiss you more than anything, but I can't. It's not right."

"Because you work for me?" She searched his eyes, a tiny frown wrinkling her forehead.

"Partly."

Her eyes widened. "Are you married?"

"No."

"Have a sweetheart?"

It would be an easy way out, but he refused to compound his deception with more lies. "No." He brushed her cheek with his thumb. "There isn't anyone else." He doubted there ever would be. "But I'm not the man for you, Anna."

"How do you know?"

"I just do." He lowered his hand and let her straighten. When she moved her hand from his arm, a chill raced down his spine. He looked away, turning his face toward the prairie, remembering the longing in her eyes.

"And I have no say?" she asked indignantly.

"No." Now was the time to tell her the truth, to destroy the respect he had worked so hard to gain. He took a slow, deep breath, but dread made him hesitate.

A rider came into his field of vision.

"We've got company." Trent pushed to his feet, looking away so she wouldn't notice his relief. "Do you know him?"

"It's Shane Parker."

Her best friend. Trent had heard plenty about Parker from Anna and the kids. He suspected the man would gladly be more than a friend if given the chance. He wanted to knock out a few of his teeth.

Anna scampered down the hill without a backward

glance. Trent hobbled along behind her, swearing under his breath at the sharp pain in his foot and the ache in his heart. By the time he approached them, Parker had dismounted, and they were discussing her stock.

"Do you think I should sell right away or wait until next month?" she asked, looking up at Parker as if he were the wisest man in the world.

Trent frowned. She hadn't asked him for his opinion on the matter. And what was she doing standing so close to the rancher? Or straightening a collar that wasn't crooked in the first place? Then he realized Parker stared at her with a bemused smile.

"I wouldn't wait more than a couple of weeks. Let them fatten up a bit, and I'll buy them. I'll give you the going rate." Parker glanced at Trent, one eyebrow lifting slightly. He nodded in greeting and held out his hand. "Shane Parker."

"Trent Malloy." Expecting less than a friendly reaction, he waited a second before uncurling his fist and shaking hands.

"You the one caught in the blizzard?"

Trent nodded.

"The good Lord must have been watchin' out for you that day. Looks like you're healing up."

"Not as fast as he thinks he is." Anna glanced at Trent with a frown, then crossed her arms and glared at him. "I believe you were going back to the house now?"

"Uh-oh," said Parker, laughing. "The mama hen's got her feathers ruffled. You'd better do what she says, Malloy, or you won't have any peace and quiet."

"Don't have it anyway," grumbled Trent.

"Then eat in the barn," snapped Anna. "I'll send Duncan down with your supper so our noise won't bother you."

"Fine." Trent started toward the wagon, then stopped and looked back at Parker. "Nice to meet you."

"Same here," the rancher said with a grin. "I'm having a few folks over for a party Friday afternoon. Celebrate the return of the grass and survival. There will be plenty of food, music and dancing. Most of the folks around here are coming. Even if you're not up to dancin', you might see some old friends and make new ones. Be glad to have you."

"Thanks. I'll keep it in mind. Depends on how I'm feeling." Trent continued on to the wagon. He had no intention of going to the party. Obviously Parker didn't recognize his name, but there was bound to be someone at the dance who would either know him or remember all about him. Besides, he didn't think he could stomach watching Anna dance with Shane Parker. "Or anybody else she decides to turn up sweet," he muttered to himself.

Anna watched Trent painfully make his way toward the wagon. "That has to be the stubbornest, most mule-headed man I've ever met. He has no business working so hard when he can barely walk. I don't know what he did this morning, but he's limping worse than he has in three or four days."

"Anna, look at me," Shane said quietly.

She glanced up impatiently. "Maybe you can talk some sense into him. I can't."

"Well, I'll be." Shane searched her face as she watched Trent climb into the wagon. "You're falling for him."

"Don't be silly." She turned away. "I just don't want him crippling himself for life. Nobody will hire a broken-down cowboy."

"You did."

"He needed a job, and I need a hand. His injuries were temporary, but they won't be if he keeps this up."

"Jobs have been mighty hard to come by the last few years. I expect he's intent on keeping this one. He knows how to mend fence." Shane studied the section Trent had repaired.

"And how to do every other kind of ranch work," Anna said with a sigh. "He's good with the horses."

"And with you?"

"He's not interested in me."

"That explains it."

"What are you talking about?" She frowned at him, resting a hand on her hip.

Shane settled his arm across her shoulders, urging her toward her horse. "Why you were flirting with me. I enjoyed it, but I did wonder why you suddenly turned all soft and womanly on me."

Stricken, Anna met his gaze. About a year earlier, Shane had suggested courtship, but she had rejected the idea. He was her dearest friend, but she couldn't imagine marrying him. She hadn't thought his feelings ran beyond friendship, but the trace of regret in his voice told her she might have misjudged him. "Shane, forgive me. I can't believe I was so thoughtless."

He smiled and squeezed her shoulders. "Don't worry about it. I'm not wasting away from a broken heart, though my pride wishes I could light a spark in you like he does."

"He's not interested."

Shane stopped and turned her to face him. "You can't believe that."

"He told me as much. He very clearly said he's not the man for me." *And I practically begged him to kiss me,* she thought in shame, lowering her gaze.

"Honey, you're talking about two completely different critters. Malloy is interested, otherwise he wouldn't have come down that hill ready to knock me on my backside.

Take a look at things from his angle. He's a down-on-his-luck cowboy. He has a horse, a saddle, the shirt on his back, and maybe a spare. I suspect he's the kind of man who needs to give his woman something of value, to show her he can provide for her. But he has nothing to offer you.''

"I have the ranch. I don't need him to give me anything.'' She looked back at Shane.

He minutely raised his eyebrows. "Nothing?''

"Himself…and his love.''

"Then help him believe that's enough. And be patient. I have a feeling life has been hard on Trent Malloy.''

"You saw it, too? The sadness in his eyes?''

Shane nodded. "Even when he's angry.''

"Or happy. It never completely goes away. Thank you for the advice and for putting up with my foolishness.'' Anna hugged him. "I don't know what I'd do without you. You're the best friend I have.''

"For now,'' he said with a smile, hugging her in return.

That evening Trent lay in his bunk staring at his swollen, aching foot. The skin had split open again on his little toe, even worse than before. It was well past time to show more sense than pride and take Anna's advice. If he didn't rest it for a few days, he might always walk with a limp.

He closed his eyes, sighing heavily. It didn't matter if he was out on the range or cooped up in his room, his mind wouldn't let him be. Over and over, he pictured Anna sliding her arms around Parker, the big man holding her tenderly. Trent had been a fool to look back at them as he went over the rise, and a complete idiot to stop and watch until they stepped apart.

"It's better this way,'' he said to the barn cat who had adopted him. The big gray tabby opened his eyes and blinked as if questioning his statement. The tomcat stretched, then hopped up on the bed and rubbed his head against Trent's hand. He scratched the cat behind the ears, too miserable to smile as the animal purred in appreciation.

"I had to turn her away, Sam. I couldn't let her feelings for me grow and then have her find out about me. Maybe I ought to sneak out of here tonight. I could probably get a job at the stockyards in Fort Worth if I used another name. 'Cept I'd forget to answer to it half the time."

A knocked sounded at the door. "Supper," he whispered to the cat. "Come in."

Anna opened the door, carrying a covered plate. She stared at the cat. Sam quit purring and sized her up, bumping Trent's hand again with his head when he stopped petting him. "How did you catch him?" she asked, moving slowly into the room, leaving the door ajar.

"I didn't. He decided to join me all on his own. Though the scraps I've been sneaking to him might have something to do with it."

A tiny, uncertain smile hovered about her lips. "Don't let Dig see you with the cat or the scraps. His feelings will be hurt, and he's liable to chew up your boots."

"Better the boots than my hide." Trent scooted up to a sitting position, leaning against the wall. "Thanks for supper." He wondered why she brought the food instead of sending Duncan down with it, but he didn't ask. He didn't want to remind her of their cross words.

"You're welcome. It's chicken and dumplings."

"My favorite."

The cat jumped to the floor and pranced across the room, sniffing at the plate.

"Sam's fond of it, too," said Trent, grinning at the feline's antics.

She laughed. "Everything Rachel cooks is your favorite, and Sam eats anything."

"True on both counts. Haven't tasted anything worthy of complaint yet."

"She is a good cook. Better than me." Anna walked across the small room and handed him the plate, looking just past his ear at the wall. "Well, I should go on back. The boys are extra rowdy tonight." She turned away, but gasped when she saw his foot. Her gaze flew to his. "How long has it been like this?"

"Probably since I dropped a post on it early this morning. I didn't take my boot off to see." When Sam sprang up on the bed, Trent held his supper plate away from him.

"I may wring your neck," she mumbled, leaning over his foot for a closer view. "At least you cleaned it. Did you soak it?"

"Enough to get the dirt and lint out of the cut."

She straightened, shaking her head in disgust. "I'll get some bandages and ointment. Don't even think about working tomorrow."

"Yes, ma'am."

She looked at him in surprise. "You mean you've finally come to your senses?"

"About a few things." He tried to ignore her wince. "Come back after supper. It won't get infected while you eat." He shoved Sam off the bed. "Wait your turn, cat." Sam calmly sat down on the floor, watching him intently.

Anna glanced at his foot again. "Do you need anything else?"

You. But he didn't mention it. "Nope. We'll do fine."

"I won't be long."

He almost wished she wouldn't return. Being alone with her in the small room made him more aware of her than ever. "Give me time to eat," he said gruffly.

She did—barely. Sam was licking the last dollop of sauce from the plate when Anna knocked on the door. Trent called for her to enter, and she bustled in, her cheeks flushed from her haste.

He frowned at her. "Did you eat?"

"Yes, even my cobbler."

"Cobbler?" He spotted a small bowl in her hand. "What kind?"

She smiled and set the bowl on the two-person wooden table by the black potbellied stove. "Does it matter?"

"No," he said with a grin. "But some kinds deserve more anticipation than others."

Her eyes twinkled. "Peach."

"My mouth's waterin' already."

She laughed. "You do know how to make the cook happy. Is there any food you don't like?"

"Cabbage."

"Not too fond of it myself." Anna sat down on the bed and picked up his foot, resting it on her lap. "This may hurt," she said, her voice shaded with regret.

Trent clenched his teeth as she gently spread the petroleum jelly over the open wound on his toe.

"The skin is very dry and irritated along here, too," she said, smoothing the salve along the side and top of his foot. Her brow wrinkled in a concerned frown. "Your toe must be awfully sore."

"It is."

She looked up at him. "Stay off of it for a few days, please."

The tenderness in her eyes was almost his undoing. "I will."

"I'll wrap it to keep it clean." She pulled a strip of soft white sheeting from her pocket, efficiently rolled it up, then carefully wound it around his foot. Tearing it partway down the length, she tied it securely.

"You're gettin' good at that."

"Between you and the horses, I've had plenty of practice." Anna tucked the jar in her pocket and moved up to sit facing him. "I don't think you should wear a boot for a couple of days."

"I'll work on the saddles or something so I won't go stir-crazy."

She nodded. "We'll be working around here tomorrow, too. We brought in a couple of heifers that are ready to calve anytime. They probably won't need our help, but I like to stay close just in case. Sometimes the Durhams have more trouble than the longhorns."

"Holler if you need me."

"I will, but only if it's absolutely necessary. That foot needs to heal before Shane's party."

He scooted up a little higher. "It won't matter. I'm not going."

"Why not?" she asked, clearly disappointed. "It would be such a good opportunity for you to meet the neighbors. And you might even see some of the cowboys you've worked with, or at least some you know."

That's what he was afraid of. "I'd rather not go."

She glanced over his worn clothing. "Duncan has a pair of new pants you could wear. They're a little long for him, but I think they'd fit you. He was growing so fast last fall I figured he'd be into them before winter was over, but his spurt slowed down. I have a shirt in the trunk that should fit you, too."

Trent shook his head. "Anna, I don't want to use Edwin's clothes. I appreciate you givin' me his boots. I'd be in a world of hurt if I had to wear my old ones, but I'm not wearing his shirts."

"It isn't his. Edwin's aunt sent it to Duncan last year for Christmas, but it's so big, he'll probably never grow into it. Your shoulders are much wider than his." Her gaze drifted slowly across his shoulders and chest, an appreciative gleam lighting her eyes.

His heart did a double back flip.

"It's dark green and would look very nice on you."

Trent felt his resistance slipping—and not just about going to the party. His gaze dropped to her lips. They parted slightly, and the room suddenly seemed much too small.

"I ought to give you a haircut," she said softly, brushing a long lock back from his forehead. "You're lookin' a little shaggy, cowboy."

"Startin' to look as mangy as Dig." He leaned toward her a little, then pictured her in Parker's embrace. "Parker wouldn't take too kindly to you giving me a haircut," he said, shifting back against the wall. *Or being here with me now.*

She blinked. "Shane? Why should he care?"

"I saw him holdin' you this afternoon."

"Oh, that." Anna waved her hand as if casting aside his concern. "It was just a hug between friends." Anna met his gaze directly, her eyes clear and guilt free. "He's my best friend, Trent, and he gave me some good advice." She shrugged. "I'm an affectionate person, so I hugged him. There was nothing more to it."

"I'm not so sure he thinks so."

"I am. We've been through a lot together so we're very close. He knows he will never be anything more than a friend."

Her expression softened and her eyes grew tender as she looked at him, her lips lifting in a tiny mysterious smile. Was she trying to tell him that he could be more than a friend if he wanted to be? Or did she already know how smitten he was?

Neither Shane nor Anna had heard of him. Was it possible no one in the area knew of his past? At least no one besides the sheriff? The peace officer struck him as a fair man who would keep the knowledge to himself as long as Trent stayed out of trouble.

It occurred to him that if he remained at the Double Deuce while Anna and the kids went to the party, her friends and neighbors would wonder why. By hiding, he would sow distrust anyway. Trent impulsively decided he would keep his secrets and take his chances. If nothing else, he would have a few more days with Anna and the family. Precious days he could shelter in his heart in the years to come.

His hand trembled slightly as he lifted it to her cheek, caressing her soft skin with the back of his fingers. She closed her eyes with a tiny sigh. "I'll go to Parker's if it will make you happy," he said quietly.

"It will," she murmured, looking at him.

The longing in her beautiful gray eyes made his heart ache. He slid his fingers into her hair, cupping the back of her head, and drew her closer. "Would a kiss make you happy?"

"I don't know." She rested her hands on his shoulders, leaning toward him. "But I'd like to find out," she whispered.

"So would I." He touched her lips with reverence, wanting to show her how deeply he treasured her. But he was the one who felt treasured. A silken thread of tenderness entwined through the chains that bound him to the past, softening a link here, forging a crack there. For that brief moment, the hurt faded away.

The faint sounds of approaching laughter and little running feet forced them apart. Trent searched her eyes for regret but found only a soft glow.

In the distance, Rachel summoned the boys to the house. Nearby, Davy yelled back. "Soon as Mitch and me tell Trent good-night."

Anna laid her hand against Trent's face, her fingers gently stroking his jaw. "Thank you."

A lump formed in his throat as he nodded. He owed her more than he could ever repay, and she meant more to him than he could ever reveal. Trent leaned down, giving her a hard, quick kiss. "I don't want to hurt you."

The boys' giggles told them they were right outside the door. A frown creased her brow, but there was no time for a reply. She moved to a chair seconds before Mitch and Davy burst into the room.

"We raced," said Mitch, panting. "I almost beat him."

"It was close." Davy winked at Trent. "How you feelin'?"

"Right this minute, pretty good." Trent glanced at Anna with a faint smile. "Your mama put some ointment on my foot that was real soothing." *And her kiss made me feel good all over.* "It hurts, but not as bad as it did earlier."

"You gonna be able to go to Mr. Parker's party?" Mitch asked eagerly.

"I expect so, if I take it easy for a few days."

"We'll fetch things for you and stuff," Davy said with a big grin.

"I'd be obliged. Is Duncan gonna read to you tonight?"

Both boys nodded vigorously. "He got another book about Denver Dan and the Dead Shots," said Mitch. "Mr. Parker brought our mail when he came by today."

"Then you'd better hug my neck and head on back to the house." Trent opened his arms.

The boys did as he asked, then dashed from the room.

A second later Mitch stuck his head back through the doorway. "You comin' with us, Mama?"

"Yes, honey, I'll be right there." Mitch disappeared, and Anna chuckled as the cat crawled out from under the bed. "I wondered where Sam went."

"He doesn't like crowds." Trent smiled lazily at Anna. "You goin' to hug my neck, too?"

"I don't think that's a good idea," she said with a shy smile, handing him the bowl of cobbler. "Enjoy your dessert."

He gave her a wink. "I already had dessert."

Her cheeks turned pink, but she smiled saucily and moved toward the door. "Good night."

"Good night, sugar."

After she left, he leaned back against the wall and tried to quell the yearning that nurtured hope.

Sighing heavily, he closed his eyes. *Lord, how many miracles am I allowed?*

Chapter Six

On Friday afternoon, Trent drew the team and ranch wagon to a halt near Shane Parker's white wooden ranch house, pulling in next to ten other vehicles of various shapes and sizes.

Acid burned Trent's stomach. *This was a mistake.*

Duncan stopped the buckboard beside them. It barely quit moving before the boys scrambled down and raced off to see their friends. Rachel laughed at their excitement.

Trent set the hand brake and glanced at Anna. Sitting next to her all the way to Parker's would have been pure pleasure if he hadn't been so worried about what might happen when they got there. "Parker must be expecting a lot of folks."

Anna looked around and nodded, her eyes sparkling. "Shane knows practically everyone in the county, and we've all waited a long time for this reason to celebrate." She turned, smiling at Rachel as Duncan helped her down from the buckboard. "Rachel, if you would take a basket of food, I'd appreciate it. Trent and I can get the rest. Have a good time. Try not to let the men fight over you," she added with a grin.

Rachel blushed but smiled. "I don't think that's going to happen."

"Most of them will take one look at you and be tongue-tied," said Trent. Her rose pink party dress was a perfect color for the blue-eyed blonde. The fitted bodice, short puffy sleeves and full skirt showed her figure to perfection. The tiny scoop of the neckline revealed her throat and a hint of shoulder without being the least bit immodest. "You're pretty as a picture tonight, Miss Rachel. If any of these boys get obnoxious, you let me know."

"I will." She glanced nervously at a group of young cowboys watching her arrival. "I'm the one who'll be tongue-tied."

"You'll do fine, honey. Just be your sweet self." Anna gave her a proud smile.

"I'll do that, too," said Duncan with a grin.

Anna laughed. "You mind your manners and stay away from Mary Beth."

"But Anna, she's sweet on me." Pure mischief danced in his eyes.

"She's sweet on everybody." Her expression grew serious, and she lowered her voice. "I mean it, Duncan. I don't trust her or her father. She's the kind to get a young man in a compromising position so her daddy can jump out from behind the mesquites with a shotgun. Stay away from her."

Duncan sobered. "Yes, ma'am." He reached over the sideboard of the wagon and picked up a basket, handing it to Rachel. "You two cooked enough for half the folks here."

"We brought extra, but I expect you and the boys will put away your share." As Duncan unhitched the horse from the buckboard, Rachel walked toward the food table. Anna watched her with a tender smile. "I'm going to miss Rachel when she marries."

Trent scanned the crowd. Even men with the settled-in look of being happily married watched the pretty young woman in admiration. The single men practically drooled, and a few stared at her with seduction obviously in mind. He made a mental note to keep a careful eye on those ones.

Another man, bearing a strong resemblance to Parker, kept glancing in Rachel's direction. He was well dressed in a crisp white shirt and expensive black suit cut in the Western style. His feelings were so carefully masked that Trent figured he was halfway in love with her already. "Is that man at the end of the porch kin to Shane?"

Anna followed his gaze. "Yes, that's his younger brother, Ian. He graduated from law school two years ago. Moved to Antelope Springs a couple of months back and opened up an office. I hear he is an excellent attorney. He already has several of the big cattlemen as clients, but he's done work for folks that can't pay much, too.

"They say he defended a young cowboy for free down in South Texas because he believed the man was innocent. The cowboy was charged with killing a storekeeper. It turned out the prosecution's main witness was actually the murderer. Ian tricked him into confessing on the witness stand."

"Sounds like a good man to have for a friend. Or a son-in-law." Trent grinned when Anna looked startled.

She quietly watched the attorney for a few minutes. Ian was careful to pay attention to the other young women, but his gaze went back to Rachel again and again. "He's certainly noticed her."

"Yep, and he's already sized up every man here who might give him trouble. I expect he's more than a match for most of them."

"Well, of course he is. He's handsome, with a good character, and has a promising career and an excellent income."

Trent chuckled. "I meant in case he had to fight them."

She looked at him in consternation. "Do men always do that?"

"Fight?"

"No, size up the other men just in case."

"Most of the time. It pays to know where you stand." He noticed several men looking in their direction. A few studied him with thoughtful frowns, but most were focused on Anna. He didn't blame them.

Like Rachel, she was something to see all decked out in her party duds. She wore her hair in the usual long braid, except she'd added some wispy curls around her face. Her plum-colored silk dress made her gray eyes prettier than ever. The plum overskirt had clusters of tiny white flowers woven into the lightweight fabric. The gathered skirt seemed to float around her when she turned. The short, puffy-sleeved bodice had vertical rows of creamy lace running from the round neckline to a wide silk band at the waist.

The style accented her bosom and narrow waist, but her pleasing curves weren't achieved by being cinched up in a corset. When he lifted her into the wagon earlier, he'd felt no stays beneath his hands. He was already jealous of every man who would dance with her.

"You're always pretty, Anna, but today, you're beautiful," Trent said.

Pink tinted her cheeks as she smiled. "I'm happy. I guess it shows."

"I wish you could stay that way forever," he whispered. *Or even another day.* "Sit still. I'll come around and help you down." He forced a smile. "Even if you don't need it."

Anna watched Trent carefully climb down from the wagon and walk around to her side. Sitting beside him, their shoulders rubbing together with every little bump, she had sensed his tension all the way there. She didn't know if he was nervous about the party, or if their closeness had heightened his senses as much as it did hers. He glanced toward a group of cowboys, his lips tightening into a thin line.

She stood and leaned over, putting her hands on his shoulders as he curved his hands around her waist. He easily lifted her from the wagon. He held her gaze for a breathless heartbeat; golden fire flashed through his amber eyes. The second her feet were settled on the ground, he released her. She knew he was protecting her reputation but still wished his touch had lingered.

"Don't be nervous. Everyone will welcome you," she said quietly.

"Likely not everyone." His expression was grim.

She looked at the cowboys, noting a few with frowns. Most appeared merely curious. One of them, Hank Newell, had been a friend of Edwin's. He watched Trent with a mixture of happiness and concern. "Do you know Hank?"

Trent took a food basket from the wagon and handed it to her, slanting a glance in the man's direction. His expression relaxed slightly. "We go way back. He's a good man."

"I'd say he thinks the same thing about you."

"Looks like maybe we're still friends." He picked up a large box of food. "I'll drop this off at the table, then make myself scarce."

"You don't have to, Trent. I'll be happy to introduce you to the neighbors." Anna smiled to herself, thinking that the women would be dying to meet him. The dark green shirt was a perfect color for him, and both it and the pants fit well. She hadn't given him a haircut after all, but wearing his black hair a little too long didn't detract from his appearance. If anything, it added a hint of mystery, a sense that beneath his polite demeanor hid a trace of a renegade.

"I expect we'll get acquainted soon enough. Stayin' too close to the boss lady wouldn't look right. You have a good time visiting and dancin'. I'll go parlay with Hank and the boys."

"It's too bad your foot isn't up to dancing. The women will be disappointed." *But not nearly as much as I am.* She knew he probably wouldn't have asked her to dance anyway, but that still didn't stop her from wishing.

He chuckled. "They won't miss much. I usually manage not to stomp on anybody's toes, but that's about as good as it gets."

"I wouldn't mind judging for myself."

"Not tonight." He was silent for a few steps, then said softly, "But maybe another time."

They walked to the food table without speaking. Trent set the box on the table, then nodded to the women standing nearby and touched the brim of his hat. "Afternoon, ladies." He turned to Anna. "Let me know when you're ready to load your things back in the wagon, Mrs. Caldwell."

"I will. Thank you."

"You're welcome. Enjoy yourself, ma'am." He nodded and turned away, the wariness in his eyes belying his polite smile.

Troubled by his uneasiness, Anna moved around behind the table so she could see what kind of reception he received from the other cowboys.

"Anna, who is that good-looking man?" asked Lizzie

Spencer. About thirty-five, Lizzie and her husband, Josiah, owned the mercantile in Antelope Springs. He was also the mayor. Lizzie was always involved in some community project. She had headed the drive to raise money for a school and church and had organized the town's first women's club. They had two boys, Patrick and Stephen. One was a year older than Davy; the other, a year younger.

"He's our new ranch hand. His name is Trent Malloy. He was caught in the blizzard and found our place during the storm. Dig heard him ride up but he had fallen off his horse and was unconscious by the time we reached him. His hands and feet were frostbitten."

"Oh, my goodness! How lucky for him that he reached your house." Lizzie grinned slyly and slipped her arm around Anna's waist in a conspiratorial hug. "And how fortunate for you. If I were you, I wouldn't mind seeing that handsome face across the table every morning."

"Well, I think it's disgusting." The high nasal voice dripping with disdain belonged to Othelia Upton, the banker's wife and town busybody.

Anna cringed. "Actually, I don't have much time to notice if he's at the breakfast table or not," she fibbed. "I'm busy keeping my boys in line and trying to teach them some manners." She took a bowl of fried chicken from the box and set it on the table, surreptitiously glancing in Trent's direction. He shook hands with Hank, who greeted him with a broad grin. Some of the other men smiled, but a few appeared ill at ease.

"You shouldn't have someone like him staying in your house, Mrs. Caldwell," said Mrs. Upton. "It just isn't right."

Anna kept taking things from the box and handing them to Lizzie, who set them where she thought appropriate. "He only stayed in the house when he was ill. As soon as he was able to walk, he moved to a room in the barn. Of course, he eats with the family, like most cowboys on small ranches.'' She moved to one of the baskets and began emptying it. ''He's an experienced ranch hand and a hard worker. I'm thankful to have the help and to know I can trust him to work alone and do the job correctly.''

''Well, I still don't think it's proper to have such a virile young man working for a young widow.'' The busybody frowned sternly.

''Should she have a virile old man working for her?'' asked Lizzie with a laugh.

''A real lady wouldn't be running a ranch in the first place,'' said Mrs. Upton.

''A real lady doesn't go around sticking her nose into other people's business and passing judgment on things she knows nothing about.'' Lizzie glared at the other woman. ''Go find someone else to annoy, Othelia. Come with me, Anna. Let's find a shady spot and visit a spell. Once the dancing starts, I won't have a chance to say a word to you.''

Anna went with her friend, sneaking another peek in Trent's direction. He stared at the ground, his expression somber as Hank spoke to the other men. She and Lizzie found two empty chairs beneath the light green, lacy foliage of a mesquite and sat down. Anna discovered she could easily observe Trent while keeping an eye on her boys.

''I thought you might like sitting there,'' said Lizzie with a knowing smile. ''So, where does this cowboy of yours come from?''

''Lizzie, he's not my cowboy.'' Anna felt her cheeks grow warm. She saw that someone else in the group with Trent had picked up the conversation. Out of the corner of her eye, she noted Duncan leading the wagon team toward the barn.

"Well, he ought to be. Goodness, he's fine looking. Is the limp from the frostbite?"

"Yes, so I think it will go away in time. He's doing much better than he was a few days ago." She shook her head. "He dropped a post on his foot and split the toe open. The bullheaded man wouldn't quit until I ordered him to, though he could barely walk. Why do men try to be so tough?"

"Maybe to impress us? Or to prove to themselves that they're stronger than other men? My Josiah is the same way. He thinks it's a sin to be sick." Lizzie scanned the crowd, smiling affectionately when she spotted her balding but dapper husband. "So where is he from? You never did say."

"I don't know." Anna frowned thoughtfully. "He said he came to Texas when he was fifteen and started working on a ranch. I can tell he's had plenty of experience. There hasn't been anything I've asked him to do that he couldn't handle. He did say he hadn't had anything steady or done ranch work in quite a while. But considering how rough things have been the last several years, that isn't surprising. He was a little off on his roping the first few times he tried, but afterward he seldom missed.

"He is wonderful with the horses. He handles them with the same gentle respect that Edwin did. If I didn't know better, I'd say my husband taught him. Some things are different, of course, but he watches what I do and adjusts his method. Usually. He's taught me a few things, too."

"Has he now?" asked Lizzie with a teasing gleam in her eyes.

"Lizzie!" Embarrassed, Anna laughed and glanced around. Thankfully, no one was near enough to hear their conversation.

"Sorry. I can't help it. I'm so happy to see that sparkle

in your eyes. It's been too long.'' Lizzie's gentle smile held understanding and sympathy.

"I am lonely."

"Of course, you are. What do Duncan and Rachel think of him?''

"Rachel likes him. She finds reasons to give us a few minutes alone now and then, which isn't easy with the boys around. Duncan is polite but cautious, even resentful. I think he's worried that Trent might start giving him orders. Duncan is also afraid the boys will forget about Edwin.''

"It's probably hard for him to see you attracted to someone besides his father," said Lizzie.

Anna nodded. "I've tried to assure him that I'll always love his father, but I don't know if he believes me.''

"Duncan will come around over time. He inherited Edwin's sense of fairness.'' Lizzie looked up at the porch where Duncan leaned against a post, talking to a pretty redhead. "He sure is growing up. He's not a boy any longer. Sally Johnson doesn't think so, either.''

"Sally is seventeen. She's too old for him.''

"You'd better tell her that.''

Anna turned toward the porch with a frown. Duncan laughed and made a comment. Sally bantered back, then flounced over to sit by Tim O'Brien. Duncan grinned and walked across the porch to greet two other friends.

Childish laughter drew their attention to Mitch, Davy, Lizzie's boys and a couple of others about the same age as they raced across the yard. Mitch and Davy ran up to Trent to show him something. Anna couldn't tell what it was, but Trent grinned and knelt down on one knee for a closer look. Mitch handed it to him, then draped his arm casually across Trent's shoulders while they talked. Her heart melted at the sight.

"Well, your littlest certainly approves of him," said Lizzie softly.

"Davy does, too, but Trent and Mitch seem to have a special bond. Maybe it has something to do with his blanket."

"Whose blanket?"

Anna told her about Mitch sharing his blanket to wrap around Trent's feet. "It was a very special gift. I don't think Trent has been around children much, but he realized how important it was and made a point to thank Mitch for it."

The boys took off again. They hadn't gone far when Mitch stumbled, hitting the ground hard. At his scream of pain, Anna bolted out of the chair and ran toward him. Trent reached him first and picked him up. Cradling Mitch in his arms as the boy bawled, he turned to Anna.

"Mitch, honey, calm down," she said, trying to talk over his cries. "Tell me what hurts."

He stuck out his hand.

Anna gasped as blood dripped between his fingers. "Let me see, honey."

He opened his hand, revealing a perfect but blood-smeared arrowhead and a jagged cut across his palm.

"Couldn't lose that arrowhead, could you, cowboy?" Trent shifted him to more of an upright position.

Mitch shook his head and struggled to quit crying and be brave in front of his friends. "I-It's special."

"It sure is." Trent nodded solemnly.

"Let Davy keep the arrowhead for you." Anna gently lifted it from his palm and handed it to Davy.

"I'll take good care of it and give it back when Mama's got you fixed up," said Davy, a worried frown creasing his forehead. "I promise."

Anna closed her hand around Mitch's. "I'm going to hold your hand tight to keep it from bleeding so much."

Mitch nodded. "Mr. Parker said the arrowhead was Kiowa."

"Gen-u-ine," said Trent as they walked to the house. "I used to have a collection of arrowheads, Kiowa and Comanche. Got them directly from the Indians."

"They just gived 'em to you?" asked Mitch.

"Not exactly." He leaned his head a little closer to Mitch's. "They were trying awful hard to stick 'em in me."

The boy's eyes grew round. "You were in a real Indian fight?"

"Three of them. When I first started cowboying. They didn't take too kindly to us driving cattle across their land."

"Were you ever shot with an arrow?"

"No. I was lucky. After we scared the Indians off, I picked up all the arrows that landed close by and saved the arrowheads." Trent smiled wryly at Anna when she looked at him. "I was just a kid."

Anna led Trent through the front room of the ranch house and into the empty kitchen. She grabbed a chair and placed it beside the dry sink. "If you'll sit here and let Mitch sit on your lap, he should be just about the right height to wash his hand."

Trent sat down and settled the boy on his knee. "Did you know your mama can read minds?"

Mitch shook his head, eyeing her skeptically. "I don't think so."

She almost laughed at his expression but turned her back, quickly pumping some water into a small basin.

"Well, she knew I needed to take the load off my feet, and I didn't tell her. Did you hear me say anything about being tired of standing?"

"Nope." Mitch transferred his wary gaze to the basin of

water. "I think she just wants you to hang on to me." He swallowed hard. "Is it gonna hurt?"

"It might, but she'll go as easy as she can," said Trent softly, meeting her gaze over the little boy's head. "She has a gentle touch."

Anna's heartbeat quickened at the warmth in his eyes. It was her turn to swallow hard. She looked down at her son's hand. "The cut doesn't look dirty. But we'd better get the rest of your hand clean. The water may sting a little."

Mitch flinched as she lowered his hand into the water. His lips puckered up and began to tremble.

Trent tightened his arms around him and bent over, resting his cheek against the little boy's. "You're doin' real good, son."

Anna glanced at them as she gently washed the area around the cut. Mitch watched her every move, his left arm curled beneath Trent's chin, his hand resting against the cowboy's jaw in love and trust. Trent's eyes were closed, as if he were drawing strength from Mitch instead of the other way around. The longing on his face tore at her heart.

"That should be clean enough," she said softly. Anna lifted his hand from the water and gently dried it with a clean dish towel that had been draped over the side of the dry sink.

"I'll hold the towel against it while you find some bandages." Trent shifted slightly, looking at Mitch. "How you doin', pardner?"

"It don't hurt as much now."

"It's not too deep, but it may be sore for a while." Anna walked across the kitchen to the freestanding cupboard where Shane kept his medical supplies. As usual, he had a stack of various-sized bandages and rolled strips to hold them in place. She picked out what she needed, closed the cabinet door, and turned around, meeting Trent's speculative gaze.

"This isn't the first time we've needed something to cover a scrape or cut while we were visiting," she said with a smile.

"With three boys, I reckon it's a common occurrence." Trent glanced around the clean but simple kitchen. "Parker ever been married?"

"No. He says he's always been too busy to look for a wife." Anna checked Mitch's hand. "Good, the bleeding has just about stopped. This should take care of it." She folded a pad in half and laid it over the cut. When Trent put his finger on it to hold it in place, she smiled at him. "Thanks."

He nodded as she quickly wrapped a strip of cloth over the pad and around Mitch's hand, looping it over his thumb to keep it from slipping before tying the ends together. "That should do it, honey. If it starts bleeding again, you come tell me."

"I will, Mama. Can I go play now?"

"Yes, but keep the arrowhead in your pocket."

Mitch nodded and scrambled down from Trent's lap, racing out the door.

Trent rose with a grin, but his smile faded when he realized how close he stood to Anna. He curled one hand around her waist. "Are you okay?"

A shiver raced down her back. She took a deep breath, releasing it slowly. "I hate it when they get hurt."

"I know. You're a good mother, Anna. Your boys are lucky to have someone who loves them so much." He hesitated for a second. "My mama was a lot like you."

She met his sad gaze. "Was?"

"She died when I was about Davy's age." He glanced

away. "Maybe I would have turned out better if she'd lived."

"I think you turned out pretty well."

He shook his head. "I've made some real bad choices, done things I'll regret the rest of my life." His hand tightened at her waist. "But I'll always treasure my time with you and your family."

The soul-deep sorrow in his eyes sent fear rushing through her. "Trent? What's the mat—"

He gently placed his finger across her lips, silencing her. "Thank you for all you've given me and for proving there is still good in the world." He released her, turned abruptly and hurried from the kitchen, leaving her staring at him in bewilderment.

Chapter Seven

The crowd doubled in the next hour, filling the yard with happy chatter and loading down the tables with food. After Shane asked the blessing, lines formed on each side of the tables.

Rachel helped Davy dish up what he wanted. Duncan carried plates for himself and Mitch while Anna filled them and her own. Earlier, she had spread a quilt in a flat spot beside the house so they had a clean, comfortable place to sit. Duncan brought them glasses of lemonade before going off to sit with his friends.

"Did Trent get something to eat?" asked Mitch, standing on tiptoe, looking through the throng of people for him.

"I'm sure he did. Davy took him a plate and silverware a little while ago." Anna glanced around, spying Trent sitting on the outer edge of the yard with Hank Newell. "There he is," she said, nodding in his direction. "His plate looks almost as full as yours."

"How come he isn't sittin' with us?" Frowning, Mitch plopped down on the quilt and crossed his legs.

Anna carefully set his plate on his lap. "Can you balance it?"

"Yes, ma'am. How come he's over there?"

"He and Mr. Newell are old friends. I expect they haven't seen each other in a while, so they have plenty of visiting to do."

Mitch appeared satisfied with her answer. "I'm glad I didn't cut this hand." He held up his left one. "Woulda been hard to eat." He picked up a chicken leg. "Is this your fried chicken, Mama?"

She looked at it. "No, but it looks good."

Anna and Rachel compared the different foods on their plates, trying to figure out who brought what so they could ask for the recipes, particularly the spiced peaches, the chowchow and three or four kinds of pickles.

Every so often, Anna sensed Trent watching them. She looked up and met his gaze, but he was too far away to tell what he was thinking.

The boys soon declared they were stuffed and hurried off to play cowboys and Indians in the pasture with their friends. Anna finished eating and gathered up their half-empty plates. "It's a shame to waste all this food. I knew they'd never eat all they thought they wanted."

"That's the trouble with potlucks. Everything looks too good to resist. Dig and Sam will enjoy it."

"Dig will gobble it down so fast, he won't even taste it." Anna went to the table for one of her empty pots, taking it back to where they had eaten. "Your potato salad disappeared in a hurry." She grinned at Rachel. "And just now, Ian Parker was trying to talk Hank out of the last piece of your coconut cake."

"He was?" Rachel's cheeks turned pink as she glanced toward the table.

"Hank wouldn't give it to him since Ian already had a half-eaten piece on his plate."

Rachel's eyes grew wide. She peeked toward the table

again, her blush deepening when Ian glanced at her and smiled. "Anna, what will I do if he comes over here?"

"Talk to him. You've done it before."

"But it was never just the two of us."

"Ask about his work. Men like that." Anna grinned and emptied the food from the boys' plates into the pot to take home to the dog and cat. "Are you finished?"

Rachel handed her the almost empty plate. "I can't eat another bite. What is he doing?"

"Going over to talk to Shane."

"Oh." Disappointment flickered over Rachel's face before she hopped to her feet and forced a smile. Anna put her arm around Rachel's shoulders. "Don't worry, he'll ask you to dance."

"I doubt it. I'm too young for him."

"You may be a little young in years, but you're very mature. I think Ian knows that, too. He's kept his eye on you all afternoon. Ian is handsome and very nice, but he may not be the right one for you. Just enjoy the party and give the other fellas a chance."

A mischievous twinkle lit Rachel's eyes. "Is Trent's foot well enough to dance?"

"He said it wasn't."

"Too bad."

Rachel left to visit with her friend, Claire. Anna gathered up the dirty dishes and silverware, tucking them in a basket. She stopped by the table and collected her empty pans and serving bowls, putting it all in the box and baskets she had set under the table.

"Hungry cowboys don't leave many leftovers," said Trent, stepping up beside her. "Especially when the ladies go all out to bring extragood food."

She laughed, her gaze skimming along the table at the

rest of the dishes. There was barely a crumb left. "We'd probably be insulted if they didn't eat everything in sight."

"Can I help you carry those to the wagon?"

"That would be nice."

He picked up the two baskets. "Set the box in my hands."

Anna did as he asked. "You don't have to carry it all."

"They don't weigh much empty."

"Are you having a good time?" she asked as they strolled toward the wagon.

"Yes, I am. Had a good visit with Hank. I haven't seen him in quite a spell. He speaks highly of Parker. Says he's a fair man and a good boss. There are a few others here that I've worked with at one time or another." A tiny smiled lifted one corner of his mouth. "They're as cantankerous as ever."

"I can think of any number of men who fit that description. But you certainly caused a stir without being ornery at all," she said, with a teasing smile.

A scowl darkened his face, and he slanted her a wary glance. "How?"

It wasn't the reaction she had expected. "Simply by being here." His shoulders tensed. "I don't know how many women asked who the handsome man was that came with us. Most of them thought I was fortunate to have you working for me."

"Not everybody felt that way?" He relaxed slightly.

"The banker's wife says you're too young and virile."

Trent grinned. "Her husband's the short fat one?" When she nodded, he chuckled. "Maybe she's jealous."

"I think so." Laughing, Anna took the box from him, holding it while he put away the baskets. When he reached for the box, his fingers brushed against hers, and awareness jolted through her. His gaze held her motionless as he slowly moved the tip of one finger down the back of hers; his gentle touch and the yearning in his eyes wrapped her broken, lonely heart in tenderness and stirred her senses.

When she shivered, he inhaled a deep, ragged breath and lifted the box from her hands. Turning aside, he set it in the wagon. "Enjoy the rest of the party."

"You, too." Anna turned away with a sigh, wishing they were back at the Double Deuce and away from prying eyes. She looked for the boys and caught a glimpse of them moving quietly through the tall grass in the pasture, pretending to be Indians sneaking up on the cowboys.

Duncan had wandered over to sit with Ian, Shane, and some of the other ranchers, listening intently to whatever they were discussing. Rachel, Claire, Sally and half a dozen other girls stood across the yard chatting, glancing at various handsome young men now and then.

Anna joined Lizzie and several ladies on the long porch, sitting in the chairs Shane had provided from the bunkhouse dining room. They shared recipes and stories about the blizzard and perused a copy of the latest *Ladies Home Journal* that Lizzie had brought.

A short time later, the men fastened two wagon sheets to the ground, pounding long stakes in the hard clay to hold them in place. The makeshift dance floor provided a smooth surface and kept down the dust. When Tom Kent, a cowboy with one of the ranches north of town, tuned his fiddle, folks gathered around, ready to dance.

Shane appeared at Anna's side. He glanced at her wagon, where Hank and Trent had claimed a seat with a good view. "Got a partner for the first dance?"

"No. I was waiting for you to ask me." She smiled at him. "You are asking me, aren't you?"

"Yes, ma'am." He grinned and put his hand at the small of her back as Tom struck up the first tune, a two-step called a redova. Shane was a good dancer, so they moved with ease, allowing conversation. "Trent's not dancing?"

"No. His foot is still too sore, but he won't ask anyway. He's afraid people will talk."

"And they would." They turned in a gentle circle. "I've heard some speculation already."

Anna looked up at him with a slight frown. "Such as?"

"One of the first things most lonesome cowboys think about. They wondered if he's sharing your bed. 'Course they don't have the nerve to say anything to his face."

"But they did to you?" she asked in surprise.

"No, I just happened to be walking by."

Anna searched Shane's eyes. "You know I wouldn't sleep with him, don't you?"

"Of course. And I told the men as much. Don't pay them any mind. They're jealous because he sees your pretty face every day instead of mine or Kingsley's."

"He also puts up with two rowdy boys."

"And enjoys every minute."

Anna laughed as Shane maneuvered her around a cowboy with two left feet. "Not every one. There are times he'd like to wring their necks, but he just clenches his teeth and doesn't say a word."

"He loves those boys, Anna. I saw how he went to Mitch when he got hurt." A deep frown creased his forehead. "But I have the feeling some of the men know something about him that they don't want us to find out."

The music stopped and Anna slipped her hand around his arm, gently drawing him to the edge of the crowd. "What do you mean?"

"A couple of times today, I've heard his name mentioned as I walked by, but when the cowboys noticed me, they quickly changed the topic of conversation. I'm judging from their expressions as much as anything. They looked edgy, like they were hiding something. I didn't push it. I figure if Hank thinks I need to know, he'll tell me. The fact that he obviously counts Trent as a friend says plenty in my book.'' He glanced at a large man plowing his way across the wagon sheet in their direction.

''Looks like my turn is over. Here comes George to claim you for his polka.'' Shane winked and tugged gently on her long braid. ''Have fun.''

Anna rolled her eyes, then turned with a smile to the bewhiskered, middle-aged man. The cowboy had worked on Shane's ranch for years and loved to dance. He never missed a polka, though she was not always his partner. By the time the song ended, she'd be tired but laughing at his enthusiasm.

A young red-faced cowboy escorted Rachel onto the dance floor, and Duncan led Mary Beth by the hand, stopping next to his sister. Over the young woman's head, he winked at Anna and mouthed, ''Don't worry.'' Anna supposed he had to dance with the girl or risk offending the family.

The afternoon passed quickly, filled with music, dancing and laughter. Twilight fell, and Shane lit a couple of coal oil lanterns on the front and back porches. Hank lit others and hung them in the three mesquites around the house and from some specially built poles. They cast a soft glow across the yard.

Since the men outnumbered the women three to one, Anna danced every dance. Most of the cowboys did not have many opportunities to spend time with ladies, and they thoroughly enjoyed themselves. She noted that Ian danced with Rachel once during the afternoon and again shortly after dark, but he didn't seem to be favoring her with his attentions.

A cowboy named Rich Peters did, however. He was a

handsome charmer in his midtwenties and escorted Rachel out onto the dance floor as often as possible. She seemed to enjoy his company, though Anna caught her glancing in Ian's direction several times.

Robert Kingsley politely asked Anna for a waltz. Though they had been neighbors for years, she did not know him well. Like Edwin had done, she considered him an acquaintance rather than a friend.

"How did you fare in the blizzard?" he asked, guiding her around the wagon sheet with a grace unexpected for his large size.

"We lost five calves and ten cows. How about you?"

"Twice that. Would you be in the market to sell part of your herd? They came through the winter better than any I've seen. You were wise to buy the extra hay last fall."

Anna couldn't hide her smile. "That's not what you said at the time."

"Like most of the men around here, I arrogantly thought I knew best." Smiling, he bowed his head. "You proved us wrong."

Anna laughed. "Mr. Kingsley, I'm surprised that you would admit such a thing."

"You are a brave and beautiful woman, Mrs. Caldwell. I find it easy to be honest with you." He swept her around in a turn, drawing her closer, his eyes filled with warmth. "I will even admit that I have wanted to come calling for some time, but with the economic situation, it seemed prudent to wait. Now, I feel reasonably assured I will have something to offer you." A twinkle lit his eyes. "And I'm not just trying to buy your cattle at a good price."

Oh, dear! She'd had no inkling of his interest. "I will only be selling a few head, and I've promised those to Shane."

Kingsley's expression sobered. "Have you made him any other promises?"

"No. We are friends, nothing more." Anna took a deep breath and met his gaze. "Mr. Kingsley, I'm flattered, but you must remember I have four children."

"And fine children they are. Rachel is growing up to be a beautiful young woman—almost as lovely as her mama. Duncan is already practically a full-grown man." Kingsley stopped dancing and stepped off the wagon sheet, his hand pressing gently against the small of her back. "Walk with me, please."

They moved away from the crowd, stopping at the end of the row of buggies and wagons. It gave them privacy, but Anna was relieved when he did not attempt to go farther from the others. She rested her hand on the back of the buckboard next to them. "Mr. Kingsley, you've been a good neighbor to me, and I appreciate it. But I'm not looking for a husband."

"The young boys especially need a father, and I have a fondness for children." He covered her hand with his. "I greatly admire you, Anna. Not only your beauty, but your strength and intelligence as well. You have succeeded where most would have given up."

She carefully eased her hand from beneath his. "Because I'm very stubborn. Since Edwin died, I've become very independent and set in my ways. I'm not exactly even tempered, and neither are you."

"I would be if I had a sweet woman to keep me happy."

"Perhaps." Anna looked down at the ground, then slowly raised her head, meeting his gaze in the moonlight. "I'm deeply touched by your interest and admiration, but I wouldn't make you a good wife. It would be best if you don't come calling, Mr. Kingsley."

"You won't even give me a chance?" he asked with a dark frown.

"It would be a waste of your time," she said gently. "I'm sorry."

"So am I." He looked away, a muscle tightening in his jaw. A minute later, he held out his arm. "We'd better go back before the cowboys string me up for taking you off the dance floor."

Anna slipped her hand around his arm. "Thank you for understanding."

"I see the way of it, but I don't like it."

"I wouldn't expect you to right now."

In spite of dancing to almost every tune, Anna kept an eye on the younger boys. As soon as the sun went down, they promised to stay close to the house. For a while they played marbles beside the porch beneath one of the lanterns, then moved inside to play dominoes and tell stories. When she went to check on them around eight-thirty, Davy was still playing, but Mitch was nowhere to be seen.

"Davy, do you know where Mitch is?"

"Yes, ma'am. He's with Trent out back."

"Thanks. Your eyelids are lookin' mighty heavy. Are you ready to bed down?"

"Not yet, Mama." Davy yawned and sat up a little straighter. "I'm not sleepy."

She smiled and ruffled his hair. "I made a pallet for you boys on the floor in Shane's bedroom, so you go on in when you want to." She figured it wouldn't be long until he gave up the fight.

Anna walked through the house and out the back door. A dimmed lantern hung near the porch steps, leaving the rest of the area in shadows. Trent sat in a rocking chair at one end of the porch, his foot propped up on the railing, holding her sleeping son in his lap. Mitch snuggled up against him in contentment and security. "Has he been asleep long?" she asked softly.

"Maybe twenty minutes. He wore himself plumb out."

"Thanks for taking care of him."

"No problem." A trace of huskiness tinted his voice.

"I put some quilts down in Shane's bedroom for the boys. I don't know if we'll stay all night, but they will both be asleep before Duncan and Rachel are ready to leave."

"I'll carry him inside." He gently lowered his foot from the railing and stood gingerly so as not to wake the little boy.

"You don't have to move too carefully. About the only way you could wake him up would be to drop him."

Anna led the way to Shane's bedroom and the temporary bed. Three other small children were already asleep in another corner of the room.

Trent knelt down and eased Mitch onto the pallet, resting his head on a pillow. "Do you want his boots off?" he whispered.

"Yes." She stood back and let Trent tend to the little boy, touched by his gentleness. He slipped the boots from Mitch's feet and set them next to the wall. Spreading a blanket over him, he tucked it around him. Every movement revealed his love for her son.

When he stood, he gazed at Mitch for a minute, his expression tinged with sorrow. "Thank you," he said softly, looking at Anna.

Seeing the depth of his emotion, a lump threatened to clog her throat. "For what?" she whispered. She should be the one expressing her gratitude.

"For letting me hold him, put him to bed." He drew a deep breath, sighing heavily. "For trusting me with him."

"You've never given me any reason not to trust you."

Anna thought she saw him flinch. ''You've been so good for him. After Edwin died, Mitch didn't talk for months, not a single word. I've always wondered if it was because I yelled at him to be quiet,'' she said with a shudder.

Trent's hand touched her bare forearm. She stepped farther back into the dark corner, awareness rippling through her as his fingers closed around her arm, and he followed her.

''In time, he returned to a talkative little boy, but it seemed as if he were afraid to get too close to anyone except me. He loved the other kids, but he always held something back until you came along. I almost cried the first time I saw him standing next to the rocker, leaning against your arm. Somehow, you set him free from his fears.''

Trent cleared his throat. ''I didn't do anything in particular. He was the one who kinda latched onto me. Not that I mind. I'm mighty fond of the little guy.''

''You love him like a son,'' she whispered.

His fingers flexed against her arm before he released her and silently walked from the room and out the back door.

Anna looked down at her sleeping child, thinking of his kinship with Trent. *One wounded soul reaching out to another.*

Leaning against the wall, she wondered if she was doing the same thing. Then she closed her eyes, remembering the touch of his hand, and the kisses they had shared a few days earlier—one sweet and gentle, one hard and quick, hinting of passion beyond anything she had ever experienced.

She shivered again. This time from longing.

Chapter Eight

Anna stopped on the front porch, taking a much needed rest. She spent the next half hour talking to the new school-teacher, an intelligent and practical woman in her early twenties. Though not a beauty, Myra Alexander had a wry sense of humor that often put a delightful sparkle in her bright green eyes.

"Lizzie tells me you've been to Europe, Miss Alexander," said Anna. She couldn't help wonder why someone who had traveled so extensively would settle in such a small town as Antelope Springs.

"Please call me Myra. It makes me feel less like a newcomer. I visited a handful of countries in Europe two years ago, though I wasn't able to see nearly as many sites as I longed to. I went as a hired companion to a middle-aged spinster from New York." Myra rolled her eyes and grinned. "She disliked practically every place we visited. I finally asked her why she had ventured across the sea in the first place."

"What did she say?"

"She wanted something new to discuss at dinner parties, which meant she had run out of things to complain about.

Still, I am indebted to her for choosing me to accompany her. I never would have been able to go there on my own."

"What country did you enjoy the most?"

Myra considered the question thoughtfully. "I found them all wonderful in one way or another. Southern France and Greece had the best climate, and the coast along the Mediterranean Sea is beautiful. I loved the food in Italy, and touring the ancient ruins there and in Greece was a dream come true. But I think I enjoyed England and Scotland the most."

She laughed, absently running her fingertip along the porch railing. "I could understand the language most of the time, in England anyway. It is lovely, so neat and green, with beautiful flowers and history every way you turn. Practically every village and town has buildings hundreds of years old."

Anna glanced across the yard, noting that Kingsley was no longer dancing. He stood on the sidelines, wearing the expression of a man who wished he were some place else. "And Scotland? What did you like there?"

"Everything. The people, scenery, food, music, their deeply held sense of nationalism, though they are no longer a completely independent country. I found them intriguing." Myra sighed softly. "And in all my travels, I never found anywhere more beautiful than the Highlands.

"In an odd way, my love of that rugged countryside is partly why I came to Texas. I wanted to live where I could feel that same vastness and freedom."

"Have you met Robert Kingsley?"

"I don't know. I've been introduced to so many gentlemen today that I've forgotten half their names."

Anna surreptitiously looked in his direction, silently thanking him for making himself particularly visible at that moment. "His mother came from the Highlands. He's the red-haired man walking toward the refreshment table."

Myra glanced his way, her eyes widening slightly. "The one in the white shirt and black suit?"

Anna nodded. "He owns the ranch that runs next to mine. I don't know exactly how big it is, but it's much larger than the Double Deuce."

"A man that size needs plenty of room." A smile played across the schoolteacher's lips. "I do believe I'm in need of a cup of punch."

"I'm rather thirsty myself." Anna smiled, hoping she was doing a kind turn for both the schoolteacher and Robert Kingsley. "I should warn you that he sometimes has a hot temper. Though since my husband's death, he has been a good and kind neighbor."

"My brother has quite a temper, so I can probably hold my own. I'd prefer not to be too obvious," said Myra as they walked down the porch steps.

"Stop and talk to Lizzie for a minute. I'll see if I can lure him over your way."

Myra giggled. "Poor man. We sound as if we're setting a trap."

"We are." Anna grinned and proceeded toward the refreshment table.

Kingsley handed her a cup of punch when she stepped up beside him. "I don't suppose you've changed your mind?" he asked gloomily.

"No, but I just met someone who might cheer you up."

He shook his head. "Not now, Anna. I'm not in the mood to attempt polite conversation."

"I think you would find her interesting." Anna took a sip of the fruit punch. "Her name is Myra Alexander. She's the new schoolteacher in Antelope Springs."

"And she'll rap my knuckles with a ruler the first time

my grammar slips. I can't see me calling on a school-marm.''

"Not even if she has visited Scotland, and thinks the Highlands are beautiful?'' Anna looked up at him over the rim of her cup.

Kingsley's gaze darted to the schoolteacher. "She's been to my mother's homeland?''

"Two years ago. Would you like to meet her?''

He nodded. "But only to talk about Scotland." He looked down at Anna, anger and passion flaring in his eyes. "You're the one I want.''

Uneasiness quickened her pulse. "Robert, I'm sorry I hurt you, but it would be cruel to encourage you when I know we would make a poor match.''

"You don't know me well enough to be sure we would.''

"But I know myself,'' she said gently. "I could never make you happy. I'm used to running my ranch and my life in my own way. You deserve someone who can love you with all her heart." Anna held her breath, hoping he wouldn't insult the schoolteacher by refusing to meet her.

He glanced at Myra and frowned. "I suppose she's expectin' me to go over there.''

"Not exactly." Anna wondered if her timing had been way off. "But I think she would be pleased if you did, as long as you could muster a smile instead of a scowl.''

"You mean I can't test her mettle by glaring at her?'' A tiny smile hovered about his mouth.

Anna chuckled and set her empty cup on the table, picking up a cup of punch for Myra. "I have a feeling she just might pass your test anyway, but it would be kinder not to.''

They joined Lizzie and the schoolteacher, and Anna made the introductions.

Myra smiled up at Kingsley, her green eyes sparkling with a hint of mischief.

Anna and Lizzie slipped away as the schoolteacher and the rancher shared their love of Scotland. "What are you up to, Anna?" asked Lizzie. "Earlier, I could have sworn Kingsley was looking at you like a man bent on courtship."

"He wanted to come calling, but I told him not to."

"Why not? He has plenty of money."

"He's a nice enough man, but I can't see myself marrying him."

"Because you have your eye on someone else. Trent and Kingsley are opposites in looks and temperament. But Kingsley has something to offer. Trent doesn't."

"I have everything I need, as far as the ranch goes. I don't find Kingsley the least bit attractive. He just doesn't appeal to me."

"And Trent does. He has a way about him, if you like the quiet type."

Anna smiled ruefully. "He doesn't need to talk a lot. He can set my heart to racing with a look."

Lizzie grinned, a knowing twinkle in her eyes. "Kingsley could be a difficult man to get along with."

"We'd be at each other's throats within a week. Trent and I work alike most of the time." Anna looked around for him, tenderness warming her heart as she thought of the way he treated the horses. He'd be just as gentle with a woman. To her disappointment, she didn't see him.

She couldn't find her stepdaughter, either. "Lizzie, do you see Rachel anywhere?" Anna stood on tiptoe, looking across the dancers, hoping she had simply missed her.

"No, I don't. Maybe she went in the house. I'll go check."

As Lizzie hurried toward the front door, Anna walked around the yard. Spying Rachel's friend, Claire, on the dance floor, Anna waited a couple of minutes until the song ended, then stopped her before the music started again. "Do you know where Rachel is?"

The young woman glanced around with a frown. "She's not back yet?"

"Back from where?"

Claire caught her bottom lip between her teeth, looking uncomfortable.

"Where did she go?" Anna grabbed her arm. "Tell me."

"For a walk down by the corrals with Rich. Just to catch her breath and cool off from all the dancing."

"Lord have mercy. Why did she have to go with him?" Anna scanned the yard for Trent or Shane. They were nowhere in sight. Neither was Duncan. *Where's a man when you need him?*

Claire shrugged. "Rich is sweet."

"He's trouble." Anna quickly headed toward the barn and corrals, praying that Rachel wouldn't fall prey to the silver-tongued charmer. The girl didn't know a thing about men.

On the way, she went by a small cluster of cowboys sharing a bottle of whiskey. She didn't want to think about what might happen if Rich had been drinking. Nearing the barn, she spied a man hovering in the shadows. Anna slowed, holding her breath. A moment later, he stepped into her path, clearly visible in the moonlight. *Trent!* Anna's breath came out in a rush. "Have you seen Rachel?" she asked softly.

He nodded, reaching for her hand and drawing her into the darkness beside the barn. Trent pointed toward the north side of the corral. "She's over there talking to Peters," he whispered. "I saw them leave together, so I followed."

Relief almost brought tears to her eyes. She squeezed his hand. "Thank you. I should have kept a closer eye on her."

"She's a woman, Anna. You can't watch her every minute."

"You did."

"Got nothin' better to do. Besides, I knew Peters might be trouble. So far, he hasn't tried anything."

"I should go get her before he does." But Anna hesitated. She didn't want to embarrass Rachel, and like it or not, the girl needed to learn to handle potentially dangerous situations. *Oh, Edwin, I wish you were here.*

"Might be better to see how it goes," whispered Trent. "She'll have plenty of help if she needs it. Ian took off after them before I could get around the dancers. He's on the other side of the granary."

Which meant he was closer to Rachel than they were. "I wish I could hear what Peters is telling her."

"I don't think they'll notice if we go on down to the end of the barn—if we don't talk."

Anna nodded. Holding her hand, he led the way to the corner of the barn. From their new vantage point, they could hear Rachel and the cowboy and see them clearly in the moonlight.

"Don't you get lonesome out here by yourself?" asked Peters, edging closer to Rachel.

"Usually, I'm too busy to think about it." She looked up at him. "Anna runs the ranch, so I take care of the house and the younger boys."

"You work too hard."

"I enjoy it. I like to cook, and Anna doesn't expect the house to be spotless." Rachel laughed softly. "That would be impossible with two boys and a dog running in and out."

"You're a special woman, Rachel." Peters caught hold

of her hand and lifted it to his lips, dropping a kiss on her knuckles.

Anna tensed, and Trent's fingers tightened around hers. Did she imagine it, or was Rachel leaning a little closer to the handsome cowboy? There probably wasn't a girl at the party who didn't wonder what it would be like to kiss him.

Peters slipped his arm around Rachel's waist, pulling her closer. "Have you ever been kissed, sweet Rachel?"

She shook her head, then slowly looked up at him.

Trent started to move, but Anna laid her hand on his chest and leaned up to whisper in his ear. "Let her have her first kiss. If he tries anything else, we'll pounce."

He nodded, releasing her hand. A second later, he slid his arm around her waist, holding her against his side. Anna suddenly felt like a young girl sneaking off from the party with her beau. Forcing her attention back to her stepdaughter, she was relieved to see that the cowboy's kiss was gentle and short.

Rachel shyly glanced away. "We'd better go back."

"Not yet."

Startled, Rachel looked up.

Rich jerked her against him, his kiss rough and hard. Struggling, she hit him with her fists, but he held her fast.

With a small cry, Anna took a step forward, but Trent tugged her back. Wrapping both arms around her, he held her close, her back against his chest. "Let Ian do it," he whispered in her ear.

Anna tried to pull away, until she saw that Ian had already reached Rachel.

He clamped down on Peters' shoulders with both hands, ripping him away from her. Ian threw the cowboy against the corral fence. "Stay away from her!" he ordered in a hushed but deadly voice.

"Hey!" Peters straightened, doubling up his fists. "We were just having a little fun."

"The lady doesn't think so. Get out of here before I break your jaw."

"I'm not afraid of a highfalutin lawyer."

"You should be." Ian moved with lightning speed, landing a powerful punch in Peters' stomach.

The cowboy doubled over with a groan.

Ian shoved him back against the fence. "The only reason you aren't a bloody mess right now is because I don't want anyone asking questions. You breathe a word about being here with Miss Rachel, and I guarantee you'll regret it. Understand?"

Holding his stomach, Peters nodded.

"Now, apologize to the lady."

Rich glanced at Rachel, who stood off to one side, fighting back tears. "Sorry." He took a shallow, wheezy breath. "Shouldn't have done that."

She nodded curtly and turned her back on him.

Ian rested his hands on his hips and stared at the other man. "Leave."

Peters stumbled away, swearing at Ian under his breath as he passed Trent and Anna. He didn't even notice them.

Anna ached to go to Rachel but knew she should let Ian take care of her. The experience was bad enough, but Rachel would be mortified if she learned they'd had an audience.

Ian put his arm around Rachel, speaking so quietly Anna couldn't understand him. Rachel shook her head. He spoke louder, suggesting they walk around the granary to the spring house. They moved away, and Anna wondered if he knew she and Trent were beside the barn.

"She's safe now," whispered Trent.

Greatly relieved, Anna nodded, her temple brushing his

cheek, sending a spark through her. They were alone in the darkness, his hard body touching hers from shoulder to thigh. His strong arms held her firmly against him, and the faint scent of shaving soap and clean, masculine skin teased her nostrils. Longing swept through her, a need so intense, it made her reckless.

Closing her hands over his, she kept his arms around her. She felt his sharp breath as his chest expanded against her back. When he kissed the side of her neck, Anna gasped softly and let her head fall forward. The warmth of his lips on the nape of her neck sent a shiver racing down her spine.

In one smooth motion, he turned her to face him, taking her mouth with a hunger that made her knees weak. Anna clung to him, weaving her fingers in his soft, black hair, her passion matching his. He kissed her again and again, his hands roaming over her, his restless but tender touch stirring her desire until she whimpered with need. Tears of pure joy sprang to her eyes and slid down her cheeks, one salty drop slipping between their lips.

Trent froze, then abruptly raised his head. He looked away, swearing softly, his voice rough, his breathing ragged. "I'm no better than Peters. Anna, forgive me." He slumped against the wall of the barn and closed his eyes.

Anna stared up at him in a daze, thankful he hadn't released her. If he did, she'd wind up sitting on the ground. "What are you talking about?"

He looked at her, his expression reflecting despair and self-contempt. "I made you cry."

She smiled and nodded, resting her hands on his shoulders. "Tears of joy. You make me feel alive, like a woman, not a cold, empty shell."

He shook his head, a bemused smile drifting across his face. "Sugar, there is nothin' cold about you. I've got scorch marks."

Anna giggled. "We are a little rumpled."

"I may not be worth much, but I'm not so rotten that I'd undress a woman where somebody might walk by any minute," said Trent quietly. He straightened with a grimace. "Instead, I practically make love to you. I'm being mighty careful of your reputation," he said in disgust.

"It wasn't very smart of us, but I don't regret it one bit."

Trent groaned softly. "Woman, you'd better leave before I drag you up to the hayloft."

Anna wrinkled her nose. "Hay is prickly and itchy."

His eyebrows shot up. "How do you know?"

"Because I work with it every day." She laughed and smoothed his hair.

Trent ducked and stepped aside. "I'm goin' back to the party. You'd better go water the horses or something."

"I look that bad?"

He caught her hand and pulled her out into the moonlight. Shaking his head, he traced her swollen lips with the pad of his thumb. "You look that good."

Ian escorted Rachel to the springhouse, keeping his arm firmly around her waist. Trembling, she sank down on a wooden bench outside the door.

He rested his hand on her shoulder, his expression tender. "Would you like a drink of water?"

"Yes, please." Rachel closed her eyes and leaned her head against the stone building. It would take more than water to wash away the bitter taste of Rich Peters. Hot tears seeped from beneath her lashes, burning a trail down her cheeks. *How could I have been so stupid?*

Earlier, when Ian didn't show her as much attention as she wanted, she had encouraged Rich's flirting. It made the evening fun. She went walking with him, knowing he would try to kiss her. She'd wanted him to. Though he was good with the sweet talk, he acted like a gentleman and the first kiss was sweet and tender. But the second one.... Rachel shivered, remembering the crush of his arms, and how he ground his mouth against hers, forcing her lips apart.

"Here's some water." Ian handed her a dipper of sweet, cold springwater. As she drank, he removed his jacket. "Lean forward a little." When she did, he draped the coat around her shoulders. "Better?"

She nodded, finishing off the water in the dipper. The jacket, still warm from his body and smelling lightly of spicy cologne, slowly dispelled her chill. But the tears could not be stopped so easily.

Ian took the dipper from her hand and laid it inside the springhouse, shutting the door. He sat down on the bench, putting his arm around her, and handed her his handkerchief. "Rachel, don't cry."

"I—I can't help it." She wiped her eyes with the soft, white linen. Her tears still flowing, Rachel sighed heavily. "You must think I'm a foolish child."

Ian smoothed a strand of hair back from her cheek and gently pushed her head against his shoulder. "No, I don't. You're a beautiful woman who has had little experience with men. And that suits me just fine."

"I should never have come down here with him."

"No, you shouldn't have." He shrugged lightly. "But, then I wouldn't have been able to come to your rescue and show you how noble I am."

"I'm so thankful you were nearby." She looked up at him, the tears slowly subsiding. "Were you checking on the horses?"

"No, I followed you down here."

To see how I'd behave, what kind of woman I am. Rachel's stomach rolled, and for a second, she was terrified she would disgrace herself even further. "To see how shameful I am?" she whispered, looking down at her lap, fresh tears stinging her eyes.

"To keep you safe." He nudged her chin up so she met his gaze. "It's natural for a young woman to want to be kissed."

She looked away from the tenderness and understanding in his eyes, anger and renewed fear surging through her. "It was disgusting! If that's what kissing is all about, I don't want any part of it. I'd rather be an old maid."

"That would truly be a waste." He rested his hand at her side. "When a man cares for a woman, his kisses— even the passionate ones—make her feel cherished."

She shook her head. "Just the thought of it repulses me."

He was quiet for a minute. "Rachel, do you trust me?"

"Yes," she said without hesitation.

"Are your lips sore?"

Her heart began to pound, both in fear and excitement. Thinking she was losing her mind, she licked her lips, testing them. "Not much."

"Look at me, sweetheart," he whispered.

Rachel slowly raised her head, meeting his gaze—and almost ran. Desire smoldered in his eyes. As if sensing her fear, Ian's hand tightened on her shoulder, his grip firm but gentle.

He cradled her jaw in his other hand, caressing her cheek with his thumb.

She swallowed hard, held captive by the mixture of tenderness and passion in his eyes.

"You are beautiful, with your cheeks like roses and little golden wisps of hair curling around your face like lacy sunshine. I want to kiss you, Rachel. I want to show you how it is when a man cares for a woman. May I?"

Rachel's heart and mind fought a battle between longing and fear. How often had she imagined him holding her just this way? Well, not quite like this. He was always so polite and controlled around her, she'd never dreamed of the passion simmering below the surface.

"I'd never hurt you, Rachel."

"I know." She let her eyelids drift closed and tilted her face, holding her breath.

Ian kissed her with exquisite tenderness, as if she were a priceless treasure to be revered. The memory of Rich's taste and touch vanished in a heartbeat. Rachel slid her hands around Ian's neck, leaning against his chest.

His arms tightened and the pressure of his lips increased, but there was no pain, no fear. Only pleasure, a rush of desire, and a deep, profound feeling that he cherished her more than anything in the world. He eased his hold and brushed several tiny kisses across her mouth before finally lifting his head.

She looked up at him, knowing her face and eyes glowed with happiness and newfound pleasure. "Thank you," she whispered.

"No more fears?" he asked with a smile.

"Never with you."

He brushed a strand of hair behind her ear. "How do you feel?"

Heat rushed to her face. "Cherished."

"Good." His smile deepened. "And how else?"

"Like I just ate a bowl of chili peppers."

Ian threw back his head and laughed. "I have a feeling this is going to be a very short courtship."

"Why, sir, are we courting?" Rachel looked up at him with feigned innocence.

He tightened his arms as his expression sobered. "Yes,

ma'am. It is my intention, Rachel Caldwell, to make you my bride.''

Joy filled her heart. "My, you're confident."

"Lawyers usually are." A frown creased his brow. "If there's no hope, tell me now. I'll not run the race if there is no chance to win the prize."

Rachel caressed his cheek, surprising herself by her boldness, and gave him a tiny kiss. "A man can't run against himself."

"But he can cause his own defeat if he moves too quickly," he said, releasing her and standing. "I came down here to make Peters behave and keep your reputation intact. And here I am, risking damaging it myself."

Rachel smiled happily as he held out his hand and pulled her to her feet. "I don't think it would damage my reputation at all if someone caught us. I expect they'd figure I was pretty smart."

Chapter Nine

"Here comes trouble." Staring in the direction of the corrals, Hank slowly straightened, moving away from the porch railing. "I'd hoped Bender would stay occupied in town all night."

Trent followed his friend's gaze to the man storming across the yard toward them, and his heart sank. His sins were about to be exposed. Ned Bender had worked at the Williams' ranch when he did. They had never been friends but had managed to work together without a problem—until Rosie, Williams' wife, decided she wanted Trent.

Bender had been head over heels in love with Rosie, but she was the kind of woman who quickly tired of her conquests and looked for a new one. Trent did everything he could to dissuade her politely. Unfortunately, she liked a challenge.

Trent and Hank walked off the porch to meet him. The man's abrupt entrance had already attracted attention. There was no way to avoid a confrontation. Trent prayed it was only a verbal one. Bender wore a gun. Trent didn't.

"Malloy, you got no right to be here," Bender said loudly. He stopped a few feet in front of Trent and gave him a shove.

Trent stood his ground, but it cost him. For a second, he clenched his teeth against the pain in his foot. "This isn't the time or the place, Bender."

"Why not? Afraid people will find out you been in Huntsville? You should have been hung for what you did to Rosie."

Several women gasped, and the men hustled them back away from Trent and Bender.

"I didn't do anything to her," said Trent, trying to keep his voice calm.

"You tried to rape her!"

More gasps and angry murmurs buzzed in his ears. "No, I didn't."

"Ned, you know that's not the way it was," said Hank, staying by Trent's side.

"You had her pinned against the wall. Her clothes were half torn off." Bender edged his hand toward his pistol, his fingers twitching.

"Move over, Hank," ordered Trent. When his old friend hesitated, he reached up and shoved him aside, not taking his gaze off Bender. "I was trying to protect her from the old man and his bullwhip. If her clothes were torn, he did it."

Shane silently moved behind Bender. Trent carefully avoided looking at him, so he wouldn't accidentally warn the cowboy of his presence.

"Her dress was open halfway down the front. He couldn't have done that with the whip. You forced her, and she left because of it," shouted Bender, reaching for his gun.

Shane grabbed him before he could touch the revolver and twisted his arm around behind his back. "Hank, take the gun."

Hank plucked the pistol from the holster and stepped

back beside Trent. "Ned, don't be a fool. Rosie was more than willing, and you know it."

When Shane released him, Bender rubbed his arm and glared at Hank. "You can lie about what Malloy did to Rosie, but you can't deny he stole Williams' horses. Not when they caught him red-handed."

The news stirred up the onlookers like throwing a nest of yellow jackets into the middle of the crowd. "Horse thief!"

"How many did he steal?"

"He attacked that woman!"

"How could Mrs. Caldwell hire him?"

"Imagine, a man like that around her and Rachel."

"Outlaw."

"Don't they hang horse thieves?"

"Naw, they don't hang horse thieves much any-more…not if the law catches them." Bender sneered at Trent. "You're stupider than I thought, Malloy. Did you think you could keep it a secret forever?" He looked right at Anna. "He spent five years in prison. Ain't been out but a couple of months."

Angry comments erupted all around her, but Anna barely heard them. A quick denial sprang to her lips, but she held back the words when she met Trent's gaze. Stark despair filled his countenance. *I've made some real bad choices, done things I'll regret the rest of my life.*

Anna thought she might suffocate. Though she saw the truth in his eyes, she shook her head in disbelief. The other words he had spoken earlier whispered in her mind. *Thank you for all you've given me, for showing me that there is still good in the world.* She drew a shaky breath. Only something terrible would have driven him to steal. She looked away, not wanting him to see her hurt, desperately wondering why he hadn't told her.

"He paid the penalty for his actions," said Hank. "He deserves another chance."

Anna's heart agreed, but her mind protested. *He's a horse thief! A convict. A liar.*

"What about attacking that woman?" asked Mrs. Upton.

Anna clenched her hands to stop them from trembling and looked at Trent. Denial burned in his eyes. She thought of his gentleness and compassion and the moments they had been alone when he could have harmed her and didn't.

"Trent Malloy would never force himself on a woman." Anna was relieved that her voice was clear and strong, not exposing the betrayal and agony she felt.

Mrs. Upton ignored her. "It doesn't sound as if anyone did anything about that."

Everyone started talking at once.

Anna wanted desperately to rush back to the Double Deuce where she could hide, cry and yell at Trent. But at the moment, the growing number of angry neighbors and townspeople gathering around him and Shane was her main concern.

Trent had hated himself for a long time but never as much as at that moment. He glanced at Duncan, and the expression in the boy's eyes cut him to the quick—hurt, confusion, distrust and anger all rolled into one.

"Malloy, I ought to beat the livin' daylights out of you," said Parker in a low, deadly voice.

Trent forced himself to look at Anna's friend. "Yeah, you should, but I doubt that would make her feel any better."

"It's a little late to be thinking about Anna's feelings." Parker glanced around at the crowd, his frown deepening.

"I figured if somebody recognized me there would be talk and eventually she'd hear it. I didn't expect her to find out like this."

Suddenly, she was in front of him. Trent's chest constricted at the pain in her eyes, and he held his breath, bracing for her anger. Though she had defended him, she had every right to rail at him. She held his gaze for a moment, then silently stepped beside him, standing against her friends and neighbors. His heart pounded even harder. "Anna, go back to the porch."

"No."

Shane moved to his other side, facing the guests. "Keep calm folks. Don't let this get out of hand."

"I don't take kindly to a horse thief livin' next to me," said Kingsley. Trent hadn't met him, but Hank had pointed him out, mentioning that he had a hot temper.

"I'm not interested in your horses, Mr. Kingsley. Or anybody else's."

"Is it true, Trent?" Duncan's voice vibrated with anger. "Did you steal those horses?"

"I did. At the time, my reasons seemed justified, but they weren't. It was wrong and the stupidest thing I've ever done. I paid for it with five miserable years." Trent looked slowly around the crowd, meeting first one angry gaze, then another. "I won't ever do anything that might send me back to prison. All I want is a chance to live a normal life, working on a ranch and thanking the Almighty each day for my freedom."

"What about attackin' that rancher's wife?" asked a man from town. "How do we know Mrs. Caldwell and her daughter—or our wives and daughters—are safe with you around?" More angry murmurs followed his question.

An icy knot hardened in Trent's stomach. "I did not attack Mrs. Williams."

"I was with Williams when he found his wife and Trent," said Hank. "It was common knowledge that she had been with some of the other cowboys, and the old man had to suspect it. But he didn't want to believe the kind of woman she was.

"She'd been after Trent for weeks, but he avoided her. It was clear to all of us that he didn't want anything to do with her. When we walked into the barn, she was kissing him, holding on to his neck and the back of his head for all she was worth. He was trying to pry her hands loose and pull free."

Trent's gaze raced over the crowd. He figured most of them knew Hank was an honest man. A few listened to him with thoughtful expressions. Most were still riled up.

Hank continued. "Williams never said a word. Just laid that bullwhip across Trent's back and split it open. Then he swung it again, yelling at his wife that he was goin' to cut her up so bad no man would want her."

Several of the women gasped and covered their mouths with their hands. A few men shook their heads.

Trent knew they would come nearer believing Hank than him, and the truth needed telling. But it was hard to hear it, harder still to remember those horrible moments. He tried to block out the sound of Hank's voice, filling his mind with thoughts of Anna, wishing he knew how to explain, to heal the hurt he had caused her.

"Trent pinned her against the wall all right, protecting her," said Hank. "He shielded her body with his so the old man couldn't get to her with the whip. I tried to stop Williams, but he was a big man, and he knocked me down. It took three of us to wrestle that bullwhip away from him. By that time, Trent's back was sliced all to pieces. He hung onto consciousness until he knew we had the old man subdued, then he passed out and fell to the ground. Rosie was crying and carrying on. She went running to her husband, sayin' Trent attacked her. It was plain as day that he hadn't, but Williams chose her story over the truth.

"He told a couple of the men to take Trent out on the prairie and leave him for the coyotes. They were afraid of what the boss might do to them if they refused, so they followed his orders—"

"Merciful heavens!" exclaimed Rachel, her eyes pooling with tears. Lizzie put her arm around her.

"If they hadn't told me where they took him, he would have died during the night in a way no man should have to suffer."

A stunned silence fell over the crowd. Trent felt Anna's arm brush against his as she shuddered. He had to explain what happened in private. But how? When her trembling didn't stop, he decided to get her away from the others, even if he had to fight his way clear.

"Mama?" Mitch's sleepy, frightened voice cut through the still night.

"No...." breathed Trent. He and Anna spun toward the house.

The wretchedness in that whispered word told Anna more about the man beside her than anything Ned Bender shouted to the world.

Mitch stood on the porch, rubbing his eyes, his lower lip trembling. Davy was behind him, resting his hands on his brother's shoulders. His wide-eyed gaze darted back and forth from Anna to Trent and the men closest to them.

Anna hurried to Mitch, kneeling down in front of him, wrapping him in a hug. "It's all right, honey."

"Why are they yellin' at Trent?" Mitch put his arms around her neck, but looked at Trent.

"There's been a misunderstanding." She touched Davy on the hand in encouragement, then picked up Mitch and turned to her neighbors and friends. "Please, stop this for the sake of my children. Duncan, hitch up the horses. We're going home."

Duncan nodded and rushed off to where he had tethered the horses.

Anna looked at Rachel. "Help Davy gather up their things."

"Yes, ma'am." Rachel moved to the porch and held out her hand to Davy. He gripped it tightly as they went inside the house, glancing back once at the crowd.

"Don't you want to know the truth, Mrs. Caldwell?" asked Mrs. Upton.

"Hank has told us what happened. Anything more, I'll learn from Trent," said Anna, not completely certain she would. He had already deceived them. Would he try to again? She glanced at him, and seeing the abject misery in his face, doubted it.

"You mean you'd believe him?" The banker's wife snorted. Several others quietly expressed similar thoughts.

"That's up to me, not you." Carrying Mitch, Anna walked down the steps and stopped beside Trent, hoping he would come with them. It didn't take many angry men to turn a party into a mob. "I need you to see us home."

Anna then looked from one face to the next, studying the troubled and angry expressions of her neighbors, friends and acquaintances. She hated them for believing Ned over Hank, for instantly passing judgment on a man they didn't even know. Yet, she understood the fear behind their actions, fear for her safety and well-being—and their own.

"What I've heard tonight and what I know about Trent are very different things. Hank is an honest and truthful man, and he says Trent didn't attack Mrs. Williams. But even if Hank didn't stand up for him, I could never believe that Trent Malloy would force himself on a woman. He has treated Rachel and me with complete respect and courtesy.

"He almost died during the blizzard. When we got to him, he was unconscious. His face, hands and feet were frostbitten. One foot was so bad, I was afraid he might lose some of his toes.''

She shifted Mitch's weight, supporting him with her other arm. ''The day after the storm stopped, Duncan and I rode out to check on the cattle. It took us longer than expected, and when we returned, Trent was getting ready to go look for us. The man could barely walk, both from weakness and his injuries. Putting boots on his swollen, aching feet had to be pure agony.'' Her voice caught, and she paused to clear her throat. ''But he was willing—determined—to risk his life to make sure we were safe and to keep Davy and Rachel from going out in the snow.

''As far as stealing my horses, or anyone else's, Trent could have taken them dozens of times over the past couple of weeks, but he hasn't. Tonight would have been perfect. He could have ridden off with the whole herd while we were here. He paid for his crime. He deserves the chance to make a new life.'' A few people nodded, others seemed to carefully consider her words. Some, like Kingsley, remained hostile. ''Trent started helping at the ranch before he was able, doing a full day's work even though he was in constant pain. We've never had anyone do a better job. Now, I understand why he tried so hard to prove he was reliable.''

''Shane, you gonna let him go with her?'' asked one of the cowboys from a neighboring ranch.

Shane glanced at Trent and Anna, then looked back at the men and women standing around them. ''Anna makes her own decisions. If she wants Trent to go back to the ranch, that's her business.''

Davy came out the front door, carrying a small cloth bag of marbles and Mitch's shoes. Rachel was behind him, holding two quilts.

''You'll wish you'd stopped her when you start losin'

horses," said Bender. He motioned toward Rachel, lust glinting in his eyes. "Or when he lifts that pretty little honey's skirts and takes a sample."

Anna barely saw Trent's movement as he landed a hard, swift punch to Bender's jaw. The man stumbled backward, and Duncan's friend, Tim, obligingly stuck out his foot to trip him. Breathing rapidly and clenching his fists, Trent glared at Bender. "Watch your mouth in front of the women."

Ian stepped between them and hauled the cowboy to his feet. "Don't talk that way about Rachel." He drove home his point with an uppercut to the other side of Bender's jaw.

Bender staggered backward but managed to remain standing. "I was just warnin' them about Malloy," he mumbled, holding his face.

Kingsley looked at his foreman. "Riley, see that he goes back to the ranch and stays there."

"Yes, sir, Mr. Kingsley. Come on, Ned."

Bender sent Trent a scathing glance as he walked by. "This isn't finished, Malloy."

Trent sighed and looked at the ground. When he raised his head, he met Shane's gaze. "Hank can tell you all of what happened five years ago. Maybe it would help if he explained it to your guests. I'm sorry to ruin your party. I didn't want to cause any trouble."

Shane studied him for a minute. "No, I don't think you did." He turned to Anna. "You'd better get these tired young'uns home to bed."

"Yes, we should. Trent, would you take Mitch?" she asked quietly. "He's too heavy for me to hold any longer."

Surprise flashed through his eyes. He swallowed hard and held out his hands to the little boy. Mitch went to him without hesitation, curling his arms around Trent's neck and laying his head on his shoulder. A flurry of whispers swept through the crowd as folks moved aside, opening up a narrow pathway. Shane walked with them to the wagon.

Ian waited for Rachel and Davy. When they stepped off the porch, he took the quilts from her, accompanying them.

Shane drew Anna aside while Rachel and Ian made a bed for the boys in the back of the wagon. ''Do you want us to ride home with you?''

''We'll be fine,'' said Anna. ''Bender is the only one I'm worried about, and Riley will keep a close eye on him.''

''What about Trent? He deceived you. I saw your face when Bender was talking. You didn't know a thing about Trent's past.''

''No, I didn't, and that hurts. But we'll talk about it when we get home.''

''He admitted taking those horses, Anna. Working as a cowboy, he'll only make enough to get by. Can you be sure he won't steal from you?''

''He won't take any horses.'' She wished she could be as certain of her heart.

Chapter Ten

Both the younger boys were fast asleep when they reached the Double Deuce. They carried them inside, and Anna and Rachel put them to bed while Trent and Duncan unloaded the wagon. Trent drove the wagon to the barn and tended to the team. Duncan took care of the buckboard and horse. When Trent finished his chore, he blew out the lantern, and walked out of the barn.

Duncan was waiting for him. He studied Trent thoughtfully. "How many horses did you take?"

"Two. A stallion and a mare." Trent closed the door to the barn and turned to face Duncan.

"You stole them because he tried to kill you?"

"That was part of it." Trent spotted Anna coming toward them, the light from her lantern casting eerie shadows in the waning moonlight. "I'm sorry you had to find out the way you did. I wish I'd had the courage to tell you earlier."

"I wish you had, too." Duncan heard Anna approach and turned toward her.

"I'd like to talk to Trent alone, please," she said quietly.

"Yes, ma'am." Duncan looked back at Trent. "You'll tell me the rest of it?" It wasn't exactly a request.

"Before I leave."

Duncan frowned but said nothing and walked toward the house.

"You're leaving?" asked Anna, stopping in front of him.

"Come daylight. I've caused you enough trouble."

"You owe me an explanation."

"Yes, I do, but it's a long story."

"The night's turned cool. I'd rather sit in a chair than in the barn."

Trent opened the door to his room, remembering the last time she had been there. He glanced at her face as she crossed the threshold. If she was thinking about the kisses they'd shared there, it didn't show.

Anna set the lantern on the table, pulled out one of the ladder back chairs, and sat down, crossing her arms.

Wanting to keep some distance between them, Trent settled near the foot of the bed, facing her. He leaned forward, resting his forearms on his thighs, staring at the floor. "I can't tell you how lousy I feel about today. I should have been honest with you long before now."

"Yes, you should have. Why didn't you tell me? I can understand why you didn't say anything at first, but not later, after we got to know each other."

He released a long, heavy sigh and glanced at her. Then wished he hadn't. A tear rolled down her cheek, and she angrily brushed it aside.

Trent looked away. "I tried half a dozen times, but I'd picture what I see on your face right now—revulsion, anger, hurt. Since neither you nor Shane knew about me, I got the crazy notion that maybe nobody around here did. That maybe you wouldn't find out."

"Secrets have a way of coming out in the open."

"Keeping my secret gave me a little more time with you. I selfishly wanted that time, needed it to become civilized again. After I got out of prison, I looked for work at every ranch I came to. Most of the time, all I had to do was say my name, and the rancher or his foreman had me escorted off the property. If they didn't recognize me right away, someone else would, and men who'd been pleasant enough a minute before turned hostile.

"I washed dishes in restaurants for a meal or swept out a saloon now and then to earn enough to buy a plate of beans. I shoveled stalls in livery stables and loaded freight on railroad cars, but it was all temporary labor, barely enough to keep from starving."

He stood, walking over to the window. Resting his hand on the wall beside it, he stared out at the dark prairie. "I'm a cowboy, Anna. It's not just a job, it's who I am. Sometimes we weren't allowed out of our cells for days, maybe weeks. I thought I'd go stark raving loco if I couldn't get outside and see the sky." He glanced up at the stars. "I didn't care if it was sunny or pouring rain, hot or cold. I needed to see more than ten feet in front of me, breathe clean air and feel it on my face."

"Is that why you sleep outside so much of the time?"

He nodded. "I haven't figured out why some nights are worse than others. Sometimes I can't fall asleep indoors at all. Other times, I go to sleep, but wake up and feel like I'm suffocating."

"It's not easy to wrestle with demons," she said softly.

A fragile seed of hope took root in Trent's heart. She knew how it was to be broken, to be chained to the past by guilt, though not shame. "Being with you and the kids has been more than a job. I'm like a wild animal that's been locked up in a cage so long he doesn't remember how to be free.

"It's hard to know how to act around decent folks. I've had to work at it. It's the little things that catch me, like wrapping an arm around my plate and hunching over my food so no one will try to take it. Almost moaning out loud in pleasure the first dozen times I washed my face in hot water. Or opening my mouth without a whole bunch of swearwords spewing out. Men don't exactly use clean language in prison.''

Warmth touched her eyes. ''That's why you clamp your lips closed so tight when the kids act up?''

''Yep. Blisterin' their ears isn't going to help any. But it's a good thing nobody was within a mile or two of me the morning I dropped that post on my foot.''

''I expect most of us would have aired out our lungs under the circumstances. You've done fine. You've never embarrassed me or made me ashamed to have you around the children.''

''Until tonight.'' He sighed heavily. ''I can barely remember the last time I went to a party. I wanted to hear the music. I missed that a lot in prison.''

She reached across the small table and briefly touched his hand. ''Tell me what happened five years ago. All of it.''

He took a deep breath, determined to be completely honest with her. ''My main job at the Williams' ranch was to break and train the horses. Williams bought a prized stallion for himself and a pretty little sorrel filly for his wife. Neither of them had ever been ridden, so he asked me to saddle break them.

''Training the filly didn't take too long, but she was skittish on the open range. A gust of wind rustling the grass would send her sidestepping, which earned her more than one cut from Mrs. Williams' quirt. She was a sweet little horse, and except for that one problem, tried hard to please.

''The stallion was ornery, but I finally got him to accept the saddle.'' He leaned against the back of the chair and straightened his leg out beneath the table, relieving some of the pressure on his foot. "Once he was saddle broke, he didn't give me much trouble, but he hated that old man— for good reason. Williams had a hot, quick temper. If the horse didn't instantly do what he wanted, he'd light into him with a quirt. Then the horse would really act up. More often than not, the old man would bring him back to the corrals and tie him to the railing and go after him with the bullwhip."

She shivered. "I've never understood how anyone could be so cruel—to man or beast. Didn't he know he was ruining the horse?"

Leaning forward, Trent rested his forearms on the table again, absently rubbing his index finger back and forth across a short gouge in the wood. "I tried to tell him, but he wouldn't listen. He'd just order me to take care of the wounds and teach that cussed horse to obey.

"One afternoon I was working with another horse in the corral. I thought I was the only one around headquarters. The men were scattered over the range, and Rosie, Williams' wife, had supposedly gone into town."

It was too difficult to sit across from Anna and tell her about the other woman. Trent stood and walked around the small room, but that made his foot ache more. He sat back down on the side of the narrow bed, stretching his right leg out in front of him, staring at the toe of his boot.

"She was young, pretty and a temptress. Half the men on the ranch said they'd been with her. I expect some weren't telling the truth, but I knew for a fact of four or five who had met her at a line shack or spent an occasional night at the ranch house when her husband was away.

"When I was done with the training for the day, I turned the horse loose and carried my saddle to the tack room. Rosie was waiting for me when I came out. She'd been flirting with me for weeks. The training had gone well, and I was in a good mood. I stopped to tease her back.''

''A big mistake.''

He glanced up, and seeing understanding in her eyes, nodded. ''I didn't have any idea how big. I'd never seen Rosie in action, and before I knew it, she had half the buttons on her shirtwaist undone. I was so busy staring, I hardly noticed when she put her arms around my neck. She got my attention quick when she started kissing me.

''I didn't come to my senses right away. I kissed her, Anna, more than once, but I swear that's all I did. When I realized I was being an idiot, I tried to pull away. Unfortunately, convincing Rosie to stop was a lot harder than I expected. Neither of us had any idea anyone else was around.''

Moving his foot back toward the bed, Trent rested his hands on his thighs and closed his eyes. For years he had kept the memories locked away in the deepest recesses of his mind, only allowing them to escape when he slept. Over time, other nightmares dominated the darkness, but this one still haunted him, always the same, repeating the events of that afternoon in excruciating detail. Now, at last, it found the light of day.

Rosie's soft, willing body pressed against his, her teasing mouth luring him to greater pleasure. The whisper of air along the nape of his neck. Fire across his back. The crack of the whip. Rosie's screams. Men yelling. Searing pain. *Don't move.* The strike of the lash, again and again. *Protect.* Agony. Blessed darkness.

A shudder wracked him. And another. He couldn't quit shaking even when Anna put her arms around him.

''Don't think about it,'' she cried, sitting beside him, holding him close. ''Don't put yourself through this. Look at me. Please, Trent, look at me.''

He felt her work-worn hand upon his cheek, and, as on the night of the blizzard, her touch and gentle voice set him free. Turning his head toward her, he opened his eyes and looked into hers, his throat tightening at the sorrow he saw there. Tears sparkled on her lashes. Tears for him. One slipped to her cheek. His finger trembled as he caught the precious drop. "I haven't let myself think about it in a long time."

"I shouldn't have asked you to tell me."

When she lowered her hand, he wanted to grab it and hang on forever. He didn't move, but took comfort that she kept her other arm around his back. "I want you to know. Like Hank said, I passed out, and Williams' men took me out on the prairie. I came to once and heard a coyote howling in the distance. The next thing I remember is waking up at the doctor's office in town a few days later. I didn't know too much for quite a while.

"Hank quit his job and went to work for another rancher on the other side of town. He checked on me every few days. When he decided I was strong enough, he told me that Williams had piled up my belongings—clothes, bedding, the picture of my mother, saddle, rope, anything that would burn—and had himself a bonfire."

"He destroyed everything you owned?"

"Not quite. He didn't shoot my horse. Sold him and my pistol and rifle to a vaquero headin' back home to Mexico. But Williams wasn't finished. He sent word to every rancher within two hundred miles that I tried to rape his wife. And to make sure some bachelor didn't hire me, he said I'd treated his stallion so bad that he was almost worthless."

"Anyone who had ever seen you work horses knew that was a lie," she said angrily.

He shrugged. "There were some who didn't believe him about the horse."

"But they believed the story about his wife? How could they if they knew you?"

"Most men look out for womenfolk, theirs and their neighbors'. By the time I healed up, no rancher would hire me. He took everything—my possessions, livelihood, reputation and dignity. I figured that stallion and filly would even things up a mite."

"It doesn't come close." Frowning, she shook her head. "He owed you a lot more."

"Yes, he did, but that didn't make it right for me to take what wasn't mine. At the time, it made sense."

"The horses were probably happy to go with you."

He smiled wryly. "They were. I think they knew I wasn't going to bring them back."

She fussed with the overskirt of her dress, smoothing out a wrinkle. Slanting a glance up at him, she asked, "How were you caught?"

"Three days' ride from the ranch, the filly threw a shoe."

"And you took her to a blacksmith." Anna shook her head with a smile. "You wouldn't leave her behind, even at the risk of getting caught."

"Couldn't." He paused, unable to return her smile. "I'd tasted the fear of being hurt and helpless and hearin' a coyote call my name. We might have made it out of Texas, except a brand-new railroad went through that little town, and they'd just installed a telegraph four days before. Word of the theft was one of the first messages they received."

"Did the jury hear all the facts? Were they told what he did to you?"

"No."

"Why not?" she exclaimed.

"They all knew the story, his version and mine, thanks to Hank. But it didn't matter, Anna. I pled guilty. I couldn't deny it when they caught me with the horses. And I wouldn't have anyway. What I did was wrong. I broke the law."

"So did he!" She hit the mattress. "He tried to kill you and stole everything you had."

"I was the one on trial. Not him. Since I pled guilty, all the jury had to do was decide the sentence. Most of them were ranchers. Even if they believed my side of the story, they couldn't condone a man stealing from one of their own. They had to make an example of me. I figure they took the circumstances into consideration. According to the judge, the sentence could be between five and fifteen years, so I got the minimum."

She scowled and picked at a loose thread on the quilt. "Most horse thieves around here get five years."

"The harsher punishment goes to somebody who takes a man's only horse, or who puts him in danger by taking it. I was lucky to be arrested by the county sheriff and taken back. If Williams had caught up with me, he would've had a necktie party."

"Is he still a threat?"

Trent figured she worried about her and the kids being caught in the middle of a fight. "No. Hank said Rosie left less than a month after I went to prison. Ran off with a drummer who sold ladies' underwear. Williams started drinkin' heavy. About a year later, he fell down the stairs and broke his neck. I doubt Rosie stayed with the drummer long. She's probably got herself a rich man by now."

"More likely two or three." Anna kept messing with the quilt, smoothing wrinkles he couldn't even see.

She's going to tell me to leave. He didn't see how she could do anything else. He took a deep breath, releasing it slowly, trying to stifle the pain in his heart. "I know you don't want the kids around a jailbird. And your neighbors won't draw an easy breath as long as I'm here. Like I said earlier, I'll leave tomorrow."

Anna looked up in surprise as a sharp pain pierced her heart. He stared at the toe of his boot, his comment as casual as if they were talking about the weather. Anyone else would assume leaving didn't bother him. She knew differently. The thought had to bring him the same ache and panic she felt.

He had not lost his integrity, only misplaced it for a while behind a wall of bitterness and pain. He needed their trust and respect to restore his honor. When she first learned of his past, the hurt and feeling of inadequacy that came with his distrust hit her like a physical blow. To face such a thing daily had to be almost unbearable.

Davy and Mitch adored him. He needed their love, and hers, too, if she had it to give. Anna studied his ruggedly handsome face, aged beyond his years by all he had gone through. *Lord, I don't know if I love him, but I want a chance to find out. Please let him stay.*

"The kids have been around you for weeks. I don't think there is a danger of them growing up to be outlaws just because they know you."

He looked at her, unable to hide his longing, though he tried. "Anna, I'm a criminal."

"No, you're a man who made a mistake, and you're trying to make a fresh start. I can't think of anyone better to help me teach the boys about the consequences of breaking the law. They need to learn about right and wrong, but they also need to learn about forgiveness and acceptance. You shouldn't have to keep paying for your crime forever. I know you are a kind, honorable man who will try harder than most to do what is right."

"Your neighbors won't agree with you."

"Shane will. Even though he doesn't know you, he respects Hank. If Hank calls you friend, that's good enough for him. Given time, the others will forget about your past and grow to trust you."

"From the way some of them were looking at me, I'll be an old man before that happens." He shook his head. "I don't want to cause you trouble."

"I can handle my neighbors." She stared across the room, focusing her gaze on the empty wall. "The boys are happier now than they've been since before Edwin died. You've been good for them, especially Mitch. You're the first man he's let himself love since he lost his daddy. It will tear him up if you go."

"I don't want to hurt him, but it might be worse if I wear out my welcome." He stared at the floor for several seconds. "I'll think on it."

Anna considered trying to persuade him with a kiss but decided against it. If passion flared between them the way it had earlier in the evening, she might be too tempted to stay right where she was—beside him on his bed. She rose and walked to the table, picking up the lantern. When she reached the door, she smiled back at him. "Just remember I'll never find anybody who can handle horses the way you do. At least not for what I'm paying you."

He stood, and for a minute, she thought he was going to walk over to her. Heart pounding, she waited, unsure of what she would do if he touched her.

Finally, he jammed his hands in his pockets and stayed by the bed, a slow smile spreading across his face. "So you want me to stay because I'm cheap."

"Partly." Flashing him a smile, she went out the door, leaving it open.

"Anna," he called softly.

She stopped and looked back. He stood in the doorway. "Yes?"

"What's another reason?"

"I like your smile." *And everything else.* "Good night, Trent." She turned toward the house, silently ordering her feet to move in the right direction.

His quiet chuckle wrapped her in warmth. "Good night, sugar."

Chapter Eleven

At dawn, Anna put her green-and-yellow print cotton wrapper over her nightgown, slid her feet into a pair of dark green knitted slippers, and wandered out into the kitchen to stoke the fire so they could cook breakfast. Worried that Trent might decide not to stay after all, she had barely slept. Yawning, she looked out the kitchen window and saw him walking toward the house. Polecat was saddled and tied to the hitching post by the barn.

Fear that he was leaving sent her flying out the door and across the yard. She stopped short of throwing herself into his arms, but came close.

His gaze moved slowly over her, all the way from her loose, tangled hair to her feet and back up again.

Anna blushed, suddenly very aware that only a light-weight wrapper covered her nightgown. When he first came to the ranch and stayed in the house, he had seen her in a heavier robe, but it hid far more than the one she now wore. Since going to work for her, he never came to the house before breakfast. She suspected it was to give her plenty of time to dress before he knocked on the door.

"You're out early," she said, trying to regain some semblance of composure, a difficult chore under the heat of his slow, thorough appraisal.

He looked out across the prairie. "Thought I'd ride over and check the cattle in the hill pasture. I figured you probably need to explain things to the kids." He turned back to her, keeping his gaze on her face. "It would be easier on both of us if I wasn't around when you do."

She glanced at Polecat. No bedroll was tied behind the saddle. Anna breathed easier. "So, you've decided to stay?"

"I'm not sure yet." He pulled his brown leather gloves from his back pocket, slipping them on as he talked. "Tell the kids about me. See how they react. Find out what Duncan and Rachel think about me staying. If anyone has a problem with me being here, I'll go."

"I'll talk to them. Don't you want something to eat?" Anna frowned when he shook his head. "At least take some of the corn bread left from dinner yesterday."

"I wouldn't mind a little corn bread."

"I'll get it. Why don't you wait on the front porch? That way if one of the boys wakes up and goes to the outhouse, he won't pester you with questions."

An ache touched Anna's heart as they walked quietly to the house. Early morning had been a special time for her and Edwin. He always climbed out of bed first, stoked the fire and put on a pot of coffee. Then he tended to the stock while she cooked breakfast. She often waited for him on the porch or walked down toward the barn to meet him, cherishing those quiet moments alone with him.

Some things seemed the same. Golden rays radiated across the pink and purple sky. Coolness lingered before the sun warmed the day. Only the rooster's crow, the quiet jingle of spurs and the crunch of boots upon the hard earth broke the stillness. The scent of leather, horse and man mingled with the fragrance of flowers in the air.

But on this clear spring morning, the spurs played a slower tune. The cadence between footsteps was longer, lighter. The man next to her smelled clean but without the subtle hint of lavender from her sheets. Yet the feeling was there, the sense of belonging by his side.

She glanced at him out of the corner of her eye. He wore his hat low to block the first beams of sunlight. His black hair lay along the collar of his green work shirt. Dark stubble shadowed his jaw. *Desperado.* The word no longer meant mystery and romance, but pain and sorrow. More than ever, Anna wanted to love away the hurt of his past.

He caught her looking at him and rubbed his jaw. "Reckon I look a little scraggly."

"I don't mind."

A tiny smile touched his face. "You would if I got too close."

She reached up and ran her finger across his whiskers. "They are a little rough."

"Too rough to touch soft, pretty skin like yours," he said as they reached the porch.

Anna's cheeks grew warm, both from the compliment and the mental image his words evoked. "I'll be right back," she said, hurrying into the house.

She wrapped the corn bread in a clean blue-checked napkin, bringing the corners to the middle and tying them. It would be better if he had some milk to go with it, but he couldn't easily carry it with him.

When she returned to the porch, he waited on the bottom step. She handed him the small bundle. "This will keep you from starving."

"I ate enough yesterday to last a week." Sadness drifted

over his countenance. "I wish the kids hadn't seen that ruckus last night. And that you hadn't been involved."

"I wish it hadn't happened, either, but it did. Now, we'll deal with it." She slipped her hands into the pockets of her wrapper.

"Will it give you enough time if I come back around noon?"

"I expect you could come back in an hour and two. The boys won't sit still for more than five or ten minutes to discuss it. Duncan and Rachel may need longer."

Trent searched her face. "And their mama? Does she still want me to stay?"

"Yes," she said firmly. "I meant everything I said last night."

"Then I'll be back in a while." He hesitated, looking down at the step. "If you want me to talk to them later, I will. Little boys sometimes get the notion that being on the wrong side of the law is just a big adventure. It's not."

"Thank you. It might be helpful. I'd better get breakfast started. They'll be up in a few minutes."

"Thanks, Anna." He met her gaze, his expression dark and troubled. "When it comes to those kids…" He looked away, swallowing hard.

"I know. Have a good ride. Let it clear your head. We'll see you at dinner."

He nodded and turned, walking toward the barn.

Anna watched him untie Polecat's reins, climb into the saddle, and ride away with ease and grace. He had been born to spend his life in open country, as free as the wind. She ached at the thought of all those years he was trapped in a prison cell. Every minute must have been pure torture. Walls no longer held him, but he remained a prisoner of distrust and fear—and perhaps worst of all, his own self-contempt.

His image became smaller and smaller, and as he disappeared from view, she whispered the cry of her heart. "Please, God, help me set him free."

The children awoke soon afterward, full of questions. Anna put off answering them until after breakfast. Then they all sat down together, and she explained about the events at Shane's and what happened five years ago.

Duncan and Rachel knew about him being accused of attempted rape, and Williams whipping him and having him left on the prairie to die. Because of the younger boys, she chose her words carefully and did not go into great detail about those events. She tried to relate everything else as closely as possible to the way Trent told it.

She hoped she sounded convincing.

"If anybody who wanted something could just take it, or one man could kill another without having to worry about what might happen to him, nobody would be safe," said Duncan. "That's why we have laws to protect us and our property."

"What's property?" asked Mitch, crawling up onto Anna's lap.

"The things that belong to us. Your toys and clothes are your property." She put her arms around him and gave him a hug. "It's different with people, though. You belong to me, but you aren't my property."

"So, it's the stuff we got." Mitch looked at his oldest brother.

"That's right. Land is called property, too." Duncan smiled at Mitch. "Although I don't think it can be called *stuff.*"

"When Trent took those horses, he was very angry and wanted to do something to make Williams feel bad," said Anna. "But later, he realized that what he had done was wrong. That's why he admitted his guilt to the judge and jury, even though he knew he would go to prison. Being in the penitentiary was very hard on Trent. He was locked in a tiny room with no windows for days at a time. Sometimes weeks went by without being allowed outside. He was in prison for five years.''

Mitch frowned. ''That's how old I am.''

''That's right. Most of the time since you were born, Trent was locked in a room smaller than your bedroom.''

''I'm not gonna be an outlaw,'' Davy said solemnly. ''I don't want to go to the pen. Mama, when we do something bad, you give us a spankin' or make us stand in the corner or stay in our room all day or something. But when we're done with the punishment, we aren't in trouble anymore. How come those people were so mad at Trent last night? Why did Mr. Kingsley say he didn't want a horse thief living next to him? He ain't a horse thief no more.''

''Often when someone does something like Trent did, people think they'll do it again. Because they are afraid, they decide he's a bad man and might steal something of theirs. Hopefully, if Trent stays with us, and the neighbors get to know him, they will see that he's a good man who made one bad mistake,'' Anna said carefully.

Mitch looked up at her, his expression filled with worry. ''He's not gonna go away, is he?''

Like Daddy did. The little boy didn't say the words but she suspected he was thinking them. ''I don't know, honey. He might.'' She looked at Duncan and Rachel, then the younger boys. ''Trent wants to know how you feel about him. If you don't want him here, he'll probably leave this afternoon.''

''No!'' cried Mitch, tears welling up in his eyes. ''Trent's my bestest friend. You can't make him go away.''

Anna held him close. ''I don't want him to go, either.

But it's not up to me. You all have a say in this. So does he.'' She looked at Duncan, worrying that this might have increased his resentment toward Trent. ''What do you think?''

''I'm angry because he didn't tell us about his past, but I guess I can understand why he wouldn't want to talk about it. I don't think he would steal again, but it will take me a while to get to where I trust him.'' He glanced at Anna, and she held her breath. ''But he cares about us. That was clear last night.'' He paused, as if wrestling with the decision. Taking a deep breath, he met Anna's gaze. ''If he wants to stay, it's all right with me.''

Anna's breath came out in a whoosh. ''Thank you.'' She looked at Davy. ''What do you think?''

The youngster shrugged. ''He loves us. We love him.''

Anna's throat tightened. There was nothing like the pure, unselfish love of a child.

Finally, Anna turned to Rachel.

''He needs us,'' said Rachel, meeting her gaze, speaking to her as one woman to another. ''And we need him.''

Anna breathed a sigh of relief. ''Thank you for your understanding.'' She looked at each of them. ''All of you. You're very wise.''

''I hope so,'' said Duncan solemnly as he stood. ''I'd better go milk Daisy. She's probably about to bust.''

''Can we go play?'' asked Davy, jumping off the sofa.

''Yes, you may. Don't wander too far.''

Mitch and Davy rushed out the back door, discussing things to do as they went. Duncan sauntered after them.

''And I'd better gather the eggs before all the hens decide to sit on them,'' said Rachel. ''Will Trent be back this morning?''

''Around noon.''

"I think I'll make some molasses cookies. He's particularly fond of them."

Anna laughed. "Honey, Trent is fond of everything you cook." She quickly sobered. "Now, I understand why. When I think of how he must have suffered in prison, I feel sick."

"You're in love with him, aren't you?"

Anna carefully considered the question. Earlier, when she thought he was leaving, her heartache had been almost beyond bearing. "Yes, I love him. Am I that obvious?"

"Probably just to me," said Rachel with a smile. "Since I'm suffering from the same affliction, it's easy to detect."

"Ian is a much better choice than Rich."

"Yes, he is." Rachel picked up the egg basket but instead of going to the back door, she came around the end of the sofa and sat down next to Anna. She hesitated, her cheeks turning bright red. "I did a very foolish thing last night. I went for a walk with Rich down by the corrals."

Anna decided it might be easier on Rachel if she admitted seeing the whole thing. "I know. When I missed you, I talked to Claire. She told me you were with Rich. I went tearing down there, but Trent stopped me before I sent you back to the house like a misbehaving schoolgirl. He pointed out that you two were merely talking."

The flush spread down Rachel's neck. "Trent was there, too?"

"He saw you leave and followed, although Ian was ahead of him. Trent wanted to keep you safe."

"How long…how long were you there?"

"The whole time." Anna shook her head. "This is one part of being a parent I don't think I handled well. When Rich started acting like he was going to kiss you, Trent was ready to stop him. Rich seemed gentle enough, so I decided maybe it wouldn't hurt for you to kiss him. I still remember my first kiss. I thought it would embarrass you terribly if we interfered.''

Rachel stared at her. "You watched?"

"Not exactly." Anna smiled wryly. "I was a little distracted because Trent had his arm around me."

A sparkle lit Rachel's eyes. "Did he hold you close?"

"Uh-huh. But I noticed when Rich got rough. I was going to claw his eyes out, but Trent held me back. He knew Ian was nearby, and he thought we should let him rescue you."

Rachel shivered. "Anna, it was awful. I was so thankful when Ian pulled Rich away. I wanted to crawl in a hole somewhere. I was so ashamed. But Ian was sweet and understanding." Her eyes widened slightly and she continued, "I was so disgusted with the way Rich kissed me that Ian just had to show me how nice it could be." Rachel's smile held a hint of mischief. "That wasn't what I had in mind when I spouted off about how awful it was, but he had a very pleasant way of making me forget about it. Ian said that when a man truly cares about a woman, she'll feel cherished, even when he kisses her passionately. He kissed me very sweetly at first, then, well…you know."

Having a very good idea what Rachel meant, Anna frowned. To think she had trusted her stepdaughter with that rogue. "I'm going to have a talk with that man."

Rachel laughed softly. "Now, don't get in a tizzy. He only kissed me." Her smile faded, but happiness shone in her eyes. "It was just like he said it would be. I felt cherished, like I was the most precious thing in the world to him."

Anna hugged her, tears of joy and sadness moistening her eyes. "Honey, I'm so happy for you."

"He didn't exactly propose, but he said that he intended to make me his bride."

"He will make you a good husband."

"I think so, too. Though I expect it will be a short courtship, we have to get to know each other better before I agree to marry him. I'm always amazed when I think how you met Daddy one day and married him the next. Weren't you afraid?"

"Oh, yes." Anna leaned her head against the back of the sofa. "I had only a vague idea what happened between a man and a woman behind the bedroom door. But he had such kind eyes, I knew he would be good to me. I still miss your father. I guess I always will. No one can take his place. I'll always love him. What I feel for Trent isn't the same, I suppose because he is so different from Edwin. But it's strong and deep."

"He's been hurt so badly and thinks so little of himself. It may be hard to convince him that you truly love him."

"I know. Somehow, he has to put his past behind him and prove to himself that he is a good and decent man. I hope we can help him see that."

"I hope so, too." When a horse nickered in front of the house, Rachel hopped up and hurried to the window. "Mercy! Ian and Shane are here!" Eyes bright and cheeks pink, she flew toward her bedroom. "Why does that man always catch me when I'm working and wearing my everyday clothes?"

"Maybe he likes you that way. Edwin always complimented me when I dressed up, but he said he liked seeing me in my regular clothes the best. He said it reminded him of how close we were. We didn't have to put on airs or fancy duds to be attracted to each other or enjoy being together." A knock sounded on the door. "You don't have time to change."

"I know. I just wanted to smooth my hair."

"I'm going to the door," Anna called softly.

Rachel rushed out of her room, carrying the egg basket.

Anna grinned to herself. Ian would probably take one look at Rachel and volunteer to help her gather the eggs. She opened the door, smiling at her friends. "Good morning, Shane, Ian. Please, come in." Stepping back, she opened the door wide.

"Good morning." Shane smiled at her as he walked in, then at Rachel. "You both look like you survived the party."

"I'm tired and a bit sore from all the dancing," said Anna. "Funny how I can work hard around the ranch every day and still discover muscles I didn't know I had when I dance half the night."

"It's worse when you sit at a desk most of the time." Ian smiled quickly at Anna before his gaze settled on Rachel. His eyes glowed and his smile grew tender. "Good morning, Rachel."

"Good morning." She smiled shyly, her gaze flickering to Shane. "Hello, Shane. Was there any more trouble after we left last night?"

"No. With Bender gone, things settled down. Hank told us about Trent. Folks chewed on it for a while, and then Tom struck up his fiddle again." He yawned and tossed his hat on the kitchen table. "More than half of them stayed for breakfast."

Since parties were few and distances far, that often was the case. He had the party on Friday night instead of Saturday so those who attended church felt like going on Sunday morning.

"Don't let me interrupt you," said Ian, glancing at the egg basket. "I'd be happy to help you gather the eggs."

Rachel smiled, blushing prettily. "I didn't think attorneys knew anything about chickens."

"Even attorneys have to eat. Besides, I grew up on a

ranch. I've tangled with more than one scrappy hen." As they walked toward the back door, he looked at Shane. "Whistle when you're ready to go."

"I won't be long."

Ian grinned and winked at his brother. "Don't hurry on my account."

"I figured you could help bust a few broncs," Shane said lazily.

"Not today," said Ian with a laugh. "After my siesta, I'm going back to town."

"Never can get any work out of that boy. You'd better watch him, Rachel. His reputation is going to his head. He's turnin' plumb lazy."

"That will be the day." Her smile told them all she adored the young lawyer.

After they left, Anna sat down in the rocker. Shane poured himself a cup of coffee. "Want some?"

"No, thanks. I've had enough."

He sat down across from her. "There will be a wedding as soon as she wants it," he said quietly. "Ian's bitin' at the bit." He blew gently on the coffee to cool it. "The first time he saw her, he told me he was going to marry her."

"And you kept that to yourself?"

"Yep. Since she has some say in it, I figured I'd better let matters take their course."

"She wants to get to know him better." Anna looked out the back window, smiling when she saw Ian lean down close to Rachel's ear. "But I don't think that will be long. I expect we'll be kinfolk within a few months."

"So, will that make you my gran-sister-in-law?"

"Heavens, I'm too young to be gran-anything. I don't think there's a name for a sister-in-law's stepmother."

Shane took a sip of coffee. "I could call you Mama."

"You do and I'll call you Ormerod." Anna tried not to

smile. Shane hated his middle name. She was one of the few people who knew what it was.

"I'd never speak to you again," he said with a grimace. He stretched his long legs out in front of him, crossing them at the ankles. "Is Trent still around?"

"Yes. He rode out to check the stock this morning. We had a long talk last night." She quietly related the things Trent said led to his prison term.

"That agrees with what Hank had to say. If I'd been on that jury, I don't think I could have sent him to prison. Williams was the one who should have been on trial."

"If the man wasn't already dead, I think I could shoot him!" Anna jumped up, pacing around the kitchen. "He almost destroyed Trent. I don't know how many mornings I've seen him rolling up his bedroll outside the barn. Most nights he can't bear to stay inside his room. The walls close in, and he almost goes loco. He gets sick if he tries to stay in there."

She stopped pacing and looked at Shane. "He asked me to tell the kids what happened five years ago. I'd planned to anyway, but he couldn't bear to be here and see their reactions. He was especially worried about what Duncan and Rachel think. Thankfully, none of them want him to go." She briefly closed her eyes. "I don't think I could stand for him to leave."

"You're taking a big risk. You may wind up with a broken heart."

"It's been broken before and I survived."

Shane stared thoughtfully at his cup. "Hank said before Trent had that run-in with Williams, he was the most honest man he'd ever met. He called Trent a good man who made a bad mistake. I value Hank's judgment probably more than anybody I know. I've also seen Malloy work." He looked up with a smile. "I watched him a few times when no one knew I was around."

"Are you going to always look after me?" Anna didn't know what she would have done without Shane since Edwin died. He'd been her lifeline.

He shrugged. "As long as I can. You do the same for me. Malloy's a lost soul, Anna, but worth saving."

"And you think I should try?"

"You're the only one who can. Though those two rascals of yours will help. They've sure taken to him."

"Most of the family has. Even Dig and the cat."

Shane laughed. "Then you know he's all right. Animals have a way of seein' a man's true character."

Chapter Twelve

When Trent rode up to the barn shortly before noon, no one was in sight. Worried that they might still be talking, he glanced at the position of the sun, confirming the time. He dismounted and led Polecat over to the water trough, holding the ends of the reins so they drooped in a big loop.

The time alone had not eased his confusion or brought him peace. The soft breeze whispered accusations, mimicking the angry, hushed words of the neighbors and townspeople the night before. The expansive vista of prairie and hills taunted him with the reminder that some prisons had no walls. He would never be welcome in the Texas he loved. The horizon beckoned him to a distant land where no one knew his face or his name.

But a woman's gentle smile and tender touch bound him to this ranch, this family. His mind told him to go. His heart bid him stay. Even though he believed the best thing for Anna and the kids would be for him to follow the wanderer's call, he would remain as long as she wanted him to. He glanced toward the house, thinking maybe she had already changed her mind.

Polecat finished his drink, swinging his head around to

nudge Trent in the shoulder. Patience was not one of the horse's greatest attributes. "Hungry, fella?"

Polecat turned slowly and started toward the corral, clearly expecting Trent to follow before the reins grew taut. Trent let the horse lead the way, wondering which one of them was really in charge.

He dropped the reins and opened the corral gate, smiling a little as Polecat moseyed inside and looked back expectantly. Trent closed the gate and unsaddled the horse, carrying his rig to the tack room. He hung the saddle over the rack and spread the saddle blanket on top of it to dry, then hung up the harness, bridle and reins.

Stopping in the doorway, he watched Polecat roll in the dirt, wiping away the sweat from the hard ride. The horse wiggled this way and that, waving his feet in the air, then stood and shook hard, sending dust flying in all directions. His coat shone as if he had been hand rubbed.

Trent scooped up a bucket of oats in the barn and took it out to his horse, dumping it in the feed trough. After pausing to rub Polecat's neck a few minutes and thank him for the ride, he took the bucket back to the barn.

While he debated whether or not to go to the house, Anna came out the back door, walking toward him. He watched her for a minute, squinting against the bright noonday sun, but couldn't see her expression.

Mitch came barreling around the end of the barn. "Trent!" The little boy skidded to a halt against Trent's leg and threw his arms around him, almost knocking him down.

"Easy, pardner." Trent bent down and picked him up, surprised to see tears pooling in his little friend's eyes. "What's this?" he asked gently, settling him on one arm, his other hand firmly supporting Mitch's back. "Did you hurt yourself?"

Mitch shook his head, his lips turned down at the corners. A big tear slid down one rosy, round cheek. "I thought you weren't coming back."

"Didn't your mama tell you I just went for a ride?"

Mitch nodded solemnly. "But you were gone so long." He threw his arms around Trent's neck, clinging to him as never before. "Don't go away. You're my bestest friend." A shudder wracked his small body from head to toe. "We want you to stay. We 'cided."

Trent closed his eyes, tightening his arms around the boy. His throat ached and tears burned his eyes. "All of you?"

Mitch nodded, his head rubbing the side of Trent's neck. He had his mother's hair—the same color, the same silky softness. "We love you."

"I love you, too, Mitch," whispered Trent. He opened his eyes, blinking back the mist. Anna stood before him, moisture shimmering in her eyes. *I love all of you.* He cleared his throat, meeting her gaze. "I'll stay as long as your mama wants me here, or until my being here stirs up too much trouble. I won't risk any of you getting hurt because of me."

Mitch leaned back and looked at him. "Folks just gotta get to know you, that's all. Then they'll see you wouldn't steal nothin'."

"I hope that's all it takes." Trent gave the boy a hug and set him on the ground. "You'd better go wash up for dinner. Your mama and I'll be along directly."

Mitch nodded and looked uncertainly at his mother.

She smiled gently. "We won't be long."

"What are we havin'?" he asked, walking backward.

"Ham and fried potatoes. Rachel made some molasses cookies, too."

That put a grin on the little boy's face. He spun around, racing to the house.

Trent smiled at the thought of those cookies.

"We're lucky to get dessert today," said Anna, starting slowly toward the house.

He fell in step beside her. "Your discussion run a long time?"

"No, not long. I explained what happened, glossing over a few details because of the little ones. Then I asked everyone's opinion. The decision to ask you to stay was unanimous."

"What about Duncan?"

"He's angry because you weren't honest with us, but he also understands why you didn't want to talk about it. He considered it carefully before he said he thought you should stay. So, I know he means it." She waved to Davy as he came around the side of the house, heading for the back door.

"Shane and Ian dropped by." She smiled up at Trent. "That's why we almost didn't get the cookies. Ian helped Rachel gather the eggs."

"It took a while?" he asked with a small smile.

"Considerably longer than normal. Shane told me what Hank had to say to the folks last night."

"Set your mind at ease that I told the truth?" He kept his gaze focused on the house.

"It confirmed what you said, but I didn't doubt you."

He glanced at her. The sincerity of her expression touched him deeply. Her trust was a precious gift.

She stopped, touching his arm to halt him. "I know it's important to you that all of us be comfortable with you being here, but don't let us push you into staying if you don't want to. After Bender's tirade last night, it won't be easy to settle here. Some folks will always distrust you. It might be easier to go someplace where there is little chance anyone knows you or has heard of you."

"I've considered it, and I admit it has some appeal." He watched the boys stop to wash up in a basin on the back porch, then he looked at Anna. She hadn't tamed her long hair in the usual single braid, but held it with a ribbon tied at the nape of her neck. The wind tugged a delicate strand free, blowing it across her cheek. He smoothed her hair back, letting his fingers trail over her soft skin, and tucked the wisp beneath the ribbon. "But it's not nearly so appealing as staying here."

Busy with calving and welcoming three foals into the world, the next two weeks flew past. Most of the new mothers didn't have a problem delivering their babies, but one of the horses and a couple of the cows needed a helping hand. Trent, Anna and Duncan spent a good portion of the night in the barn with the mare, convincing her they knew best. Shortly before dawn, she gave birth to a beautiful colt. Trent slipped his arm around Anna's waist, holding her gently as they watched the mother and baby become acquainted.

One of the calves was in the wrong position and had to be turned. Used to dealing with longhorns, who wouldn't allow man's interference, Trent managed the feat through strength, sheer determination and instructions from Anna. When the calf arrived, tired but healthy, Trent decided he'd never known a greater accomplishment.

A thunderstorm gave them a fireworks show one afternoon and blessed them with a good rain.

Shane came by to pick up the cattle he purchased from Anna. When he learned Trent was ready to ride a three-year-old gelding for the first time, he decided to stay awhile.

Because Anna and Trent used an unconventional, gentle method of breaking the horses, the lesson went well. Their philosophy was to slowly acquaint the animals with man and the equipment, gaining their trust—not tie them down, throw on the saddle and hang on for dear life. Their method took longer, but it was far better for both the horses and the cowboys who eventually rode them.

After the session, Trent put the rig away. When he came out of the tack room, Shane leaned casually against the side of the building, cleaning his fingernails with a pocketknife. He straightened, closing the knife, and shoved it in his pocket. "Good job."

"Thanks." Trent walked over to the pump by the water trough. He pumped the handle a couple of times until a stream of cold, clear water ran out. Leaning down, he took a long drink, then stuck his head under the stream of water and washed off the dust from the corral. He straightened and combed his wet hair back with his fingers.

"Anna tells me that when you came here, you already broke horses in much the same way as she does. Where'd you learn it?"

They walked toward the corral where Anna was saddling her horse. "Self-taught. I started bustin' broncs when I was eighteen. Did it the traditional way for about three years, and I was good. Had a reputation for hanging on when most men couldn't. Then I figured out a gentler way, one that was better for the horses and easier on me."

Shane watched Anna talk to her horse, then he glanced at Trent. "She doesn't look nearly as tired as she has the past couple of years. She worked harder than most men would have to save this ranch. I helped when she'd let me, but that wasn't often. I'm glad you're here."

Trent looked at him in surprise, studying his expression. "You mean that," he said in amazement.

Shane nodded. "But if you ever do anything to hurt her, you'll regret it."

Trent's gaze settled on Anna, love welling up in his heart. "Yes, I would," he said quietly. "More than you'll ever know."

On Friday, Sully Smith, a horse trader who worked much of West Texas, stopped by the ranch. He had been buying horses from the Double Deuce for years. Trent didn't know how well Edwin had handled sales, but he thought Anna did better than anyone he'd ever seen.

"Now, Sully, what are you grumbling about?" Anna said with a teasing smile as he mounted his horse. "You just bought my three best horses."

"Yeah, and I let you sweet-talk me into too high a price." Sully looked at Trent and shook his head. "Bats those pretty eyes of hers, and I plumb forget what we're doing."

Trent laughed. Anna had been all business. She hadn't flirted with the burly horse trader once.

"I'll do good to make a profit," muttered Sully.

"When people notice the Double Deuce brand, you'll make a good profit and you know it." Anna handed him the lead string for the horses. Feeling sad to let them go, she walked back to the first one, a dun gelding, and rubbed his nose. "Goodbye, Cactus. You be a good boy for your new friends." She moved to the next horse, a little bay, and patted the filly's neck. "Sweetpea, mind your manners, and Sully will find a kind, pretty lady to ride you."

The man glanced at Trent. "She does this every time. Makes me feel like I'm taking off with her young'uns," he said gruffly. "The way y'all treat them, I guess I am."

Anna stopped at the last horse, a sorrel mare. She rested her forehead against the animal's neck. "Magnolia, you carry yourself proud like a Southern lady, even if those cowboys call you Maggie."

''Must have been a good year for flowers,'' mumbled Sully.

Anna hugged Maggie's neck, then stepped back, giving the horse trader a wobbly smile. ''We didn't have enough rain for flowers that year so we made the horses our bouquet.''

''I should've known. Good day, Miz Caldwell. I'm leavin' before you make me all weepy.'' He nodded to Anna and Trent and rode away at a comfortable walk, leading the horses.

Anna sighed, and Trent put his hand on her shoulder. ''Nice work. You drive a hard bargain, lady.''

''We did get a good price, but I'll miss them.'' She looked up at him with a tiny frown. ''I didn't bat my eyes at him, did I?''

''No, ma'am.'' Trent grinned. ''You can't help it if Sully was distracted because you're so pretty.''

A smile warmed her eyes and spread slowly across her face. ''Thanks.''

He backed away a few steps and winked. ''You're the prettiest boss I ever had.''

''I'd better be,'' she said with a grin.

Anna was still smiling at noon when she declared they should all go to town the next day and stay until Sunday afternoon. Laughing, she let the boys whoop and holler for several minutes until she quieted them down.

''There's no need for me to go to town,'' said Trent, uneasy about going back to Antelope Springs. He hadn't endeared himself to the sheriff the last time he was there. He figured by now, everyone in town knew about his past, whether they'd been at Shane's party or not. ''I'll stay here and keep an eye on things.''

Anna shook her head. ''I've already arranged with Shane to feed the horses and chickens and check on the cattle while we're gone.'' She reached in her skirt pocket and pulled out some money, handing it to him across the table. ''I never met a cowboy who didn't want to spend at least part of his wages.''

Trent took the money, silently adding it up. Thirty-five dollars. ''Anna, there's a whole month's pay here.''

''You've earned every penny of it.''

''But we agreed I'd work for room and board for a few months.''

''That was before we sold the cattle and the horses. I can afford to pay you now. We don't have to wait a couple of months. Besides, you need some new clothes.'' She winked at him—right there in front of the kids—and he almost dropped his fork. ''If you wait another month, the seat of your britches will be worn clear through.''

He dropped his fork on purpose, hoping the others would think his face turned red from being clumsy. Bending down to pick it up, he grinned to himself. When he straightened, he glanced at Duncan. A tiny smile hovered about the young man's mouth.

While the younger boys discussed the kind of candy each one would buy, Rachel said something to Duncan. With everyone else busy, Trent looked at Anna. Her knowing smile made him wish they were off in a secluded corner of the ranch by themselves. After dinner, he escaped to the corrals and spent the next couple of hours working with the horses.

As he turned the last student out into the pasture, Mitch hollered at him from the other side of the corral. He turned, smiling at the little boy. Mitch stood on the second rail, leaning his arms over the top to hang on. ''What are you up to, pardner?'' asked Trent, walking over to him.

''Duncan and Rachel are takin' us fishing.''

''Rachel is going, too?''

Mitch nodded. "She always catches more than anybody, but she makes Duncan clean 'em."

Trent walked through the gate, grinning when Mitch hopped down and came to meet him. "Looks to me like you just had your ears lowered."

"Yep. Mama gave me and Davy a haircut. She said for me to tell you that it's your turn. She's waitin' on you."

Being alone with Anna would be heaven, but Trent didn't think it wise, especially if everyone else was gone. After their heated kisses at Shane's party, he had avoided similar opportunities. He thought she had, too. "Tell her thanks, but I'll wait and get one in town."

"She cuts hair good." Mitch frowned at Trent. "Don't my haircut look good?"

"She did a fine job, but I don't want to put her to any trouble."

"Aw, it ain't no trouble." Mitch glanced toward the house. Duncan, Rachel and Davy walked out the back door, carrying fishing poles and a bucket. Dig scampered back and forth beside them. Duncan motioned for Mitch to join them as they started down the path toward the creek. "I gotta go. See you at supper." He took off like a shot. "Mama's waitin'," he called over his shoulder.

"But what for?" Trent mused quietly. He knocked the dust off his pants with his hat, then brushed his shirt with his hands. Stopping by his room, he removed his spurs and hung them on the wall. He paused by the water trough and pumped some fresh water, washing his face and hands. All the way to the house, he talked to himself, boosting his resolve not to get near her.

Anna met him at the back door with a grin. "The barbershop is open for business. Step right on out to the front porch." Turning on her heel, she bustled through the house, not giving him a chance to tell her thanks but no thanks.

"It's shady out there, and I don't have to worry about getting hair everywhere."

Trent hesitated, not wanting to spoil her jubilant mood.

She stuck her head back through the front door. "Well, get out here. You look shaggier than Dig."

"You don't have to bother. I'll get a haircut in town." But he took off his hat and hung it on the rack as he walked by.

"Nonsense. Why pay good money when I'll do it for free? Won't take me ten minutes."

He wasn't sure he could stand to be alone with her for one minute, much less ten.

"Sit right here." She patted the back of a kitchen chair as he stepped outside. When he sat down, she whipped an old tablecloth around him and fastened it at the back of his neck with a clothespin.

Anna ran her fingers through his hair. A barber sometimes did the same thing to judge how it had been cut the last time. He didn't think she meant it to be provocative— but it was. Trent closed his eyes, stifling a groan.

"You have such beautiful hair," she said softly, beginning to trim the back. "I won't cut it too short, just bring it up so it doesn't touch your collar." Unlike most barbers, she worked silently.

Snip, snip, snip. The steady sound of the scissors soothed his taut nerves. Being outside in the open, they'd have to behave themselves. Anybody could come along, or the kids might give up right away on the fishing. No sense thinking about temptation. He opened his eyes, letting his gaze rest on the green countryside. A gentle breeze blew across the porch, further relaxing him.

Anna switched sides, and the breeze surrounded him with lavender. She bent down behind him, muttering about not wanting to cut it crooked. Her breath warmed the back of his neck, and Trent knew he'd made a big mistake. He shifted in the chair.

''Sit still or I'm liable to nick you.'' She straightened and ran the comb through the hair at his temple. ''There, the bottom is even. Now, I'll just layer this in a bit.''

He wondered if she realized her leg was pressing against his. Cutting away, she moved again, and some part of her anatomy brushed against his shoulder. He tried not to imagine which part, but the attempt was futile. He glanced up at her face out of the corner of his eye. She appeared to be concentrating totally on the task at hand, mindless of the havoc she caused him.

That annoyed him. He tried to make a mental list of the things he needed to buy, striving to ignore her as well as she ignored him. It worked for a few minutes, as she trimmed across the back and crown of his head. Then she moved around to the other side, leaning even harder against that leg. But he noticed she worked quicker.

''Almost done. I'll just shape up the front. You probably should close your eyes so hair doesn't fall in them.''

Did she sound a bit breathless? Trent closed his eyes and felt her move in front of him. *Snip, snip, snip.* The scissors went faster. She ran the comb through his hair, lifting a strand in the air. *Snip, snip, snip.* Comb. *Snip, snip, snip.* Faster still.

She shifted her weight the tiniest bit, and Trent suddenly realized she was standing between his legs. Opening his eyes, he discovered she was trying to keep her distance, but doing a good job required her to bend her arms. That brought her closer. He watched the rapid rise and fall of her chest, admiring not only the view but her diligence in finishing the chore. If he leaned forward just a little bit, he could rest his face against her lovely softness. Lost in his imagination, he barely heard her whisper that the job was done.

Trent slowly raised his gaze to hers. Deep, desperate longing burned in her eyes.

Anna dropped the scissors.

He jerked the tablecloth free, tossing it aside. Circling her waist with his hands, he stood, lifting her feet off the porch, and carried her through the open front door. She slid her arms around his neck, lifting her face for his kiss.

Stepping inside the house reminded him of where they were, but he couldn't deny her—or himself—one sweet taste. He kissed her deeply, molding her body against his, wishing with all his heart he had the right to touch her, to fulfill her desire, to love her. But he didn't. He was a fool to even dream.

Trent broke off the kiss, holding her tenderly, waiting a minute to catch his breath. "Anna…" He brushed a kiss on her forehead.

"Hmm?" She snuggled closer, kissing his jaw.

"Don't open a barbershop."

Chapter Thirteen

The trip to Antelope Springs took three hours with an occasional stop to water the horses and for the boys to stretch their legs. Rachel and the youngsters rode in the two-seat buckboard with Anna. Trent and Duncan brought the ranch wagon to haul back supplies.

When they finally reached town, Anna drew the horses to a halt in front of Spencer's Mercantile. The boys scrambled down, racing inside the store to find out where Lizzie's sons were.

The youngsters usually spent the night at the Spencers', while Anna, Rachel and Duncan rented a couple of rooms at the hotel. Trent planned to stay at the wagon yard.

Trent pulled the wagon up beside the buckboard. "Do you want to meet us at the feed store?"

"There's no need. Tell Mr. O'Brien I'll drop by later and pay him. I'll say hello to Lizzie and take the buckboard to the wagon yard. Then I'm going to Haley's." She pointed across the street to the general store. "I figure I'd better buy supplies before I look at anything else."

"I'll bring the wagon over there when we're done." Trent smiled at Duncan. "Though I'll probably lose my partner. He's been dropping hints about staying at the feed store with Tim."

"That's fine." Anna glanced at Duncan, then looked back at Trent. "Both Spencer's and Haley's have a good selection of work clothes. Their prices are about the same, unless something is on sale."

"I'll check them both, starting at Haley's," said Trent. "That way I can load the wagon for you."

"Thanks. I'll see you in a few minutes." She smiled at him, appreciating his thoughtfulness.

"Thought I might drop in and say hello to Ian," said Duncan, winking at Rachel. "Let him know we're in town."

"That would be nice." Rachel grinned at her brother. "Keeps me from seeming forward, though I'd go by his office myself if I had to."

"Uh-oh, better watch out. She's turnin' into a floozy."

"I doubt it," said Anna with a laugh. "Rachel, do you want to go ahead and browse in here?"

"If you don't mind. You know how long it takes me to decide on dress fabric." Rachel laughed when Duncan quickly hopped down from the wagon and gallantly offered her his hand as she stepped out of the buckboard. She stopped on the boardwalk, glancing casually up and down the street, waiting for Anna.

Anna smiled at Duncan as he came around to her side of the buckboard and helped her down, too. He took the reins and looped them over the hitching post.

"Let me know what you have planned." She had decided to allow him some freedom, but she did have a few limits. That morning, she had given him thirty-five dollars, normal cowboy wages. "Don't stay out too late. I want you back at the hotel by eleven. And no gambling."

"I'm too young to go into the saloons, and everybody knows it."

"You can lose your money anywhere. Remember what your papa had to say about it."

"I do," Duncan said, his expression growing serious. "And you don't need to worry. I'm not going to gamble away my pay." A lightning smile flashed across his face. "Even if what I brought is burning a hole in my pocket."

"You left some at home?"

"Fifteen dollars. I figured if I didn't have it with me, I couldn't spend it."

"Wise man." Anna smiled and patted him on the shoulder. "Wish I'd thought to do that."

Duncan stepped back with a laugh. "You don't need to worry. You always manage to hang on to money."

As Anna and Rachel started into the store, Davy and Mitch came barreling out. "Slow down, you two," chided Anna. "You know better than to come running out of a store that way. You could knock someone over."

"Sorry, Mama," said Davy. "We'll be more careful."

"Good. Mitch, will you behave, too?"

"Yes, ma'am. Mrs. Spencer said we could go over to their house, if it's all right with you. She said Mrs. Lawson wouldn't mind keeping an eye on us."

Anna glanced at Davy. "Did Mitch understand correctly?"

"Yes, ma'am. She asked us to spend the night, like always."

"Walk on over there, then. Don't run on Main Street." She handed Davy some change. "Here's your candy money. Get some for your friends, too. I'll be over later. Don't go anywhere besides the store and the Spencers' house, unless Mrs. Lawson gives you permission."

"Thanks. We won't." Grinning, Davy put the money in

his pocket. "Come on, squirt. Let's show Mama we can behave like gentlemen." They carefully crossed the street, barely controlling their excitement as they went into the general store.

"That won't last." Rachel pushed open the wooden-framed glass door of Spencer's with a chuckle.

"I'll be happy as long as they don't run up and down the boardwalk or out into the street," said Anna. "Sometimes I wonder if they're growing up uncivilized."

"You don't need to worry about those boys," said Lizzie, who was setting up a window display. "They're as good as any town kids. Better than some. You will come to supper, won't you?"

"Of course." Anna smiled at Lizzie. "You know I won't pass up a chance for one of Mrs. Lawson's meals and a visit with you all evening."

"Rachel, you and Duncan are invited, too."

"Thank you, Mrs. Spencer. May I let you know later?" asked Rachel.

Lizzie's face lit up. "You expecting a better offer?"

Rachel blushed. "I don't mean to slight your meal or your company."

"But you're hoping Ian will take you out to eat." Lizzie smiled happily, adjusting the folds of a skirt hanging in the window.

"Maybe." Rachel's blush deepened as she shrugged. "I am very fond of him, and he's fond of me."

"Honey, that not exactly what I'd call it. The man practically worships the ground you walk on. But I'll quit teasing you now. A new shipment of spring fabrics came in yesterday. Just got the last of it on the shelves a half hour ago. There are ribbons and trims to match. And we have some new ready-made dresses hanging on the other side of the hats.'' She pointed to a rack of dresses nearby. ''That pink would look especially pretty on you.''

''Thanks.'' Rachel wandered over toward the dresses, pausing to look at the display of hats on the way.

''Can you imagine the clothes that man will buy for her?'' Lizzie sighed dreamily. ''She's already the prettiest girl in the county. Oh, won't Othelia Upton have a hissy fit the first time Ian takes Rachel to Fort Worth and brings her home dressed to the nines.''

Anna laughed and shook her head. ''You must lie awake at night and think of ways to annoy that woman.''

''Well, a thought has crossed my mind in the middle of the night on occasion but more often when I see her strutting down the street. Now, my dear, what are you looking for today?''

''Supplies first.'' She leaned closer to Lizzie, talking quietly. ''I'll be back later. Might even buy myself a new dress.''

''So you can look pretty for Trent? I've been almost afraid to ask if he's still around.''

''He is. They all want him to stay. He and Duncan are at the feed store. I'm supposed to meet him at Haley's, so I'd better go.''

''If he's shopping, tell him I'll knock off twenty percent on anything he wants. Same as I do for you. Just warn him not to tell anybody else, or they'll all want special treatment.''

Anna hugged her friend. ''You're a dear. The man's clothes are practically threadbare, so he needs just about everything.''

''We'll take care of him. I'll ask Josiah to see to it personally.''

The town had an ordinance against carrying weapons, so Trent left his gun at the sheriff's office. Duncan told him that the lawman had advised Anna to keep her pistol with her for safety. A young man about Duncan's age took his revolver and gun belt, marking them with a name tag. He explained that the sheriff was out of town and the deputy was out of the office right then. Trent wondered if the man snoring in an open cell was the deputy, but he didn't ask.

Embarrassed because his own clothes were so shabby, Trent had worn the shirt Anna gave him and borrowed Duncan's pants. He had to buy some new clothes, but he was determined not to spend too much. When the day came for him to leave the Double Deuce, he intended to have some money set aside. Though he wished otherwise, he was certain he would have to go sometime.

It didn't take long to load the bags of oats and chicken feed, so he arrived at the general store ahead of Anna. He wandered around a few minutes, looking at the numerous items they carried. Most of the brands were familiar, though he occasionally spotted one he'd never heard of. Everything he owned was secondhand, sometimes purchased, sometimes given in charity. He hadn't been in a real general store since his release from prison.

A man in his early twenties stood behind a long counter, tallying up an order for a neatly dressed, middle-aged woman. Another young man stacked canned goods on the shelves, and a third unpacked a large box of shoes. A polished, gray-haired man, who someone addressed as Mr. Haley, assisted another lady in choosing some dress material.

At first, no one paid Trent any mind. Then he noticed the woman whispering to the clerk behind the counter. The man glanced nervously in his direction and hurried across the store, speaking to Mr. Haley and nodding toward Trent.

While the clerk talked, the owner continued to unfold a bolt of bright blue silk, showing it to the tall, skinny woman, but he glanced at Trent several times. The lady customer turned, plucking nervously at the fringe on her black handbag.

His expression cold, Haley studied Trent for a minute, then gave the clerk instructions. The young man hustled over to another employee, both glancing at Trent as they talked. The two women didn't waste any time, either. Within a couple of minutes, everyone in the large store knew who he was.

And they all stared.

One beady-eyed weasel peeked around the end of a high display case, losing his derby in the process. Others sidled over to sections of the store that gave them a clear view of the convict. One elderly lady suddenly developed a keen interest in the plows propped against the nearby wall. Trent would have laughed at their antics if their curiosity and obvious contempt hadn't hurt so much.

When the door opened, Trent glanced up and almost groaned out loud. That malicious old biddy, Mrs. Upton, strolled into the store as if she owned it. He figured since her husband was the banker, there was a good chance she did—or part of it, at least. Hoping she wouldn't see him, he walked around a rack of men's suits.

One of the clerks appeared at the end of the aisle, pretending to tidy up an already neat display of shirts.

Trent considered making his escape but discovered he had a bit of pride left after all—probably Anna's doing. He wouldn't let their stares and silent accusations drive him out. Earlier in the week, he had broken the largest blade on his pocketknife, so he strolled over the far wall to check a glass case which held knives and other small items.

The shoe clerk craned his neck around a stack of boxes as if expecting him to steal something. Trent was tempted to point out that he'd either have to break the glass or lean over the case and practically stand on his head to reach anything.

Trent inspected the knives through the glass, spying a bone-handled one he liked. He checked the price and decided he didn't like it as well as he thought he did. The one in front of it appeared sturdier and was less money. He looked over at the anxious clerk and forced a smile. "Would you show me a knife, please?"

The young man seemed startled that he had asked politely. "Y-yes, sir." The clerk went around behind the case. "Which one?"

"The brown one, second from the top in this row."

The clerk removed it from the cabinet and handed it to Trent, glancing nervously at Haley. Trent had already noted that the owner watched his every move. He carefully opened the large blade, then the smaller one. "This looks like it will do the job." He closed the knife and laid it on the counter, pushing it over near the other man. "I'll take it. I'd also like to look at that harmonica in the corner."

The clerk removed the musical instrument and handed it to Trent. He turned it over in his hand, admiring the etched flowers on the side. "How does it sound?"

"I don't know. Don't think anybody's ever tried it."

"May I?"

The clerk nodded, his eyes widening.

Trent wasn't sure he could play a tune, though once upon a time, he'd been pretty good. He took a deep breath and lifted it to his mouth, running through a few notes. The harmonica had a good, clear tone. He played a few bars of "Yankee Doodle," frowning when he hit a wrong note. Trent glanced at the young man across the counter. "It's been a while."

The clerk's Adam's apple bobbed as he swallowed. "I reckon so."

A harmonica wasn't a necessity, but when Trent thought of the pleasure the music would bring Anna and the kids, he decided to buy it. It would also give him something to do on the nights he couldn't sleep. He handed it back to the clerk. "I'll take this, too."

"Can I show you anything else?"

"No, thanks. This will do for now." He followed the man up to the front and paid for his purchases. Haley hovered at the other end of the counter, pouring coffee beans into the large countertop grinder.

A little girl about Mitch's age tiptoed up, stopping about four feet away, curiously eyeing Trent. "Are you an outlaw?"

"No." Trent held out his hand as the clerk handed him the change.

"That lady says you are." She pointed in the general direction of Mrs. Upton and the tall, skinny woman.

Trent figured they both had been spouting off. He put the money in his pocket. "Well, she's mistaken. I'm just a cowboy." Seeing the little girl's dubious expression, he smiled. "You don't think so?"

She slowly shook her head. "She said you took somebody else's horses. My daddy says that stealing is wrong."

"They're both right. But it happened a long time ago. It's not something I'd do again."

"Why not?"

"I learned my lesson."

"You were punished?" the little girl asked with a frown.

Trent glanced at Haley, noting that though the man toyed with the coffee beans, he hadn't ground a one. "Yes, I was."

"Did you have to go to bed without your supper?"

"A few times."

"Priscilla, stay away from that man!" The child's

mother grabbed her by the arm, dragging her backward. "He'll hurt you, do terrible things to you!" She turned, sweeping the girl in front of her, pushing her toward the door.

Trent flinched, her vile accusation cutting deep. But what hurt even more was the panic he saw in the young mother's eyes—honest, bone-chilling fear for the safety of her daughter. Stunned, he glanced at Haley and was surprised to see a hint of sympathy in the man's expression. Trent cleared his throat, struggling to keep calm. "Ma'am…"

The woman halted, her back stiffening. She turned slowly, looking at him over her shoulder.

"I would never hurt your daughter." The anguish in his voice seemed to confuse her. "Or you."

"That's not what I heard."

Trent knew she wouldn't believe anything he had to say. There was only one other person present who could defend him, one who had been at Shane's party. Even as he looked at Othelia Upton, Trent told himself he was an idiot. "Ma'am, you know the truth."

The banker's wife preened at suddenly becoming the center of attention, yet she didn't say anything—good or bad.

"Mrs. Upton, you're a woman of integrity," Trent said quietly, hoping she couldn't tell that he didn't fully believe it. "Don't let me be judged by lies."

She studied him, her eyes narrowing shrewdly. He doubted if she cared how he was judged but weighed how coming to his defense would affect her standing in the community. When she nodded like a queen granting a favor to her lowliest subject, Trent breathed easier, though her high-handed manner irritated him.

"Come, my dear, let me set your mind at ease. Hank Newell assured us at Shane Parker's party that Mr. Malloy has been falsely maligned about what happened with that woman. He is innocent—at least of that offense." Mrs. Upton put her arm around the younger woman's shoulder, propelling her and the little girl to another part of the store.

Trent picked up the knife and harmonica and headed for the store entrance without looking at anyone else. Once outside, he walked to the end of the wooden building and down the boardwalk steps into the alley. Fairly well hidden from view, he leaned against the wall and drew a deep, shaky breath. When he heard brisk footsteps coming down the boardwalk from the opposite direction, he straightened.

Seconds later, Anna stepped down to cross the alley, stopping with a worried frown when she saw him. "Trent, what's wrong?" She hurried to his side.

He related what had happened in Haley's, from the time he entered the store until he left. He figured she might as well hear it all from him before she heard it from someone else. Leaning one hand against the building, he stared at the ground, nauseated. "The girl can't be more than five years old, but her mother was terrified I would hurt her." He swore under his breath. "Anna, how could she think I'd rape a child?"

"A mother's fear doesn't always make sense. She based her belief on rumor because that's all she's heard. Thankfully, Othelia was there to set her straight." She shook her head, her expression bemused. "Though I'm surprised she did. Her husband must have had a talk with her. Once people get to know you, they'll realize that you're a good, decent man."

"Will they, Anna?" He lowered his hand, meeting her gaze. Was he fighting a battle he could never win? Would he drag her down with him? "Won't there always be lingering doubts, if not about Rosie, then that I might steal again? Will I ever be able to go into a store in this town without everyone waiting to see if I slip something into my pocket?''

''Yes, you will. Right this minute, in fact. Lizzie said for you to come up to their place.'' Anna leaned a little closer and lowered her voice. ''Not only will they welcome you, they'll give you twenty percent off anything you buy, just like they do me.''

He stared at her in disbelief. ''Why would they do that?''

''Because they like you.''

''They hardly know me.''

''Well, they know me.'' She backed up toward the street, giving him a look that would have melted a block of ice at twenty below. ''And how much I like you.''

Chapter Fourteen

Trent entered Spencer's Mercantile, not expecting them to follow through on Lizzie's promise of a warm welcome. After all, they'd had a good half hour to reconsider such foolishness. Spencer was a businessman and mayor. Befriending a notorious outlaw, as Trent was bound to be considered by now, wouldn't help his business or his standing in the town.

The minute Trent walked through the doorway, Spencer came around the end of the front counter to meet him, holding out his hand. "Good afternoon, Mr. Malloy. It's good to see you again."

Trent shook his hand, trying to act as if such a welcome were an everyday occurrence. "Good afternoon. Anna tells me you have a good supply of work clothes."

"That we do. Denim pants, cotton and flannel shirts at a reasonable price." Spencer winked as he directed him toward the men's section of the store. "I'll guarantee a much better deal than my competition will give you."

"So I understand." Trent glanced at him as they walked down the aisle past a display of children's shoes. "I'm much obliged."

"Happy to help. Anna speaks highly of you, and that's good enough for us."

Trent wound up buying two pair of pants, three shirts, a pair of drawers, an undershirt, socks and a couple of handkerchiefs. Two of the shirts were for work and one was for Sunday-go-to-meetin'.

He hadn't set foot in a church building since his mother died and didn't expect to visit one anytime soon, but Anna said the circuit rider preacher would be holding services at Shane's before long. The minister usually came through their area once a month, but he'd been laid up for a while with a broken leg. Trent figured it would please her if he went with them. And after surviving the blizzard and finding Anna and her family, he reckoned he owed the Almighty the courtesy.

"We'd like to get to know you. Why don't you join us for supper tonight? It's always good to make a new friend," Spencer said with sincerity.

"Yes, sir, it is. I appreciate the invitation and would be pleased to come. What time?"

"Around six. It's a block north of the courthouse and two blocks east. The gray house with blue gingerbread trim. You can't miss it."

Trent thanked him and paid for his purchases as a clerk wrapped everything in brown paper and tied it securely. Walking back down the street, he met Anna on the boardwalk in front Haley's General Store and watched the clerks load the supplies into the freight wagon. "I'll take it over to the freight yard," he said as a store employee hefted the last twenty-five pound sack of flour into the wagon.

"Thanks. Did you find everything you needed?"

"Mostly." He paused as the clerk walked by, going into the store. "Figured I'd better wait on a hat. Spencer invited me to supper."

"I thought they might." Anna's smile reflected her pleasure. "You are coming, aren't you?"

"Yes." He lowered his voice. "Though it makes me as nervous as a frog in a fryin' pan."

"Don't be. They're just good, hardworking folks like you and me."

He was half tempted to point out that he was unlike anyone else in town, but decided against it. If Anna and her friends were willing to overlook his past, he should let them. Unfortunately, there were far too many others who wouldn't be so generous. Trent gave himself a mental shake, pushing aside the dreary thought. He glanced at Anna, his spirits lifting at her impish smile.

"I expect Josiah is tickled to have someone new to talk politics with," she said. "He has an opinion about everything. He'll bend your ear all night if you let him."

"Maybe I'll learn something. I haven't kept up with politics in a while." He grinned as her eyes twinkled merrily. "A long while."

"That doesn't matter. Josiah will fill you in on anything you've missed, and then some. He has a knack for knowing the most obscure facts and expounding on them at length."

Anna always enjoyed the Spencers, and that evening was no exception, though Rachel's absence at supper reminded her poignantly of the ongoing changes in her life. Duncan ate at Tim's, which he often did, but she worried about what mischief the O'Brien boy would lead him into afterward. At supper, Trent cut up Mitch's meat, something that had become so routine she thought nothing of it—until she caught the look Lizzie exchanged with Josiah.

After supper the adults moved out to the wide porch that ran around three sides of the house, enjoying the sunset and cool breeze. A few minutes later, Mrs. Lawson, the housekeeper, stuck her head out the kitchen door and bade them good-night.

The boys rounded up more friends to play baseball in the empty lot next door. They had enough for one team plus a couple of extras, so they took turns batting and didn't keep score.

Lizzie and Josiah brought them up-to-date on the local news, which Anna silently thought wasn't much. There had been the typical fights at the saloons the past two weekends. The preacher's wife was expecting their second child. The blacksmith and his wife had another argument, only this time it was right in the middle of Main Street. The sheriff was out of town for a week, testifying in a trial in San Angelo. The day he left, the deputy got drunk and had been that way ever since. Only their last bit of news was of interest. Robert Kingsley had called on the new schoolmarm three times.

"He came into town two weeks ago and took her out to dinner," said Lizzie. "Then last weekend, she cooked dinner for him, and they went for a drive on Sunday afternoon. But they had a spat. They were both angry when they returned."

"Too bad," Anna said, watching Davy hit the ball and run to second base. "She seems like a very nice young woman."

"She is. As far as I know they are still at odds. Myra didn't tell me the details, but I believe Kingsley may have inadvertently indicated his interest in you. She won't play second fiddle."

"She shouldn't have to," said Anna. Troubled by the anger in Trent's eyes, she steered the conversation to how the new schoolteacher was handling her classes.

The baseball game ended at dark, and the other boys went home. Anna's youngsters went inside with Patrick and

Stephen to find something else to do. The adults retreated to the parlor, hoping to escape some of the mosquitoes.

A short time later, Ian and Rachel joined them. Her face glowed with happiness as they sat together on the sofa. Only a blind man would miss how much Ian adored her. A bittersweet pain bruised Anna's heart as she wished Edwin could see his beautiful daughter in love. Then guilt swept over her. If Edwin were there, he would take one look at Anna and know she was in love, too—with another man.

Josiah and Ian began discussing the current race for governor, particularly candidate James Hogg, who was the Texas Attorney General. Lizzie leaned over to Rachel and whispered that she'd better get used to it. Rachel smiled indulgently and tucked her arm around Ian's.

"Well, I'm going to vote for him," said Josiah. "He's made some headway in battling the railroads. I think he can do more if he's governor and sets up that railroad regulatory commission he keeps talking about."

"The rail companies do need regulating. They set rates favorable to interests outside of Texas. It's cheaper to send East Texas lumber to Nebraska than it is to Dallas," said Ian. "But I don't agree with some of the other things in his platform, such as abolition of the national banking system and free coinage of silver."

"Well, most Westerners—Southerners, too, for that matter—will disagree with you on that. I'm still studying on it. He'll carry the farm vote, that's for certain."

Ian nodded. "I'm not so sure about the ranchers. Some of the smaller ones will probably be for him, and even the large landowners will admit lower railroad rates will help them. But I've heard he wants to strengthen the antitrust law he secured as attorney general. Some say he wants to take on the beef industry and land companies."

Anna noted that Trent did not contribute to the conversation but listened intently. She supposed most of the discussion was news to him. She also knew she should pay attention to what was being said. Though a woman might not be able to vote, she certainly should be interested in the outcome of elections and legislation.

But she had personal issues on her mind, concerns she thought had been put aside. She knew Edwin would not want her to be alone. Yet guilt over her feelings for Trent weighed heavily on her heart, even as she wondered if her love alone was enough for him. Would he ever believe how much she valued him as a man, a person? Would he ever be able to return her love?

She had bought her first new dress in ages. Made of peacock blue cotton sateen, the two-piece style was all the fashion and suited her well. The full skirt draped gracefully in front and had a wide, cascading drapery in back. She even wore a long, slender bustle to achieve the right effect.

The bottom of the basque, or blouse, covered the waist of the skirt. Gathered slightly for fullness across the bosom, it fit snugly at the waist, with a high arch over the hips, and came to a point at the center front and back. The right front overlapped the left and fastened with hidden buttons and buttonholes. A frill of white embroidered lace trimmed the right front edge, ran around the high-standing collar, and back down the left front. The dress made her feel pretty and feminine, which had prompted her to pin up her hair in a chignon instead of the usual simple braid.

Trent hadn't seemed to notice. If he did, he didn't bother to tell her she looked nice, or even let his thoughts show in his eyes. She wondered if he didn't like it, or if he thought a woman who worked outdoors all day looked foolish getting all gussied up—like trying to make a silk purse out of a sow's ear.

Another thought slithered into her mind and stayed there. Maybe he didn't care for her the way she believed he did. Had she let her imagination run wild, putting feelings behind his looks and kisses when all he truly felt was desire?

After five long years without a woman, he probably would have been attracted to her if she'd been missing half her teeth.

Suddenly, the room felt stifling. "Excuse me, I think I'll get a breath of air." Anna hurried out the front door and around the porch to the side of the house next to the empty lot. Taking a deep breath, she listened to the night sounds, so unlike the stillness of the ranch. Down the street, a baby cried. A dog barked on the other side of town, and the hound dog living next door to Lizzie answered him. Rowdy laughter and tinkling piano music drifted up from the saloons, a reminder of her foolishness.

A board on the porch creaked, and Anna glanced over her shoulder.

Trent walked toward her, a dark, perplexed frown creased his brow. "Anna, what's going on with you?"

She hesitated, afraid he would think she was being silly. "I'm wearing a new dress," she whispered, thinking how much she had fussed and primped to look pretty for him.

His gaze skimmed over her. "It looks mighty fine on you."

"You don't really like it. If you did, you would have told me earlier." She stepped away from him, putting her back to the wall, and crossed her arms.

"When? At dinner? On the porch or in the parlor with everybody listening?"

"Would that have been so bad?"

"Maybe, maybe not." He stepped in front of her, resting one hand on the gray wall beside her head. "I reckon it wouldn't hurt for anyone else to hear me tell you that the color turns your eyes to sparkling, silver stars. It probably wouldn't hurt to say the style is very flattering.'' He moved his right hand to her waist, unfastening the three lower buttons, and slipped his fingers beneath the basque, caressing her side. Only a thin lawn chemise separated his hot palm from her skin.

Anna gasped softly, her heart rate tripling at the unexpected intimacy of his touch. She uncrossed her arms and lifted her hands to his shoulders.

"Should I have mentioned how well it shows off your pretty shape?" His gaze burned into hers, and his voice grew deeper, softer. "Or how it tempts me?" He lowered his left hand to her waist, sliding it, too, beneath the blouse.

Anna found it hard to breathe.

"Half a dozen times tonight, I've thought about how it would feel to touch you like this." He moved his hands up her ribs, his thumbs grazing the underside of her breasts through the chemise.

"Trent..." Anna murmured his name as she sagged against the wall.

He caressed her again. Anna caught her breath and closed her eyes. She felt him move closer. He brushed a featherlight kiss at the corner of her mouth.

She threaded her fingers through Trent's hair, loving its thick softness. A shiver of anticipation swept through her. "No one has ever made me feel the way you do," she whispered, turning her head a fraction to meet his lips. She expected, and wanted, deep hot kisses and bold caresses. Instead, he kissed her with exquisite tenderness, the gentle movement of his thumbs teasing yet soothing, making her ache even more.

When he slowly straightened, she almost begged him not to stop. Then the sound of childish laughter from a distant room reminded her where they were. "Why do you always do this when we're surrounded by people?'' she asked in exasperation.

He smiled ruefully. ''We're always surrounded by people, even if most of the time, they're little.''

She took a deep, shaky breath. ''This is torture.''

''Yes, but in some ways, it's safer. We can taste and touch but have to stop.'' He smoothed a loose strand of hair behind her ear and tucked it into her chignon, then quickly buttoned the bottom of her blouse. ''As much as I want you, sugar, I could never make love to you, then sneak back to my room and pretend nothing happened. And you couldn't, either. You aren't the kind of woman to take a lover.''

''No, I'm not.'' Anna sighed quietly. ''Though sometimes I wish I were.'' A golden spark flashed through his eyes, and Anna almost kissed him again. She eased away and walked over to the porch railing, peering past the eaves at the sky. ''It's funny how even in a small town like this, the lights block out some of the stars.''

''That's one reason I like to sleep outside.'' He moved beside her, resting his hands on the railing. ''The night sky is never prettier than out in the open, whether you're in the mountains or on the prairie.''

''I'd love to see real mountains.'' She looked at him, admiring the way the moonlight illuminated his handsome face. ''Are the ones in Colorado and Montana as beautiful as they seem in pictures?''

He nodded, hooking his thumbs in the pockets of his pants. ''Majestic doesn't seem like big enough a word, but it's the only one I can think of to come close to describing them. It's beautiful country, but I prefer to live and work in Texas. The year I spent in Montana, it got down to thirty below. One winter was enough for me. That was one reason I left Kansas in the first place.''

Anna swatted at a mosquito on the sleeve of her dress. "Is that where you grew up?"

"Yep. My grandpa had a small farm. Corn was his main crop, though he didn't work hard at raising it. He figured he had me for that. I put up with his temper, cussin' and general contrariness until my fifteenth birthday. When I woke up that morning, I looked out at the field and decided I was done with farming. Done with him hitting me whenever he felt like it. I wrapped my few belongings in a shirt, walked away and never looked back. Hitched up with some cowboys heading back to Texas from a trail drive, and mostly been here ever since."

"Do you have any other family?" She turned so she could see him better and leaned against the porch railing.

Trent shook his head. "No. Pa died in the war, fighting for the Union. Mama only lived a little while after she got word that he was gone. She was sickly to begin with, and after he died, she seemed to dry up inside. We'd been staying with her mother and father, so they kept me. Grandma wasn't too bad, though she was rough in her ways. Politeness and manners weren't real important to her.

"Neither one of them could read, and they didn't see any sense in me going to school. I'd been working on a ranch for a couple of years when I finally got up enough courage to ask one of the other cowboys to teach me to read and write. I'm not real good at it, but I get by. Another friend taught me enough arithmetic to keep from gettin' cheated."

He brushed a mosquito off Anna's neck. "We'd better go inside before you get bit. Those critters like the way you smell almost as much as I do." He leaned close to her for a second, inhaling deeply. "You have the sweetest smellin' neck of any woman I've ever known."

"You go around sniffing women's necks?" she asked with a smile.

"Just the ones I want to kiss."

Anna caught the heat in his eyes and shook her head. "Trent, you're doing it again."

"Yeah, reckon I am." He settled his hand at the small of her back and nudged her toward the front of the house, then leaned close to her ear. "Ain't it fun?"

Chapter Fifteen

Figuring Anna would like some time alone with her friends, Trent left the Spencers' a short time later. He enjoyed the evening more than he'd thought he would. Lizzie and Josiah had a knack for making a stranger feel welcome, though he couldn't relax completely. Being comfortable in someone's home had never come easy to him—except for Anna's, and that had taken time.

Trent strolled back to Main Street. Like many small western towns, Antelope Springs wasn't big enough to have a separate red-light district. Four saloons were scattered in among the regular businesses. Two others, the Red Garter and the Good Time, occupied the last buildings on each side of the street. According to Hank, if a man wanted more than a drink and a game of cards, he went to one of those. Judging from the music and rowdy laughter coming from that end of town, they did a good business.

Spying Hank through the window of the Silver Buckle Saloon, Trent went inside. He stopped by the bar and bought a glass of whiskey, then wandered across the room to where his friend and three others played draw poker.

''Evenin','' said Hank, looking up with a grin. ''I saw

Miss Rachel and Ian come out of Ivy's Restaurant earlier. Wondered if you'd come to town with the Caldwells.''

Trent nodded to the others at the table. He was well acquainted with the other two cowboys, Rooster Stevens and Gus Hall. The fourth man was Tim O'Brien's father. When they returned his greeting, he pulled out a chair from the empty table next to them and sat down near Hank. ''Figured I might as well get it over with.''

Rooster was in his midtwenties, short, and scrappy. He frowned at Trent over the cards in his hand. ''Been rough?''

''Some. Reckon it'll take a while for folks to realize I won't steal them blind.'' He didn't want to think about the little girl at Haley's and her mother's fear, much less mention it. ''The Spencers were real nice, though. Treated me like any other customer.'' *Better than most,* he thought with a tiny smile.

''Since they're so close to Mrs. Caldwell, I'd expect that.'' Hank glanced at O'Brien and tossed two dollars onto the pile in the middle of the table. ''I'll see your dollar and raise you one.''

Shrugging, Rooster slid his cards into a stack and laid them facedown on the table. ''I'm out. Y'all are too rich for me.'' He grinned at Hank and picked up his mug of beer, leaning back in the chair and taking a long drink.

''Me, too,'' said Gus, slapping his cards down on the table. ''It's up to you, O'Brien. Somebody better stop Hank's run of luck, or he'll be buying his own spread.''

''I think I'm the man to do it. I call you with triplets.'' The feed store owner grinned and threw another dollar in the pot. He spread his cards faceup on the table—three tens, a four and a six. ''And you, Newell?''

''Two pair.'' Hank laid down his cards, a pair of fives, a pair of nines and a jack. ''You got me beat.''

"About time someone did," said O'Brien with a boisterous laugh. "Glad it was me." He scooped up the money, glancing at Trent. "He's won the last three hands."

"Trent, you want to play?" asked Rooster, scooting back his chair and standing.

"No, thanks. I bought some new duds. Better hang on to what little I have left."

"I'm done, too," Hank said, as he stood and stretched his arms above his shoulders. "Can't sit any longer or my joints will start creaking."

"You creak anyway, you ol' galoot." Rooster dodged when Hank playfully jabbed at his shoulder. "Gotta catch me."

"Squishin' you ain't worth the effort, boy. Wouldn't hardly make a grease spot."

Rooster just grinned. "You comin' over to the Red Garter with us? I hear they got a new gal. A real purty one with long blond hair and a generous figure." He held out his hands in front of his chest, grinning wider.

"She's pretty enough," said O'Brien. "Though her figure is generous because she's a bit on the plump side." He winked at Rooster. "Not that you'd notice much. She's a young one, but she could teach the other gals a thing or two." He shuffled the cards with a satisfied smile. "Yes, sir, sweet little Jasmine knows how to please."

Trent frowned thoughtfully. O'Brien was married, and though it wasn't that unusual for a married man to go to a saloon gal occasionally, he had a feeling Tim's father was a steady customer. Tim probably was, too. Trent had been with a few soiled doves over the years, his first when he was Duncan's age. But the thought of Anna's stepson going to one troubled him.

Hank glanced at Trent, then looked back at Rooster. "I think I'll wander around town awhile. See who else we run into. Come on, Trent, I'll show you the sights. They got a stuffed two-headed calf over at the Longhorn.''

Rooster shook his head. "I hope I never get as old as you two. If the day ever comes when I'm more interested in seeing a two-headed calf than a pretty woman, somebody just shoot me." He shifted his gaze to Trent, a gleam lighting his eyes. "Then again, if I was with women as pretty as the Caldwells every day, I might be content to look at a freak calf, too.''

"Careful, Rooster, or you may get shot sooner than you want," Trent warned softly.

"I didn't mean no offense," Rooster said quickly, his expression wary. "It's just that spending time with fine ladies like them would make a man think twice about going to a cathouse and spending time with whores.'' His face turned beet red, and he gulped. "That didn't come out right.''

Trent glared and took a step toward him, but Hank moved in between them.

"Rooster, you're diggin' yourself in deeper every time you open your mouth." Hank grinned and clamped his hand down on the younger man's shoulder, turning him toward the door. "You'd better skedaddle before Trent gives you a whipping.''

Rooster nodded. "Come on, Gus. Let's get out of here." He glanced sheepishly at Trent. "I didn't mean that like it sounded.''

Trent nodded, silently accepting the apology. Rooster wouldn't intentionally be disrespectful of Anna even if he thought there might be something going on between her and Trent. He was a good man, but his brain and tongue didn't always cooperate.

"Sure I can't talk you into another game?" asked O'Brien.

"Nope," said Hank. "Had my fill of thinkin' for the evenin'. Since my luck's turned, I'm not anxious to get cleaned out."

"Do you know what Tim and Duncan are doing tonight?" Trent asked the feed store owner.

O'Brien shook his head and leaned back in the chair. "Tim's full-grown. What he does is his business as long as he doesn't cause any trouble or show up late for work."

Trent and Hank left the Silver Buckle, going across the street to the Longhorn. Sure enough, the baby calf was displayed prominently above the bar. Trent studied it for a few minutes, thinking the poor thing would have had all sorts of problems if she'd grown up, especially with two sets of wicked horns.

They stayed a while, visiting with acquaintances and listening to the piano music. Hank had another drink, but Trent passed. After the blizzard, he concluded that getting drunk was pure folly.

Leaving the saloon, they headed back toward the wagon yard. A few minutes later, they came across Duncan, Tim and two other town lads about the same age sitting on the side of the boardwalk between the doctor's office and the apothecary.

"Evenin', Trent, Hank. Fine night," said Duncan with a silly grin.

Trent frowned, his gaze darting around the group as one of the other boys clumsily tried to hide something beneath his jacket. "Pleasant enough."

"It's gonna get better 'fore it's over." Tim grinned and poked Duncan in the side with his elbow.

Duncan frowned, as if warning his friend to be quiet. "Uh, maybe. What ya been doin'?" he asked, slightly slurring his words.

Trent stepped into the street, moving around in front of

Duncan. The strong odor of whiskey bombarded his nostrils. Drawing back, he whistled softly. "How much have you had to drink?"

"Just a couple of swallows." Duncan motioned toward one of his companions. "Neil spilled some on my britches."

"Aren't you supposed to be back at the hotel by eleven?" Trent nudged up the front of his hat. The boy was going to get into a heap of trouble. "It's a quarter till."

Duncan's eyes grew wide. "Already? I can't go back there smellin' like this. Anna will skin me alive. You think you could get her to let me stay out until twelve?"

"That smell isn't going to disappear by then. What's on your breath won't, either."

"What are you so worried about?" asked Tim. "So she throws a hissy fit and stomps around the house for a few days. It ain't gonna matter in a week or two."

Eyes narrowing, Trent pinned the O'Brien boy with his gaze. "Duncan respects Anna and how she feels about things." He straightened his hat and looked at Duncan, holding out his hand. "Come on over to the wagon yard. I'll go talk to her, suggest you bunk down with us for the night. Maybe we can air those pants out enough so she won't notice."

"Thanks." Duncan took his hand, stumbling a bit when Trent pulled him to his feet.

Trent steadied him. "Can you walk straight?"

"I think so." Duncan looked sheepish. "But you'd better stay close. I'm feelin' a little dizzy. I'd hate to fall flat on my face on Main Street."

"You wouldn't be the first," said Hank, chuckling as he moved to Duncan's other side. "Come on, son, I'll tell you about my trail ridin' days."

"He needs to sleep, not listen to your yarns all night." Trent winked at Duncan.

"You're just afraid I'll tell somethin' on you. Come to think of it, I probably could. Let's see, which you want to hear about—the pretty little filly in Austin that chased him down the street in her petticoat or the time he got throwed in the creek and purt near drowned?"

"Both." Duncan glanced at Trent and laughed at his irritated expression. "He may give us a lickin' though."

"Ain't big enough for the two of us. We can whup him."

"Hey, Duncan, you better stay with us," called Tim.

Duncan stopped and looked back at his friend.

Trent glanced back in time to see O'Brien take a long swig from the whiskey bottle. "You keep that up, and you'll be fallin' down drunk before long."

"I can hold my liquor. He could, too, if you give him a chance." Tim shifted his gaze to Duncan. "She works you like a full-growed man. Time you took a stand and made her start treatin' you like one when you come to town instead of like a snot-nosed kid." His grin was filled with devilry. "The women over at the Red Garter won't treat you like no little boy."

"Shut up, Tim." Duncan's face turned red.

Tim shook his head. "Too bad. You don't know what you're missin'."

"Ignore him," Trent said, draping his arm around Duncan's shoulders. "He never learned to respect his mama."

Duncan turned away from Tim and started walking. "That's 'cause his pa doesn't show her any respect." They were almost to the wagon yard, when he glanced up at Trent. "He's right about one thing, though. Anna treats me like a man at the ranch and like a kid here in town."

"It's because she loves you and wants to protect you."

"Drinkin' a little doesn't hurt anything."

"Maybe a little is all right. But if you pour too much down you too fast, it can kill you. Even if you go slow, liquor robs a man of clear thinking and wise choices. It can make you act like a fool, do things you'll regret come mornin'."

"I reckon."

Trent knew he couldn't convince him. Sometimes a boy had to learn things for himself. Unfortunately, at his age, Duncan probably spent most of his time thinking about women.

"It has to be difficult on Anna without your father to help her. Give her a little more time to get used to you growin' up."

"Heck, Trent, she married Pa when she was fifteen. Met him one day and married him the next." He was silent for a minute, then said quietly, "She wasn't any older than me."

Just like he figured. "But she was his wife. There's a big difference." Trent and Duncan stopped outside the livery building and wagon yard. Hank eased away from them, going on inside, leaving them alone.

"You can't tell me you haven't been with saloon gals," said Duncan, speaking in a hushed voice.

"No, I can't."

"How old were you the first time?"

Trent hesitated. "Sixteen. I'd been on my own for a year and might as well have been for the six before that. I didn't have anyone who loved me and cared what I did.

"Waitin' isn't easy, but it would be better if you held out until you can come to town on your own. Anna will have a good idea what you might be doin', but she won't feel so responsible. She's raisin' you the best she can, Duncan."

"I know she is." He stuffed one hand in his pocket and

looked dejectedly at the ground. "But, Trent, all my friends have already been with a woman. Some of them several times. They talk about how the gals look, how it feels. It's drivin' me loco."

"Goin' to the Red Garter will only help temporarily. The need comes back." Trent ruffled Duncan's hair. "Real often for a few years. Being with that kind of woman isn't as satisfying as your friends want you to believe. A saloon gal will say most anything she thinks you want to hear, but they're empty words. You're just a way to make money. She may ease the physical ache, but you'll walk away with a hollow feeling inside. I suppose only the woman you love can fill that emptiness."

"You ever been with someone you loved?"

Trent shook his head. "I just kissed her." *And touched.* "Kissin' her was a whole lot nicer than beddin' anyone I'd ever paid for the privilege." He rested a hand on Duncan's shoulder. "It helps to occupy your mind with something else. Go on in and visit with Hank. Get him to tellin' stories. I'll talk to Anna."

"Thanks, Trent. She wouldn't listen to me, but she probably will you."

"Those apron strings won't choke you, even if they feel like they are. You'll be on your own soon enough."

Trent hurried to the hotel, afraid Anna would come looking for Duncan if he didn't show up by eleven. Sure enough, when he knocked on the door to her room, she opened it instantly. When she saw him instead of Duncan, she peered out into the hall with a dark frown.

"Duncan was supposed to be here by now. Have you seen him?"

He wanted to smooth away her worry lines with his fingertips and soothe her fears with gentle words of reassurance. "Just left him. He's down at the wagon yard with

Hank. He sent me to ask if he could stay there with us tonight and listen to Hank and some of the other men spin yarns.''

Anna crossed her arms and frowned up at him. ''Why didn't he come ask himself?''

Trent rested his hand against the doorjamb and smiled lazily. ''I reckon he figured once he was here, you'd want him to stay.'' He leaned a little closer—as much as he dared but not nearly as much as he wanted to. ''Probably thought I could be more persuasive.'' He lowered his gaze to her lips. Remembering how sweet she had tasted earlier made him restless. ''With him down there, maybe I should borrow his room,'' he said softly. ''For a little while, anyway.'' He looked back up, catching a flash of heat in her eyes before she glared at him.

''Get out of here and quit stirring me up,'' she whispered irritably. ''Duncan can stay at the wagon yard if you promise to take care of him.''

''He's too old to need takin' care of, but I'll keep an eye on him. Sleep well, sugar,'' he added in a whisper.

''Not likely.'' She shut the door the door so fast it almost mashed his fingers.

When Trent reached the wagon yard, he discovered honoring his promise would be harder than he had anticipated.

Duncan was gone.

Chapter Sixteen

"I went out behind the livery for a few minutes," said Hank, his expression apologetic. "When I came back here you were both gone. I thought maybe he went with you."

"I shouldn't have left until I knew he was with you," said Trent. "His friends have been fillin' his head with stories about wild, wild women."

"A young man sowin' his oats." Hank sighed as they started toward the edge of town. "I remember those days. Seems like a hundred years ago."

"It was." Trent smiled at his friend.

"Ever think we're too young to feel this old?"

"Most every mornin'. Wonder if city dwellers do as much creakin' and groanin' as we do."

"Depends on their occupation, I reckon. Shopkeepers and office men have it soft." Hank grinned as they stepped up on the boardwalk, their boots tapping out a steady rhythm. "And it shows. On most, that is. Ian can hold his own with us any day."

"Considerin' his age, I don't know as that's a compliment."

"Guess we'd better not mention it."

They walked the rest of the way in silence, ever mindful

that trouble might spill out of the saloons right in front of them. When they entered the Red Garter, Trent quickly scanned the room. There was no sign of Duncan, Tim, or any of their friends. He spotted Rooster at a table, leaning his chair back on two legs. The cowboy looked up lazily when they came through the door.

They wove their way between the patrons and scantily clad women to his side. Trent glanced around again. The saloon gals were more attractive than most in small towns, though only a few were truly pretty. Their low-cut, knee-length dresses left just enough to the imagination to make lonesome cowboys pant for more.

"Have you seen Duncan?" asked Trent.

"Nope. Been sittin' right here the whole time. He ain't come in."

"What about Tim O'Brien?"

"Ain't seen him, either."

"You already been upstairs?" asked Hank.

"Nope. Waitin' for my turn with the new gal."

Hank glanced around the saloon, smiling at a blonde who gave him a come-hither look. "They aren't all occupied." He nodded to the woman.

"Not now, Hank," warned Trent. "We have other things to tend to. Rooster, if Duncan comes in, try to keep him down here until we get back."

"Only 'til Jasmine calls me. After that, he can fend for himself."

Trent and Hank went across to the Good Time Saloon but didn't find Duncan or his friends there, either. They made their way back up that side of the street, then down the other, checking every saloon along the way. "They must be hidin' out somewhere, building up their courage with the whiskey."

Trent stopped in front of the Red Garter. "Go on over to the Good Time. If they show up, holler."

"How come you're sendin' me over there?" Hank peeked through the door, looking around the room. "Dang, that purty little gal ain't downstairs now."

"That's why I'm sendin' you over there. If I leave you here, you'll forget all about keepin' Duncan out of their clutches."

"You ain't as much fun since you started actin' like a daddy," grumbled Hank.

That gave Trent pause. He sometimes felt like a father to the younger boys, but not to Duncan. "Big brother. He's too old to be my son."

"Well, the other young'uns aren't. You'll make 'em a good daddy, even if you have turned into a wet blanket."

"Go do your job and quit complainin'."

Hank wandered across the street, muttering under his breath.

Trent went inside the Red Garter, pausing near the doorway. He didn't see Duncan or any of his friends. Nodding to Rooster, he stepped up to the bar and watched the reflection of the room in the large mirror hanging on the wall.

"What'll it be?" asked the tall, stout bartender.

"Whiskey."

The bartender set a clean glass on the counter and poured the drink. "Noticed you in here a while ago. You lookin' for someone in particular?"

Trent paid for the drink. "A kid about my height, a little thinner. He's probably with Tim O'Brien."

"They haven't been in, though I wouldn't be surprised to see the O'Brien boy anytime now. He's a Saturday night regular. What do you want with the kid?"

Trent sipped the whiskey. "I work for his stepmother. Promised her I'd look out for him, only he took off. I think he's with Tim, working up the courage to come here. She'll be mad enough if she finds out he's drinkin', but if he visits one of the gals and his mama hears of it, she'll be stoked up hotter than a depot stove.''

"Pick a chair. Sit as long as you like."

Trent crossed the room and sat down beside Rooster. They chatted for about ten minutes until Duncan and Tim came in. Duncan walked into a table, then bowed slightly and attempted to apologize to an empty chair.

Tim caught him by the arm and pulled him over to the bar. "A drink for my friend."

"Looks to me like he's had enough already," said the bartender, resting his hands on the polished mahogany counter.

"Think so?" Tim turned to Duncan. "You had enough?" he asked, slurring his words.

Trent started toward the bar as a buxom brunette sidled up beside Duncan, putting her arm around his waist. "Better say yes, honey. If you drink anymore, you'll fall asleep before we have any fun." She ran her hand across his chest. "And I think you and me could have a real good time."

"Not tonight." Trent stopped behind them, hoping to get the boy out of there without causing a scene.

She glanced back at Trent in irritation, then raked her gaze over him, lifting her lips in a seductive smile. "Whatever you say, honey." She released Duncan and moved over a few steps. Turning, she leaned back against the bar, her sultry expression inviting Trent to join her.

Duncan turned around, catching hold of the edge of the bar for balance, and frowned at him. "You're supposed to be talkin' to Anna."

"I took care of that a while ago. You were supposed to stay at the wagon yard."

"Changed m' mind." Duncan looked at the soiled dove

on his right, his wistful gaze resting on the exposed white skin of her ample bosom.

Tim moved over, letting a young redhead slip in next to Duncan on the other side. Duncan shifted his gaze toward her, taking a minute to focus on her face. "You're sure pretty," he said with a sigh.

"Aren't you sweet. Handsome, too." She slid her hand up his chest and around his neck, leaning against him. "Why don't you come upstairs with me, darlin'? Pearl can have your friend." She winked at Tim. "The cowboy friend. Betsy's waitin' for you, Tim."

Duncan looked at the brunette. "Do you mind, ma'am?"

She glanced at Duncan, then smiled at Trent. "Not at all."

"Come on, Duncan, we're going back to the wagon yard before your mama wrings our necks." Trent moved forward, reaching for Duncan's shoulder.

Pearl stepped right into his path. Before he could react, she draped her arms around his neck and pressed against him. "Leave the boy alone and come upstairs with me."

"Let Duncan go with Sal," Tim said. "His ma don't have to find out."

Trent shook his head and pulled Pearl's hands loose, pushing her away from him. "No, thanks. I'm not interested."

"I always figured working for a female would be downright irritating, but guess I didn't think about the side benefits," said Ned Bender from behind him.

Rage swept through Trent, but he clamped down on it, turning slowly to size up the situation. This time Bender wasn't wearing a gun, but he had a couple of friends with him. "Shut up, Bender."

"That pretty little widow must be takin' real special care

of you." Bender glanced at his companions with a nasty grin.

Trent doubled up his fists. When Bender looked around, he jabbed him in the jaw. The cowboy jerked back a step, then started swinging. Trent blocked his blows and buried his fist in the other man's stomach, following with a hard punch to the jaw. As Bender staggered backward, his friend attacked, hitting Trent in the mouth.

"Hey, that's not fair," Duncan cried, going after the second man. He landed several good punches before the cowboy caught him in the eye.

Trent jerked the man away from Duncan, throwing him aside. Bender's friend stumbled backward and crashed into the table beside Rooster, smashing it to the floor. Dazed, he raised up on his elbows, but Rooster planted his boot in the middle of the man's chest and pushed him down again, holding him there.

Bender charged, but Trent sidestepped, grabbing him as he went by, and shoved him into the bar. Trent slammed Bender's head down on the counter, knocking him out. As he slid to the floor, Trent spun, facing the third man. "You want to take me on?"

"It ain't my fight." He backed away to the other end of the bar.

Bender groaned, and Trent bent down, grabbing a handful of the man's shirt. Lifting his head and shoulders off the floor, Trent glared at him. "There's nothing going on between Mrs. Caldwell and me. She's a decent, moral woman. If I hear of you bad-mouthing her again, you'll think this was just playacting. Understand?"

Bender nodded feebly, and he released him, letting his head hit the floor. Trent dug most of his money out of his pocket and handed it to the bartender. "If this doesn't pay for the table and anything else we broke, let me know. I'll have to settle up with you next payday.''

The bartender counted the money and nodded. ''This should do it.''

Red-haired Sal fussed over Duncan. ''Oh, honey, you're gonna have a shiner, even if you are a pretty good fighter. Let's go take care of that eye.''

''He stays with me!'' shouted Trent.

Sal's lips puckered into a pout, but she moved away from Duncan. ''Some other time, darlin'.''

''Where'd you learn to fight like that?'' asked the bartender.

Trent tasted blood and wiped his mouth with the back of his hand. ''Prison.''

The man behind the counter raised an eyebrow. ''You must be Trent Malloy.'' When Trent nodded, he asked, ''You got any more enemies?''

Trent picked up his hat and jammed it on his head. Grabbing Duncan's arm, he tugged him toward the door. ''Just about everybody in Texas.''

Anna slipped out of her hotel room, quietly easing the door shut so she wouldn't wake Rachel. Reminding Duncan to meet her for breakfast in time for church was only an excuse to check on him and ask him to come back to the hotel. There was no sense paying for a room, then not using it. ''I shouldn't have told Trent he could stay with him,'' she whispered to herself as she hurried down the stairs. ''Duncan is my responsibility, not his.''

The dozing desk clerk jerked awake and looked up in surprise. ''Is something wrong, Mrs. Caldwell?''

''No, everything is fine. I left something down at the wagon yard that I'll need in the morning. I'll be back in a few minutes.''

"I don't know as it's safe for a woman to go out there alone, ma'am. There are a lot of cowboys in town this weekend, and most of them have been drinking." The clerk stood uncertainly, as if he might be thinking about escorting her.

"My son and hired hand are at the wagon yard. I don't think I'll have a problem between here and there, but if I'm uncomfortable, I'll ask one of them to see me back here."

"Very well, ma'am. Be careful."

"I will." Anna hurried down the boardwalk, glancing nervously at the door of the first saloon she came to. One of Shane's men stood outside and nodded politely.

"Where you headed, Mrs. Caldwell?"

"To the wagon yard."

"I'm goin' that way myself. Mind if I walk with you?"

"I'd appreciate it, Zack." She relaxed as he moved beside her, shortening his long stride to keep pace with hers. "I've never ventured out this late at night." Loud laughter poured out of another saloon as they walked past. "It's rowdier than I'd expected."

"Gets this way on payday. The men like to blow off steam. There's a lot of whiskey flowing tonight as usual." Nearing the wagon yard, they stepped off the boardwalk to cross the street. Zack stumbled and chuckled quietly, the scent of liquor drifting on his breath. "Probably had more myself than I should have. Lost my money in a card game last payday, so haven't been to town all month."

Anna smiled to herself. She'd known Zack for several years and had never heard him speak more than one or two sentences at a time. Whiskey not only loosened his legs, but his tongue as well.

"Yes, ma'am. They do get rowdy. Most of the boys are cordial enough, but seems like there are always a few out to make trouble, like Ned Bender. He has to be one of the orneriest men I ever met. Not that it did him any good tonight. From what I hear, him and his crony weren't any match for Trent and Duncan.''

Anna halted, pivoting on her toes to face him. ''What are you talking about?''

''Uh-oh.'' Zack scratched in back of one ear, looking sheepish. ''I better let them tell you what happened since I got it secondhand.''

Anna settled her hands on her hips. ''Tell me what you heard, Zack. Now.''

''Well, they were down at the Red Garter—''

''The Red Garter!'' *All those willing, eager women.*

Squirming, Zack cleared his throat. ''Uh…yes, ma'am. That's what I heard. Bender said something insulting, and Trent lit into him, settin' him back a bit. Then one of Bender's friend's hit Trent, and Duncan went after him.'' Nodding, he smiled in approval. ''Hear the boy done himself proud, too, before he got punched in the eye. Trent took care of that feller, then knocked Bender out when he tried again. Then I guess they left.''

''Oh?'' she asked sarcastically. ''They didn't let the *ladies* take care of their wounds?''

Zack cleared his throat again. ''Well, ma'am, I can't rightly say much about that, though I heard Sal made quite a fuss over Duncan. Reckon that's understandable.''

''Why?''

''She was the one he'd picked. Don't know why he decided to let Trent have Pearl, though. She's a right smart prettier than Sal. Guess he likes red hair better than dark brown. Or maybe he was too drunk to tell the difference.''

The picture of Trent in the arms of a dark-haired beauty flashed through her mind. Pain engulfed her, piercing her heart in a way nothing ever had. Anna moved away from

Zack, rubbing her arms against the cool air, but no warmth could touch the coldness in her soul.

She had thrown herself at him like a wanton, inviting his kisses, his touch. She trusted him, believed she was dear to him. She defied her neighbors and friends to show her faith in him. *And the first time he's in town, he goes to a whore. Oh, Lord, I'm such a fool! Such a stupid, stupid fool.*

He murmured honeyed words and left her aching, but he'd never made her any promises. She was nothing more than a convenient amusement. She wouldn't fulfill his desire, so he turned to someone who would. Someone who didn't need commitment or words of love and reassurance or the sanctity of marriage vows.

She had depended on him to take care of Duncan, when she should have been the one watching over him. The loathsome man had taken that wonderful, innocent boy to a den of iniquity. "Edwin, I failed you," Anna whispered miserably.

A sudden blaze of anger smothered the hurt, and Anna marched into the wagon yard. A lantern hung from a pole on the livery, illuminating the outdoor area in a soft light. The wagons and buggies cast blurred shadows across the yard and into the street. Quiet conversation, punctuated by an occasional laugh, drew her around a freight wagon to a group of cowboys lounging on the ground.

Spotting her, they scrambled to their feet—some easily, some with difficulty from too many years on horseback or too much whiskey in their bellies. One lone body remained sprawled on the ground, snoring quietly. Anna strode over to Duncan's peaceful form and nudged him none too gently with the toe of her shoe. "Duncan, wake up."

"Mmm?" He smiled without opening his eyes. "Not now, honey."

"Duncan James Caldwell, I said wake up." Anna bent

down and shook him, then drew back, making a face. "Merciful heavens! You reek of whiskey and cheap perfume." She leaned over him again, turning his face toward the light. His left eye was practically swollen shut and turning black. She poked him again with her shoe, but he kept sleeping.

She straightened and spun around, looking for Trent.

He moved away from the others, stepping in front of her. "Anna…"

Whiskey and cheap perfume. Pain flooded her anew, and she reacted by slapping his face. His head jerked, but he said nothing, meeting her gaze with an unreadable expression.

"How could you?" she asked quietly, her voice trembling with anger and misery. "I trusted you, depended on you to watch over him, and you took him to that wretched place, to those awful women." She drew a deep, ragged breath. "When we get home, pack your things and get off my property. I want you out of my life, Trent Malloy." She added in a broken whisper, "And out of my heart."

Anna looked back at Duncan, who had curled up on his side and slept like a baby. "He might as well stay here. Then when he's sick in the morning, no one will have to clean it up."

She paused, waiting for Trent to say something, to defend himself, but he was silent. Glancing up at his face, she felt a twinge of remorse. The lantern light clearly displayed the bright red imprint of her hand on his cheek and jaw, as well as his cut and swollen lip. When she met his gaze, the deep, raw pain in his eyes confused her. Surely, he didn't expect her to simply overlook what he had done.

"I'll be here as soon as the boys have breakfast." Turning abruptly, Anna walked out of the wagon yard and back to the hotel with her head held high. She reached her room and closed the door before sagging to her knees with a heartbroken sob.

Sick at heart, Trent retreated to the far corner of the wagon yard. How could she believe he would let Duncan get drunk, much less take him to the Red Garter? He rested his hands on the fence railing and hung his head, closing his eyes.

His time with Anna had been a foolish dream, a lie. She might hunger for his touch, but there was no hope of her ever loving him. She didn't trust him or truly believe he was a good and decent man. If she did, she would have scoffed at the idea of him taking Duncan to a whorehouse.

Hank stepped up beside him, resting his forearms on the fence. "I think I know why she thinks you took him there."

Trent slanted him a glance. "Why?"

"Zack gets yappy when he's been drinking. He was makin' conversation as they walked over here, and he kinda stumbled into it with her. Just repeated some of what he'd heard. You know how stories get all twisted up in no time. Why didn't you tell her the truth?"

"What I say won't make any difference." Trent straightened, lowering his hands to his side. "She doesn't trust me."

Suddenly, it didn't matter much whether anybody did.

Chapter Seventeen

Duncan couldn't understand why anyone would get drunk more than once. If a hangover was always this bad—and Trent assured him it was—then only an idiot would purposely put himself through such misery.

He lay in the back of the freight wagon on top of the bags of oats, cushioning his throbbing head on a twenty-five pound sack of flour. Every time they hit a bump, a barrage of cannons exploded in his brain. He even saw the gunpowder flashes. And why hadn't he ever noticed the terrible condition of the road? The ranchers needed to talk to the county commissioners about improving it.

As for fighting, that wasn't so great the day after, either. His eye wasn't quite swollen shut, but the light hurt it too much to open it. Hank said he had a mighty fine shiner, as if it were a badge of honor or something. Trent told him he handled himself well, and that he appreciated his help. It made him feel better, but Duncan figured a real good fighter wouldn't wind up with a black eye. He'd give the other guy one.

He didn't remember much about starting the trip home, except that he didn't think Anna had ever been so mad at him. She hadn't spoken to anyone. When they stopped to water the horses, she wasn't much better, curtly ordering the boys to stay close to the buckboard. He understood why she was so put out with him. He'd let her down in a big way. But he didn't know why she was so angry with Trent. She acted as if he didn't even exist.

By the time they pulled up in front of the house, the worst of the hangover had past. Duncan climbed slowly out of the wagon and lifted the sack of flour to his shoulder.

"Can you handle that?" asked Trent, his forehead creased in a frown.

"I'm shaky and a little weak, but I'll make it." He carried the flour into the house. When he went outside again, he stopped for a minute on the porch, watching Anna and Trent gather up more things to bring in. They never looked at each other. He couldn't remember a time since Trent first showed up that they'd been so close to each other and at least one of them hadn't sneaked a glance.

After the household supplies were unloaded, Trent drove the wagon down to the barn. Duncan followed with the buckboard and helped put away the sacks of oats and chicken feed. As they unhitched the teams and led them into the corral, Trent looked at Duncan. "Will you put out their feed?"

Duncan nodded, worried about Trent's hard expression. "I'm awful sorry about last night. I should have stayed at the wagon yard like you told me to."

"Yes, you should have." Trent walked out the corral gate, closing it behind him. "I hope you'll use better sense next time."

"I will." Duncan watched in growing dismay as Trent disappeared around the corner of the barn. He needed to thank him for helping him, for keeping him from doing something he might always regret. He wanted to tell him that he had no intention of ever drinking again.

He fed the horses, then walked around to Trent's room, knocking on the open door as he stepped inside. Trent was closing the flap on his saddlebags. Nothing personal remained out in the room. Duncan's heart began to pound. "What are you doing?"

"Ridin' out."

"Why?"

"Anna fired me."

Duncan's stomach rolled. He took a deep breath, releasing it slowly. "Because of me?"

Trent nodded. "She thinks I took you to the Red Garter so you could get drunk and be with a woman."

"But that's not what happened! Where in tarnation did she get that idea?"

"One of Shane's cowboys heard a distorted version of the story. I don't know why she was coming to the wagon yard in the first place, but he walked down there with her. Guess he passed on the tale."

"Didn't you explain? Tell her you stopped me?"

"No." Trent straightened, leaving the saddlebags on the bed. "If she trusted me, she wouldn't have believed it in the first place."

Duncan stared at him. "So, you're just going to leave without trying to straighten things out?"

"Yep."

"Don't leave until I talk to Anna. If you two bust up because of me, I'll never forgive myself."

Trent glanced at him, raising an eyebrow. "I had the impression you weren't happy about my interest in her."

Duncan looked at the floor. "Seeing the way she took to you has been hard. I was afraid she'd forget about Daddy and that didn't seem right. But now I know I was just being selfish. She has to find her own happiness." Distraught, he looked up, directly meeting Trent's gaze. "Please, Trent, this is all my fault. Give me the chance to set things straight.''

"I won't rush saddling his Polecat, but that's all the time you've got.''

Duncan spun around and had to grab the door frame to keep from falling over. As soon as his head quit whirling, he took off at a run toward the house. He stumbled a couple of times but didn't slow down. Throwing open the back door, he let it crash against the wall.

Gasping, Anna whirled around, almost dropping the can of peaches she was about to put in the cupboard. "Duncan! You scared me half to death!''

Rachel came running out of her bedroom. "What's wrong?''

Panting, Duncan rested his hand on the table to steady himself. "It wasn't Trent's fault!''

Scowling, Anna set the can on the table. "What do you mean?''

"Tim had a bottle of whiskey, and we started drinking after dark.'' Waiting a few seconds, he caught his breath, then pulled out a chair and collapsed on it. "Trent and Hank found us sitting on the boardwalk about a quarter to eleven.'' He hurriedly told her about going to the wagon yard with Trent. He glanced at Rachel, who had retreated back to the bedroom doorway and stood listening quietly. She nodded her encouragement.

Anna sat down at the end of the table and crossed her arms. "So, he was going to hide the fact that you'd been drinking.''

"He was trying to keep me out of trouble and keep you from getting upset. On the way there, he lectured me about the perils of drinking. After he left to see you, Tim showed up.'' Duncan's whole face turned red. "Him and Neil had been talkin' all night about the women down at the Red

Garter.'' He hung his head. "Tim has been going there regular for almost six months and tellin' me about it. Neil and Arnie have been there, too.''

Anna shook her head in dismay. Tim was older, but the other two boys were the same age as Duncan. She hadn't realized boys that young would be so interested in women.

"It didn't take much persuasion to get me to go with him, but I wasn't brave enough to go visit a woman. We hid behind the feed store and finished off the whiskey.'' To her amazement, his face grew an even brighter shade of red. "When we got to the Red Garter, Trent was waiting. He'd figured out what we had planned from some things Tim and I said.''

"He didn't go there because of you, Duncan. I smelled that hussy's perfume on him from three feet away.''

"That's 'cause one of the gals wrapped herself around him when he was trying to get me to leave.'' He frowned and glanced up at her. "Those women use awful strong perfume, and she, uh…had a lot of room to wear it. She was persistent, but he shoved her away, told her he wasn't interested.''

He looked back at the floor. "And I know he wasn't. Earlier he'd told me that being with that kind of woman leaves you with a hollow feeling inside. He said he supposed only the woman you loved could fill that emptiness.'' He straightened and met her gaze, his voice softening. "I asked him if he'd ever been with a woman he loved. He said all he'd done was kiss her, and that kissin' her was a whole lot nicer than bedding anyone he'd ever paid. I figure he was talking about you.''

Moisture stung Anna's eyes, tears of shame. Regret weighed heavily on her heart and burdened her soul. She had treated Trent horribly, shattered the very trust she had worked so hard to build. All because of jealousy. "And the fight?" she whispered, a tear rolling down her cheek.

"Bender made an insulting remark about you, and Trent nailed him. When Bender's friend hit Trent, I jumped right in the middle of it. Trent took care of him and Bender, too, when he came after him again. I've never seen anyone fight like him. He said he learned it in prison, but there was more to it than that. He was like an avenging angel."

"Defending my honor." Anna closed her eyes, sick at what she had done. "Has he left?" she whispered, tears streaming down her face.

"I don't think so. He still had to saddle Polecat."

After saddling his horse, Trent went back into his room to make certain he hadn't left anything. He bent down, looking under the bed. When he straightened, he saw Anna through the open door, walking toward the barn. "Doesn't look like she's in much of a hurry to stop me."

She stepped through the doorway, her cheeks streaked with tears and misery in her eyes. She met his gaze for a heartbeat, then looked away. "Can you forgive me?" she asked softly.

"I don't know." He pulled off his hat and threw it on the bed, raking his fingers through his hair. "How could you believe I'd take him there?"

Anna shook her head and waved her hand in a helpless gesture. "I don't know. I tried to figure that out between here and the house." She shrugged and turned away, walking over to the cold stove, keeping her back to him.

The defeated droop of her shoulders tugged at Trent's heart, but he didn't move or speak. If nothing else, prison had taught him how to wait.

She rubbed her arms as if she were cold. "When we

were at Lizzie's, I wondered if I'd misread your interest, that maybe fire was all you felt.

"I went to the wagon yard to ask Duncan to come back to the hotel. I was worried that he would be a bother to you, not that you wouldn't take care of him. He's my responsibility, not yours, and I should have been the one keeping an eye on him."

She turned around, glancing at him, then nervously shifted her gaze. "When Zack mentioned that you and Duncan had beaten Bender and his friend in a fight, I was annoyed but not terribly upset, though I naturally wanted to hear what happened. But when he said you were at the Red Garter, I barely heard the details of the fight. I thought about how the women would take one look at you and fall over themselves trying to get your attention. Then he said something about Duncan picking Sal and letting you have Pearl, which puzzled him because Pearl was much prettier than Sal."

Trent rubbed the side of his neck, sorting that one out.

"As a mother, I should have been appalled and angry because Duncan had been with a prostitute, and later, I was." She turned to face him. "But my first thought wasn't of my stepson. It was the image of you in the arms of another woman, one who was pretty and oh-so-willing to please."

Tears shimmered in her eyes as she looked away. "I can't describe how much that hurt. So many thoughts and feelings hit all at once. Betrayal. Jealousy. Failure, both mine and yours. I'd given you my heart, but you needed more. I'd trusted you, depended on you to watch over Duncan, and you took him to that horrible place. And if I'd taught him the way I should have, he wouldn't have gone there."

"So, you failed Edwin."

Anna nodded and walked back across the room, stopping in front of him. "Suddenly, I was so angry—at myself, you, Duncan, those women. Even Edwin for leaving me with such a responsibility." She raised her hand, tenderly touching his sore lip with trembling fingers. "I'm so sorry I hit you, especially in front of those men. I hadn't planned to do it, but when I smelled that woman's perfume on you…"

Lowering her hand, she searched his eyes, as if trying to see into his heart. "I've wronged you terribly, hurt you deeply. I can never tell you how much I regret it. Please forgive me."

Trent looked down at her sad, lovely face, struggling with his thoughts and emotions. "Hearing what Zack said and how you took things, I can understand why you were so angry, even why you slapped me. I can forgive you for that. But Anna, if you trusted me, you should have known what he said couldn't be right. You should have at least questioned it."

"I know," she said miserably. She caught her lower lip between her teeth for a second, worry and uncertainty reflected in her face. "Will you stay?"

"Yes."

"Thank you," she whispered on a sigh, relief washing over her expression. When she started to hug him, he caught her arms, holding her away from him. Anna looked up, clearly bewildered.

"I'll stay and work for you." *And love you till my dying breath.* "I'll help you run the ranch and look after the kids. I'll do what I can to protect you and keep you safe, but that's all I can give."

"Trent, I don't want you to work for me. I love you."

How had he yearned to hear those words, to see the love shining in her eyes. He fought the urge to haul her into his arms and kiss her senseless, to tell her what was in his heart. "But you don't trust me."

"Yes, I do. I made a mistake because of my own fears and jealousy. I won't do it again."

"I want to believe that, but I can't. I treasure your love, but I need your trust just as much, the kind you gave Edwin—complete and unwavering. Because of what I've done and who I am, I don't think you can give it. Maybe no one can. In the back of your mind, there will always be a doubt that I won't keep my word or my promises, that somehow I'll fail you."

"We all fail, Trent. We all make mistakes. I don't expect you to be perfect. You can't expect me to be, either."

"I'll work for you and be your friend, but that's all I'll risk. There can't be anything more between us." He released her and straightened, stretching the emotional distance between them.

"I love you, Trent Malloy," she said softly. "If friendship is all I can have, then I accept it gratefully." She cupped his face in her hand, stretched up on tiptoe, and touched his sore lip with a featherlight kiss. "For now." Anna stepped back, her face filled with grim determination. "In time, I'll prove worthy of your love." She turned and walked out the door, head held high.

Trent watched her go all the way to the house. As she disappeared inside, the truth hit him like a lightning bolt. He demanded something from her that he couldn't give in return.

Complete, unwavering trust.

Chapter Eighteen

During the weeks following their trip to Antelope Springs, Anna spent a great deal of time thinking about Trent's behavior since he became a part of their lives. He had kept his past from them, but everything else showed his integrity and loyalty to her and her family.

Though he declared there could never be more than friendship between them, they were already beyond that. She loved him with all her heart, and oddly, since the incident in Antelope Springs, she was more confident of his love. The effort he made to get Duncan away from the Red Garter and fighting for her honor were acts of love. The very fact that he remained at the ranch after Shane's party and after she degraded him in front of the other men spoke of his love.

Anna was determined not to fail him again, no matter what. With tenderness, patience, and most of all, her steadfast trust, he would regain his faith in her.

They had settled into much the same routine as before, with the addition of his music sometimes in the evening. He played well, always choosing lively tunes when he was with the family. But late at night, when everyone else was asleep, the sad lonely strains of the harmonica reached out to her, whispering of his broken heart and lonely soul.

Whenever they worked together, he was aloof, concentrating strictly on the task at hand. But often at breakfast or in the evenings, she would glance up and catch him watching her with heart-stopping tenderness and longing. Usually, he quickly looked away—but not always.

For almost two weeks, they'd had trouble with coyotes attacking the newborn calves. Trent had spent several nights on the range guarding the herd and killing the marauders, sometimes going out in the middle of the night because the coyotes' howls seemed particularly excited. He always told her what he found.

One morning shortly after ten, Mitch came running in, his expression troubled. "Mama, there's a bunch of riders coming down the road. They're comin' fast."

Anna dropped the pencil beside the ledger book and hurried to the front window, counting at least ten men galloping toward the house. "Mitch, where is Davy?"

"Around at the side of the house, watchin'."

"Go tell him I said to come inside right away." She hurried to the gun rack, lifting down her Winchester. "The man in the lead looks like Robert Kingsley, but this isn't a social call." Grabbing a handful of cartridges, she loaded the rifle and dropped the extra bullets into her skirt pocket. "Rachel, keep the boys inside. Load the other rifle, and be ready in case I need you."

Anna stepped out onto the porch, closing the door behind her. She stopped right above the steps and waited, holding the gun crosswise in front of her. When her neighbor and his men drew to a dusty halt near her, she smiled graciously. "Good morning, Robert. What brings you out so early?"

Kingsley surveyed the house, barn and grounds. When he looked back at her, his face twisted in anger.

Anna tensed, tightening her hold on the Winchester.

"I'm after a horse thief. Malloy cut the fence between our properties last night and took two of my prized horses."

She usually awakened at any odd night noise, and if she missed something, Dig ran in and alerted her. The dog was used to the sounds Trent and Polecat made, however, so he might not have stirred. He hadn't three nights earlier when Trent left without her hearing him. Trent had told her about it the next morning, just as he had every other time he'd left during the night.

He hadn't stolen Kingsley's horses. She'd never been more certain of anything in her life. "You're mistaken. Trent was here all night last night."

A hint of scorn crept into Kingsley's expression. He glanced at the barn, then the house. "How can you be so sure?"

"I'm a light sleeper, and our dog always alerts me if he hears something out of place during the night. I'm certain Trent is innocent."

"I don't believe you," Kingsley said flatly. He leaned forward, resting his arm on the saddle horn, and glared at her. "I should have guessed the night of Parker's party that you had something goin' with your hired hand. Otherwise, you might have been a little more obliging."

Anna glared at him. "You're mistaken again."

"I doubt it. I heard about you storming into the wagon yard and slapping him. You're too good a rancher to hit a cowboy just because he made you angry. It had to be personal."

"There he is, boss," yelled one of Kingsley's men, pointing toward the corrals.

Along with everyone else, Anna looked around, spotting

Duncan and Trent running toward the house. They'd been training horses and were unarmed.

"Get him," ordered Kingsley. Two men rode in Trent's direction as several others dismounted.

Anna fired a warning shot into the air, halting Kingsley's men. Duncan and Trent slowed to a walk but kept moving toward her. Anna raised the rifle to her shoulder, pointing it at the men closest to Trent. "I'll put a bullet in any man who lays a hand on him." She heard the door open behind her, but didn't look back. Rachel moved to her side, leveling a Winchester at the rancher.

One of the younger cowboys glanced at Kingsley. Either wanting to please the boss or show off, he started walking toward Trent. Anna fired at the ground one step ahead of him, bringing him to an abrupt stop. "Don't try my patience or test my aim. You're on my property. I don't hold with trespassers."

"And I don't hold with thieves," shouted Kingsley. "Where are my horses, Malloy?"

"Kingsley, I told you Trent didn't take them." Anna's voice was firm, her expression resolute. "He was here all night."

Trent had never wanted to hug her more than at that moment. For once, he'd slept inside all night. She couldn't know positively that he'd been there the whole time. He could have quietly saddled Polecat and taken him out the far side of the corral with her none the wiser, like he'd done before. He stepped up onto the porch beside Anna. Duncan moved around behind Rachel, and she handed him the gun.

"I didn't take your horses," said Trent. "Why do you think I did?"

"The fence between the Double Deuce and my ranch was cut. You've stolen before. This time you made off with my best stallion and a brood mare.'' Kingsley frowned at Anna. ''He has to have them hidden on your land.''

''Then they should be easy to find,'' said Trent. ''Did you follow the tracks?''

Kingsley shifted in the saddle, suddenly appearing uncomfortable. ''No. After Bender rode into headquarters and said the fence had been cut, I had some other men check the pasture. When they didn't find the horses, we came straight here.''

''By the road,'' said Anna, glancing at Trent. He wondered if she found it as odd as he did that Bender had discovered the cut barbed wire.

''Reaching your house is quicker that way.'' Kingsley frowned at Anna. ''Why else would the fence be cut if you didn't bring the horses through?'' he asked sarcastically, staring at Trent.

''Bender hates him,'' said Duncan. ''Maybe he cut it, figuring you'd blame Trent.''

''Why don't we go check the area?'' suggested Trent. ''If the thief took the horses that way, we should be able to trail them. There isn't much brush along that fence line, and it's mostly clay. Not many rocks.''

Kingsley grudgingly agreed. He and his men hovered nearby, keeping a watchful eye on Anna, Duncan and Trent as they saddled their horses and mounted. It took about half an hour to reach the site.

When they were near the break in the fence, Anna drew her horse alongside Kingsley's. ''Have your men stop here. You, Trent and I should inspect the area on foot. That way we won't disturb any prints that are already there.''

''That's reasonable enough.'' Kingsley ordered his men to halt. He waited until they were all within hearing distance before explaining what they intended to do.

Anna and Trent dismounted, handing their reins to Duncan. After swinging down from the saddle, Kingsley tossed his reins to one of his men. They approached the area of downed fence slowly, studying the area for any signs that someone had ridden through the opening.

"There are some prints," crowed Kingsley. He took a menacing step toward Trent, but Anna moved in between them.

"Those are only from one horse," she observed.

Her neighbor frowned and swore under his breath. A few minutes later he sighed heavily. "And they double back around through the fence. Must have been Bender. That idiot. He should have looked for a trail."

Trent thought the same thing about the man's boss. He glanced at Anna. She nodded toward the other rancher and rolled her eyes. Trent flashed her a grin behind Kingsley's back, then walked up to the fence, checking the ground on the other side. "There's only been one horse over here, too.

"We'll need to look along the fence lines. Whoever took them had to go out somewhere. If the wire hasn't been cut anywhere else, he went out a gate." Trent stated the obvious, but judging by the look that flashed across Kingsley's face, he could have sworn the thought hadn't occurred to the man. The rancher had been so set on him being the thief that he hadn't considered any other possibilities.

Kingsley sent two men to check the fence in one direction, kept two with him, and ordered the rest to go back to his ranch. Anna and Trent joined him and the two cowboys in the inspection of the rest of the fence line.

They hadn't gone far when one of the other men came riding back across the pasture. "We found the tracks, Mr. Kingsley." He glanced at Trent. "He went through a gate just like Malloy said. Probably took them through the pasture to the gate at the road, but we figured we'd wait on you to go see.''

Kingsley glared at Trent. ''Think you're mighty smart, don't you, Malloy? What have you done with my horses?'' he shouted.

Trent took a deep breath in an effort to remain calm. ''Nothing. Whoever stole your horses obviously wanted to make you suspect me, but maybe he's not all that smart. He had to leave prints on the road.''

''We went that way to Mrs. Caldwell's place, so we probably destroyed them,'' said the other cowboy. ''I doubt if we can even tell which way he went.''

''Check the road past the Double Deuce,'' said Anna. ''And have someone go the other way, past your ranch. There has to be some sign of his direction. We want your animals returned as much as you do.''

Kingsley snorted. ''I doubt that.''

''Then I hope someday you're accused of a crime you didn't commit and see how it feels,'' said Trent, his patience spent. ''Believe me, Kingsley, there probably isn't a man alive who wants to catch this thief more than I do.'' He turned to the other cowboy. ''Will you show me his trail?''

''Don't see what it can hurt.'' The man didn't wait for his boss's approval, but turned and led Trent across the pasture. Trent glanced back, glad to see that Anna and the others followed.

When they reached the road, Trent quickly realized he wouldn't be cleared that day. Hundreds of hoofprints and the slowly moving cloud of dust in the air past the Double Deuce put an end to his hope. He shook his head in disgust, wondering why, of all days, someone had to move a herd of cattle down the road, probably all the way to Antelope Springs to sell.

Kingsley stared at the trampled earth for several minutes. Finally, he wheeled his horse around, consternation written all over his face. "I still think you're a liar and a thief, Malloy, but I can't prove it. We'll be watchin' you." He looked at his men. "Go on back to the ranch. I'm going to see the sheriff." With another glare at Trent and Anna, he rode toward town.

Three of the cowboys turned and started toward Kingsley's ranch. The one who had led Trent across the pasture hung back. "There are some of us who don't figure you did this," he said. "You aren't the only one around who's been on the wrong side of the law at one time or another. It don't sit well to accuse a man just because of it."

"I appreciate that," said Trent.

The man nodded to Anna. "You're a mighty fine shot, ma'am," he said with a grin.

"Thanks. I keep in practice."

Returning to the ranch, they stopped by the house to tell the others what happened before taking the horses to the corral and unsaddling them. When they had everything put away, Trent motioned to Duncan, silently asking him to leave him alone with Anna.

"I think I'll head on up to the house and see if Rachel started anything for dinner," said Duncan. "I'm starved."

"We'll be along directly." Anna poked his stomach as he walked by. "Don't eat up everything before we get there."

Duncan dodged with a laugh. "Yes, ma'am."

When they were alone, Anna caught Trent's gaze.

Trent put his arm around her, drawing her to him. "Thank you for standing up for me." He looked into her eyes, allowing her to see into his soul and his heart. "Knowing you believe in me, trust me...I can't tell you how much it means to me."

''I had a problem with jealousy when another woman was involved,'' she said with a tender smile, ''but when it comes to whether you took those horses or not, I never doubted your innocence, not for one second. You're too smart to steal again. You know you'll be the first one people will blame.'' She rested one hand on his chest and put the other around the back of his neck, caressing it lightly. ''The Trent Malloy I know and love is a good and honorable man. I trust you with my life, my children's lives.'' She brushed a kiss across his lips. ''And my heart.''

''Thank you.'' He kissed her with gentle intensity, a fervent cry from his heart to hers. He gazed into her beautiful gray eyes, cherishing the sweetness of her soul, the blessings of her angel's heart. ''I love you, Anna.''

Her smile almost blinded him. ''I know.''

He pulled her tightly against him, kissing her with a hunger born of weeks of longing and self-denial. When he finally eased his hold, she smiled wistfully. ''Sweetheart, if we got married, we wouldn't have to sneak kisses in the barn.''

Trent rested his forehead against hers. ''You don't know how good that sounds.'' Straightening, he took a look at her face and smiled. ''Guess you do.'' He released her with a shake of his head. ''But as long as people are so suspicious of me, I can't marry you.''

''If you were my husband, they would realize how much I trust you. They'd see that they were wrong.''

''No, they'd think you were a fool and shake their heads over how low you'd fallen. You and your family would be shunned. I won't tie you to that kind of life, Anna. I can't do it to you and the kids. It would tear me apart.''

Chapter Nineteen

Leading a packhorse, Anna guided her mount carefully through the loose rocks of the dry creek bed and up the bank. She rode to the top of a hill overlooking the breaks— a rugged tangle of gullies, narrow canyons, boulders and areas of thick brush covering almost a full section of land, partly hers and partly Kingsley's.

A few of her cattle had a bad habit of wandering into the maze and not finding their way out again. More than once she'd been tempted to build a fence clear across it to keep them out, but during winter storms those same canyons provided the herd with the best shelter on the ranch.

Anna shifted her weight, squinting at the lengthening shadows crawling across the land. Half an hour of daylight and another of dusk—not nearly enough time to search the countless places a horse could stumble. Or a man could be bushwhacked.

During the past week, they'd had no further encounters with Kingsley or his men, but she didn't know how long she could keep Trent from confronting him. Or how long she could let her anger simmer.

Kingsley had set up a camp on a hill above the Double Deuce, with men positioned day and night to watch the ranch headquarters. Occasionally, she noticed sunlight glinting off a spyglass, and Anna wondered if the men used it at night, too, hoping for a shadow show. As a precaution, she hung sheets over the curtains in the bedrooms.

They kept up a normal routine, pretending that nothing was out of the ordinary, but even the younger boys felt the tension and reacted to it. Anna thought the kids squabbled as many times in the past two days as they did all winter.

They moved more of the horses to the corrals at night, keeping the rest in the pasture closest to the house. Though they had put them all in the pens during the blizzard, they would be much too crowded in the warmer weather. Trent and Duncan slept in the pasture where they could watch both portions of the herd.

The circuit rider preacher finally made it to Shane's on Sunday. Much to her joy, Trent went to the services with the family, but her temper was sorely tested by her neighbors. Some, like Kingsley, were downright rude. Others treated Trent—and her—with barely concealed disdain. Only Shane, Ian, the minister and a few others were cordial.

The good reverend boldly reminded his little flock not to judge or condemn unless they wanted to be treated in the same way. Some squirmed when he admonished them to remove the beam from their own eye before they tried to pull out the mote from their neighbor's.

But if Kingsley listened to the sermon, he didn't take it to heart. Rage burned in his gaze whenever he looked at Trent or Anna, and she feared the theft of his horses was only a small part of it. Her rejection and his jealousy were breeding bitterness and hatred.

Anna scanned the countryside once again and shook her head, her worry growing the more she thought about Kingsley. "Trent Malloy, why did I ever let you come out here by yourself?"

She turned in the saddle, looking at the same rough terrain behind her. Even if she headed back immediately, she'd lose the light before reaching safe ground. Her horse glanced back at her, as if asking what she had in mind. Anna leaned down and patted the little mare's neck. "Might as well keep going and hope we find him, Ginger. I don't particularly like the idea of staying out here alone."

Whispering a short prayer for Trent's safety as well as her own, she nudged the horse into motion, and the second horse, Jake, followed on the lead. They wove through thick brush and crossed another ravine, following a faint cattle trail along the edge of it. Seconds before the sun dropped below the distant hills, Anna spotted a spiral of campfire smoke about a hundred yards to the northwest.

She moved slowly toward it, wary both of the terrain and who she might find. Even in the best of times, a rider approached a strange campfire with caution. Easing her carbine out of the leather scabbard hanging from the saddle horn, Anna quietly cocked the rifle and laid it across her lap, curling one hand around the stock, a finger on the trigger.

When she reached a place that gave her a partial view of the campsite, she spotted the horse Trent had ridden, a gelding named Little Bit. She drew the horses to a halt, peering around the branches of a scrub oak. Trent was nowhere in sight, but neither was anyone else. Nor was there any indication that someone besides him might be there. "Hello in the camp," she called. "Trent, it's Anna."

He stepped out from behind a large boulder with a grin, carrying his rifle. "Well, don't just sit there, woman. Come on in." He didn't move like a man who had been injured.

Anna said a silent *thank you* to the Lord and rode around the trees, noting that Trent had picked his camp with protection in mind. The straight sides of the ridge in back of him would keep anyone from sneaking up from behind. The grove of scrub oak in front blocked the view of a shooter trying to keep his distance. If a man moved in closer, Trent could hide behind the large rocks on either side of the camp.

"Good spot," she said, dismounting.

"It'll do. If the coyotes come callin', I figured I could pick them off when they hit the clearing." He looked up at the top of the ridge line. "I reckon the horses will let us know in plenty of time if a mountain lion is around. There are a lot of small, loose rocks up there, particularly along the edge. I doubt a cat could sneak up without peppering us with a few of them."

He met her gaze and smiled tenderly. "No, I'm not hurt, but thanks for coming out to see. Little Bit slipped on some rocks. Sprained his right front leg."

Anna handed him the mare's reins and walked over to the injured horse. Little Bit looked at her with sad eyes, lifting his leg slightly as if to tell her it hurt. She patted his neck and rubbed his forehead, crooning to him softly.

Trent had brought up mud from a nearby creek and packed it around the knee, wrapping it with his neckerchief. Gently untying the cloth, she pressed lightly on the swollen joint. "When did it happen?"

"About four. I changed the plaster a couple of times. Found a bowl-like hole in that rock, so I brought some mud up for tonight." He looped Ginger's reins around a rock and hunkered down beside Anna. "I'm sorry I worried you. I couldn't leave him out here."

"I know you couldn't." She reached for Trent's face, then realized her fingers were covered with mud. When she drew her hand back, a twinkle lit his eyes. "What's the matter, cowboy?" she asked with a smile. "Afraid of a little dirt?"

"I'd just as soon not use it for war paint." He stood and held out his hand. When she held up her arm, he closed his fingers around her wrist, gently pulling her up to stand. Running his thumb across the inside of her wrist, Trent frowned. "I figured you'd come looking for me. I wanted you to know I was all right, but it troubled me to think you'd wind up staying out here alone if you didn't find me."

"I brought medical supplies and enough food for several days, both for us and the horses. I packed extra ammunition, too."

"Did you see any of Kingsley's men?"

"No. I expect they saw me riding this way, but the land gets rough sooner on his side of the fence. If someone followed, he wouldn't have been able to keep up. We're out of sight this far over."

"One followed me this morning," Trent said. "I lost sight of him while I was looking for the cattle. I didn't find them, by the way. They must be over on the far side. Little Bit got hurt before we made it that far."

"We can look for them in a few days." Anna paused beside the creek, listening to the soft bubbling tune as the clear water ambled over the pebbles and sand. She knelt down on the bank, washing her hands and the trail dust off her face while Trent watered the horses a few feet downstream. She unfastened the top two buttons on her shirtwaist. Tipping her head back to splash her throat, she glanced up to find him watching the water trickle down her skin and disappear beneath the open collar of her blouse, dampening the cloth.

For the first time, they were by themselves in a place where no one was likely to intrude. They would be alone all night, shielded from the world by darkness and miles of empty prairie. Dare she follow her heart and give in to the longing to be his?

Trent met her gaze for a heartbeat, then looked away. He cleared his throat, but when he spoke, his voice sounded strained. "Hope you planned on cookin' supper. About all I can manage is to fry a little salt pork or open a can of beans."

"Rachel made us some ham sandwiches. We'll have the salt pork for breakfast." She walked over to join him, holding out her hand for Ginger's reins. They waited a few minutes until the horses finished drinking. Trent untied a bucket and the coffeepot from one of the packs and filled them with water. He carried the bucket and Anna carried the coffeepot as they led the horses back to camp in silence.

Before unloading the packs from Jake's back, Trent let Little Bit drink from the bucket. Anna threw some coffee in the pot and set it over the fire, then unsaddled Ginger. After the horses were tethered and fed, they unrolled their bedrolls—two blankets each on top of waterproof tarpaulins—placing them side by side, their saddles at one end. Trent unfastened his gun belt and looped it over the saddle horn. Anna did the same and laid her Winchester on top of the scabbard beside her saddle. Sitting down on the blanket-covered tarps, they leaned against the saddles, ate the sandwiches, and watched the stars appear one by one.

"Everything all right back at the house?" He sipped his coffee, looking at her in the dancing firelight.

Anna nodded. "The kids were worried about you, of course. Duncan asked if I wanted him to come with me, but I thought he'd better stay there and guard the horses tonight. I don't think we'll have a problem."

"If the moon is as bright as it was last night, we'd spot him clear across the pasture."

"But in case he's watching us, I didn't want to risk it.

When I left, Davy was helping Rachel gather in the wash. I expect Duncan will read to them tonight before he goes outside. That should help.''

''How's Mitch?''

''He came down to the corrals about midafternoon, wondering when you would be back. I don't think he moved off the porch the rest of the day, watching for you. When I left, he asked me to bring you home safe.''

''I hate for him to worry,'' Trent said with a frown.

''It's one of the costs of living out here. The kids grow up learning the dangers, but I don't think they want to live in town. They enjoy visiting Antelope Springs, but they're always ready to head back home. I am, too.''

They talked some more about the kids, the ranch and the horses, and finished their coffee. After a while, Trent put his arm around her shoulders. She rested her head against his solid muscles, remembering when he'd first come to the ranch and been so thin. Staring up at the sky, Anna listened as the man beside her breathed quietly, though perhaps a bit faster than normal. She wondered if his heart raced like hers.

They fell silent, waiting, anticipating. Just when Anna had about decided she would have to make the first move, Trent cradled her face in his hand, tipping it toward him.

He searched her eyes in the flickering firelight. ''I shouldn't even kiss you,'' he whispered.

''I want you to.'' She wanted more than his kisses, but she didn't say the words. She didn't have to.

His mouth claimed hers in a searing touch. When she parted her lips, he accepted her invitation, deepening the kiss. With a low groan, he broke away from her mouth and slipped his arm beneath her knees. Lifting her, he scooted her down on the bedroll. He slid down, too, lying beside her. Trent raised up on one forearm and leaned over her, kissing her slowly and thoroughly, gently caressing her breast.

Anna ran her hands over his back and shoulders. She unfastened the buttons on his shirt, wishing the opening didn't stop halfway to his waist. Pushing the material aside, she spread her hands across his chest.

He shifted, jerking the shirt from his jeans and tugging it off over his head. She helped him free his arms from the sleeves and tossed the garment on top of his saddle. Lying back down on his side, he settled his hand at her waist as she caressed his chest. When she followed the movement of her fingers with tiny kisses, he closed his eyes and pulled her closer.

She delighted in his sharply drawn breath and soft sighs, the tiny sound he made in his throat and the restless flexing of his fingers. Kissing a path to the other side of his chest, she pleasured him there in the same way. "You don't know how many times I've wanted to touch you like this."

He chuckled quietly. "Probably not as many times as I've wanted you to." Holding her gaze, he trailed his fingertips down her throat, stopping at the first fastened button on her shirtwaist. "My turn..." He waited until she nodded, then slowly unfastened her blouse.

Easing it from the waist of her riding skirt, he pushed the material aside. In the dancing firelight, the thin white cotton corset cover—without the corset—hid little from his view. Trent's mouth went dry. Sitting, he pulled her up also, slipping off her blouse and laying it on top of his shirt.

He skimmed his fingers along the delicate skin below her throat, then dipped them beneath the lace-edged cloth. Heart pounding, he glanced at her face. Her eyes were closed; her slightly parted lips curved in a faint smile.

"You're so beautiful, Anna," he said reverently. "In

prison, a man develops a good imagination, but you're more beautiful than anyone I ever dreamed up.'' Lowering his head, he feathered kisses across the swell of her bosom. Anna gasped and arched her back. Brushing the cloth aside, he dipped lower still.

She threaded her fingers in his hair, drawing him with her as she lay back on the blankets. Stirred by her tiny whimpers of desire and fevered touch, his caresses grew more urgent, his kisses more intense. Fumbling with the button at the waistband of her riding skirt, he slipped it from the buttonhole just as the horses' nervous snorts and stamping feet broke through the haze of passion.

Releasing Anna, he grabbed his pistol from the holster, pulling the hammer back as he rolled to his knees. He listened intently, quickly scanning the perimeter of the camp. The yipping and howl of coyotes echoed across the breaks, not close enough for immediate danger, but near enough for concern.

''Can you tell where they are?'' asked Anna, drawing up the straps of the corset cover and reaching for her blouse.

He glanced at her, letting his gaze linger as she sat up and put on the shirtwaist. ''Toward Kingsley's, I think.'' The muffled sound of a gunshot ricocheted around the hills and canyons, followed instantly by frightened yaps and barks. Another gunshot resounded, and the clamor of the coyotes moved farther away.

''Well, whoever is it, he scared them away from us.'' He grabbed his shirt and pulled it on. ''Maybe that was the Almighty's way of reminding me I got no business doin' what I was doin'.''

Buttoning her blouse, Anna looked up with a smile. ''It wasn't just you. I think we were both involved.''

He grinned back. ''Yeah, reckon we were.'' Leaning toward her, he kissed her gently. ''I love you, and I'm going to make you mine. But not until it's right in the eyes of God and man.''

She tipped her head to one side, studying him thoughtfully. ''Was that a proposal, cowboy?''

Standing, he shrugged. ''I guess it was—but don't go gettin' all excited. There won't be a wedding until the thief is caught.''

She rose and slid her arms around his waist. ''Then we'd better start praying that he gets greedy and careless. And the sooner, the better.''

During the rest of the night, they took turns keeping guard, putting cold mudpacks on Little Bit's leg, and dozing. Neither of them slept much, but it didn't seem to matter. They'd never spent such a long stretch of time together and treasured simply being with each other.

At sunup, they agreed that the horse should be able to make it home if they went slowly. Anna rubbed his leg with liniment and carefully wrapped it in a bandage. Trent rode Jake, carrying his bedroll and one of the packs. Anna took the other pack and her bedroll on Ginger.

A short while after starting out, they caught sight of Kingsley's man shadowing them from across the fence. They stopped often, allowing Little Bit to rest. Eventually, the other cowboy tired of the slow pace and rode on ahead of them.

When they reached the barn, the family came running to meet them. The minute Trent dismounted and wrapped Jake's reins around the hitching post, Mitch flung his arms around him.

''You're gettin' strong, little britches. You 'bout squeezed me in two.'' Trent leaned down and picked up the little boy, his grin vanishing when he saw tears streaming down Mitch's face. ''Hey, what's this?'' he asked gently, settling the child on one arm and brushing a cheek with his thumb.

"I was scared you got hurt bad," Mitch said on a sob, burying his face against Trent's neck.

Trent held him close, resting his jaw against the boy's soft hair. "Don't you worry about me, pardner. I'm tough. I survived the blizzard, remember?"

Mitch nodded, then raised his head and solemnly met Trent's gaze. "I figured Mama could protect you from the coyotes last night, but I didn't know how she could get you home if you was hurt."

Anna smiled at her son, lightly rubbing his back above Trent's hand, then looked at Rachel and Duncan. "Any problems around here?"

"Not a one," said Duncan. He glanced at Davy with a smile. "He stayed with me in the pasture so I wouldn't get lonesome."

The younger boy grinned. "Sleepin' out under the stars is fun."

"Can be," said Trent, slanting a glance at Anna. He barely kept back a smile when delicate pink flushed her cheeks. "Unless it rains, snows or comes a sandstorm. Then it's downright miserable." He gave Mitch a hug before setting him down on the ground. "You all right now, son?"

"Yes, sir." Mitch smiled and joined the other boys.

Duncan led Little Bit into the corral while Trent and Anna unsaddled the other horses and turned them out into the pasture. They checked Little Bit's leg again before putting away the remaining supplies Anna had taken.

After dinner, the younger boys went down to the creek to throw rocks and wade in the ankle-deep water. Anna sat down in her rocker and propped her feet up on the footstool. "I need a siesta."

"Coyotes keep you awake?" asked Duncan with a twinkle in his eyes.

She met Trent's gaze with a smile. "Yeah, ornery critters. For a while we thought they were going to pay us a visit, but, from the sound of things, they dropped in on Kingsley's man first, and he scared them off."

"We took turns keeping guard in case they decided to come back," said Trent, heading for the back door. "Think I'll stretch out for a bit, too. I'll be down by the barn in the shade. If I'm not up when you're ready to work, holler."

"I'll send Dig over to give you a big kiss," said Anna.

"No, thanks." Since Rachel and Duncan were looking the other way, Trent mouthed, "Rather have yours." He winked and went out the back door. As he passed the end of the house, he spotted two riders coming up the road. Trent turned around and went back inside. "We've got company."

Anna sighed. "No nap today. Can you tell who it is?"

He walked over to the front window, frowning as the sunlight glinted off something on one rider's shirtfront. "Looks like the sheriff and another man."

Anna joined him at the window. "That's Jim Halstead with him. He owns a ranch about six miles south of here."

"How many horses do you suppose he lost last night?" he muttered.

"It only takes one, and he bought a champion stallion about a year ago that cost a fortune."

Trent and Anna walked out onto the porch. Rachel and Duncan followed. The men slowed their horses, approaching the house at a walk, stirring up a minimum of dust.

"Good afternoon, Sheriff Taylor, Mr. Halstead," said Anna.

"Afternoon, Mrs. Caldwell," said the sheriff. The other man nodded politely to Anna, then glared at Trent.

"How many were stolen?" asked Trent, figuring they might as well get to the point.

For a second, Halstead appeared startled, but he recovered quickly, scowling back. "One. A champion thoroughbred stallion. I want him. Now."

"I can't help you. I don't have him."

"Liar!" Halstead pulled the gun from his holster and aimed it at Trent. "Give me my horse!"

Heart pounding, Trent moved slowly away from Anna, sidestepping toward the end of the porch. "Take it easy, mister. You don't want to shoot somebody else by accident."

"Put the gun away, Halstead," ordered the sheriff. "I told you I'd handle this, and I will." When the rancher hesitated, Sheriff Taylor said with quiet, unquestionable authority, "Don't make me tell you again." The rancher obeyed with a irritated glance in the lawman's direction.

"Now, Malloy, where were you last night?" asked the sheriff.

"Over in the breaks. I was looking for some cattle there yesterday. I got in around midmorning." He wasn't about to mention that Anna spent the night alone with him. He'd risk going to jail before he did anything to damage her reputation.

"One of Kingsley's men followed me." Trent pointed to the hill on the other ranch. "They've been keeping watch on us night and day. I know he saw me ride into the breaks in the afternoon and out again this morning. He wasn't camped too far from me."

"How do you know?" asked the sheriff.

"Heard him shooting at coyotes."

"How do we know you didn't leave, steal my stallion

and take it back there?'' asked Halstead. ''That would be a perfect place to hide stolen horses.''

''Only an idiot would try to ride through that country at night. I value horses and my neck too much to try it. I wouldn't take a high-priced animal through there even in the daytime.''

''Unless you found a good, clear trail. A man could follow Little Draw Creek all the way to Halstead's ranch. The ground settles out about halfway through Kingsley's land.'' Sheriff Taylor's gaze narrowed. ''Why do I have the feeling you aren't telling me the truth?''

''Because he's trying to protect me,'' Anna said. Trent shook his head, but she ignored him. ''When Trent didn't come back by late afternoon, I got worried. All kinds of things can happen in that country, including one of Kingsley's men taking a potshot at him. So I took food and medical supplies and went looking for him. I found him right at sundown, camped near the creek so he could put mudpacks on Little Bit's leg. Trent couldn't have stolen that stallion. He was with me all night.''

The sheriff digested that bit of news with the lift of an eyebrow. ''What about when you slept, Mrs. Caldwell? Couldn't he have ridden to the Halstead ranch and back then?''

''We slept very little, Sheriff Taylor.''

The sheriff's eyebrow shot up again, and Halstead's eyes took on a leering gleam. Trent almost groaned out loud. ''There were coyotes and a mountain lion prowling the area.'' He hadn't seen or heard a lion, but there was bound to be one around somewhere.

''So we stood guard in two-hour shifts,'' Anna explained, with amazing composure, though her cheeks had turned slightly pink. ''He couldn't have ridden to your ranch, stolen your horse, hid him and returned to camp in that time. Besides, I would have heard him leave, even when I dozed.''

Halstead shifted in the saddle, frowning at Anna. ''That stallion would greatly improve your breeding line, Mrs. Caldwell. You could get twice the price for your stock as you do now. Sheriff, she's in on it with him. They probably had it all planned, right down to making his horse go lame so she could rescue him and give him an alibi.''

Trent bolted over the porch railing toward Halstead. ''You dirty—''

''Hold it right there, Malloy.''

The sheriff's draw was faster than any Trent had ever seen. He stopped instantly, sweat breaking out on his upper lip as he stared down the barrel of the Colt Peacemaker. ''He's got no call to accuse Anna.''

''No, he doesn't.'' The sheriff slipped his gun back in the holster and stared at the rancher in disgust. ''That's the dumbest thing I've ever heard. Mrs. Caldwell is no more a thief than I am. Besides, if she stole the horse and used it for breeding, who could she tell about the bloodline? It wouldn't do her a bit of good. If she says Malloy was with her, I believe her, which makes him innocent of this particular crime.'' He looked at Trent. ''Where were you three nights ago?''

''Here. Duncan and I have been sleeping in the pasture, trying to guard the horses. He was with me the whole time.''

Duncan nodded. ''That's right, sir. From dark 'til dawn.''

The sheriff glanced at Anna as she walked down the porch to Trent's side. ''I figured as much. One of the ranchers north of town lost a couple of mares that night. Malloy, I don't think you've taken any of them. I've had a hunch all along that you aren't the culprit. You aren't the criminal kind.''

"He could have a partner. He was caught red-handed before," said Halstead.

"It was an act of revenge, nothing more," said the sheriff. "I figure old man Williams got off lucky. If he'd treated somebody else the way he did Malloy, he probably would have been shot in the back. My advice to you, Halstead, and to all the other ranchers hereabouts, is to quit blaming Malloy and do a better job protecting your stock and trying to catch the thief. Now, go on home and quit bothering these good folks."

"You'll pay for this come election time, sheriff," said Halstead, turning his horse toward the road.

"If I'm wrong, vote me out. If I'm right, give me a raise." As the rancher rode away, the sheriff smiled. "Reckon I could talk you out of a cup of coffee, Anna?"

"Of course. How about a plate of beans and corn bread to go with it?"

Trent smiled at the sheriff's grin as he dismounted and looped the reins over the porch railing. To a West Texan, pinto beans and corn bread were akin to manna from heaven.

"Never turn down dinner when I'm hungry." Sheriff Taylor winked at Rachel. "Especially when Rachel is cooking."

She blushed and smiled back. "I made a peach cobbler this morning. I'll go warm up the beans."

"I'll water your horse, sir," said Duncan.

"Thank you, son. You're lookin' like your pa these days. Growing into a fine young man."

"Thanks. I'm trying to remember all he taught me. Having Trent around helps, too. He gives me good advice." Trent looked at him in surprise, and Duncan grinned. "Most of the time anyway." He loosened the reins from

260 For Love of Anna

the railing and led the sheriff's horse toward the water trough by the barn.

Anna laughed and went inside to help Rachel, leaving Trent alone with Sheriff Taylor. "I appreciate what you said, and you believing that I'm innocent."

"Your history speaks for you. I made some inquiries after I sent you packin' that morning in March. When that blizzard blew in, I regretted making you leave town. But it looks like it's turning out all right."

"Anna and the kids have been very kind. They've been good for me, helped me feel like I can be around decent folks again." Trent looked down, tramping a dirt clod with the toe of his boot. "Prison makes a man forget how to act."

"Do you love her?"

Trent looked up in surprise. "That's gettin' mighty personal, sheriff."

"I know. Edwin and I were good friends. Used to cowboy together before he started raising horses and met Anna. When he began having trouble with his heart, he asked me to look out for her if something happened to him. I've done what I could, but I haven't intruded much because I know Shane takes good care of her."

"As much as she'll let him."

Sheriff Taylor nodded. "She's independent. That's a fact. He was in town the week after the blizzard, and I asked about Anna. He told me you were here."

"Why didn't you tell him about me?"

"I figured as long as you stayed out of trouble, your past was your business. I rode out this way about once a week."

"I never saw you, and Anna never mentioned you stopping by."

"Neither of you saw me because I didn't want you to. I know this country better than anyone. I've watched you work in the pasture and here in the corrals with the horses. I've seen you with the kids.'' He paused. ''And with Anna.''

''What do you mean?'' Trent asked uneasily. The sheriff gazed out across the pasture, and Trent wondered if he was intentionally making him squirm.

''Mostly working together. You make a good team.'' He looked back at Trent with a lazy smile. ''I think I'll let my wife give me a haircut every now and then.''

Trent swore softly. ''I knew that was a mistake.''

The sheriff chuckled. ''Didn't look like one to me.'' His smile faded. ''Unless you don't intend to do right by her.''

''I do. When this horse thief is caught and people know it isn't me, I'll marry her if she'll have me.''

The sheriff grinned and slapped him on the back. ''Son, I don't think that will be a problem.''

Chapter Twenty

Ian picked Rachel up midmorning on Saturday for a picnic, with the promise to have her home by early evening, well before dark. Not quite halfway to town, he turned off the main road onto a narrower one.

"We don't have to go far this way." He grinned, reaching over to take her hand. "The next part of the trip goes through a pasture."

Rachel smiled back at him. "Heading out into untamed territory, are we?"

"Yes, ma'am." He lifted her hand and kissed the palm. "I was out this way on business earlier in the week and found the perfect spot for a picnic—a grove of pecan trees alongside a small creek. There is a spring with pure, sweet water among the trees. It's like an oasis out here in the middle of the prairie."

"It sounds lovely. I've always wished we had more trees around the ranch house. There are some willows and mesquites down by the creek, but it's too long a walk on a hot day."

A few minutes later, he drew the horse and buggy to a halt in front of a barbed wire gate and handed the reins to Rachel. "Your turn."

"Thanks," she said with a grin. "I thought you might want me to open it."

"And risk scratching your lovely skin?" He kissed the tip of her nose. "Never." He hopped out and opened the gate, shutting it again after Rachel drove the buggy through.

Since she didn't know which way to go, she handed him the reins when he rejoined her. They drove across the pasture, bouncing over dips and rises, passing a scattered herd of fat cattle grazing on the thick grass. Rachel studied them as they drove by. "They look healthy." A playful calf raced along with them, making her laugh. "And happy."

Ian stopped the horse right before the land sloped down to the creek and trees. "It's beautiful," said Rachel, thinking she'd never seen a prettier spot.

"It's a good ranch, not huge, but big enough," Ian said quietly. "It'll be better when we get the house built."

Rachel looked at him in surprise. "You own this?"

"I bought it on Wednesday. I should have asked your opinion of it, but there was another potential buyer and I had to move fast." He pointed to a level spot overlooking the creek and trees. "The spring is right below there. If we put the house on that flat place, we should be able to pump the water up to it. And we'll be high enough to be out of danger when the creek floods."

"We?" Rachel's heart pounded so hard, she expected he could hear it. He'd said he wanted to make her his bride, but he'd never actually proposed.

"We'll have to live in town during the week because I need to be near the office, but we could come out here on weekends and other times as well. The place I'm renting isn't bad for now. After we finish this one, we can build a house in town, or even a little way out of town if you'd rather."

"Two houses?"

"Well, we could build three, but I don't see the need for it."

"Ian…"

He looked down at her with a tender smile and twinkling eyes. "What's wrong, darlin'? Did I forget something? Like a proposal?"

Her mouth and throat were so dry, she could only nod.

"Rachel, I love you with all my heart. I want you by my side always. Will you marry me?"

"Yes." She touched his face with her fingertips. "I love you, Ian."

"You don't know how many times I've wanted to hear you say those words." He put his arms around her, kissing her gently, sweetly. "I don't suppose you could pull a wedding together in a week?"

Rachel smiled and shook her head. "You'd better give me a month," she said, kissing him back. He pulled her closer, deepening the kiss, caressing her more freely than ever before. When he finally ended the kiss, Rachel stared up at him in dazed wonder. "Make it three weeks."

"Two."

The flare of heat in his eyes sent a new shiver of awareness rippling through her. "Two," she whispered, resting her head against his arm.

"Thank you." His smile would have lit up the blackest night. "Reverend Hargrove will be coming back through that weekend, and I know he would be pleased to perform the ceremony. Unless you want to have it in town?"

"No, I'd rather have it at home. We've been on his circuit for so long, it seems as if I've known him all my life."

"It will also give us almost a month together before we have to be in Washington."

"Washington?" She stared up at him. "D.C.?"

"There may be legislation introduced in the fall that

could adversely affect the cattle industry, so several of my clients have asked me to see what I can find out. I figure we can go to Fort Worth on the first part of our honeymoon and buy you a few fancy dresses to take with us. Then we can take the train to Washington and see some of the sights before I have to work. Would you like that?''

''I guess so.'' She looked down, toying with a button on his lapel. ''I haven't been to Fort Worth in a long time. And I'd like to see the country and especially the Capitol. But I wouldn't know how to behave if you take me to fancy dinners or parties.''

He gently tipped her chin up until she met his gaze. ''Just be your sweet, beautiful self. Everyone will be enchanted.''

''I doubt that. What if I use the wrong fork or something?''

''I'll show you what to use before we ever get there. My grandmother was always giving elaborate dinner parties, and she trained us how to behave. Now, don't fret about it. We'll have plenty of time to practice. Right now, we have more important things to do.'' Ian pulled a small wooden box from his pocket and handed it to her. ''I want everyone—especially the men around here—to know you're promised to me.''

Rachel opened the box with trembling fingers, gasping when the saw the size of the diamond solitaire mounted in a gold band.

''Like it?''

''It's beautiful,'' she said softly, watching numbly as he took the ring from the case. He curled his hand around her right one and slipped the ring on her finger. At their wedding, it would be transferred to her left hand and worn with the wedding band. She stared at it for a minute, then threw her arms around his neck, hugging him fiercely. ''Thank you.''

"My pleasure, love."

She sat back in the seat, holding her hand out in front of her, watching the light sparkle off the diamond. "Where did you find such a wonderful ring?"

"I picked it up the last time I was in Fort Worth."

Rachel glanced up at him with a small frown. "But you haven't been there since Shane's party."

"True. But I had met you." He shrugged, his eyes twinkling. "I like to be prepared."

"And what if I hadn't been interested?"

The light faded from his eyes. "Then it would have remained in my safe for a very long time. I knew you were the one I wanted the first time I saw you."

"I felt the same way about you, but I didn't want to admit it to anyone. I kept telling myself I was foolish to hope you'd be interested in me."

"How could any man not be interested in the most beautiful woman in Texas?"

Rachel giggled and shook her head. "You'll bite your tongue if you keep up such flattery." She hesitated, then met his gaze. "The ring is beautiful, but it must have cost an awful lot. You don't need to spend so much on me." She wondered how he could afford the ranch, but didn't want to take away from their joy by asking, even though they tried to be open with each other. He represented some rich, powerful men, and lawyers made good money, but she didn't see how he could make that much money so early in his practice.

"The ring is only the beginning. I'm a wealthy man, Rachel. My grandfather was an extremely successful businessman. When he died, he divided his fortune between Shane and me. Shane established his ranch. Since I wasn't ready to purchase land then, I invested mine in various stocks and bonds.'' He smiled wryly. ''After buying the ranch, my bank account isn't as plump as it was, but there is still plenty left to spoil you shamelessly.''

''Ian, you don't have to spoil me. Being loved by you is enough. If you were to lose all your money, I'd still be happy. I'd still love you.''

''I hope it never comes to that, but it's reassuring, just the same.'' He picked up the reins, gently flicking them against the horse's back. ''My stomach is growling, so it must be time to eat.''

They parked in the shade by the creek and spread a quilt out on a level, grassy spot. Ian had stopped at Ivy's Restaurant for the meal, which consisted of fried chicken, corn on the cob, tomatoes, biscuits and peach tarts. They drank cold, fresh water from the spring and talked about the house they would build there.

After they put away the remnants of the picnic lunch, they moved the quilt to follow the shade. Rachel leaned against the trunk of a giant pecan tree while Ian stretched out lazily, resting his head in her lap. They talked, dreamed and planned their future.

After a while, Ian sat up, facing her, and they shared long kisses and slow, sweet caresses. As the afternoon wore on, Rachel's respect for him grew even more.

Glancing at the position of the sun, he whispered that it was time to go, then kissed her with the promise of wonderful things to come. ''Two weeks.'' He brushed her chin with his fingertips. ''An eternity, but worth the wait.''

''I appreciate your restraint.''

''It isn't easy, but anything less wouldn't show you how much I honor and respect you. Now, my love, let's go wave that ring in front of Anna and see if she notices.'' He stood and pulled her up beside him. ''Think she'll be impressed?'' he asked with an impish grin.

* * *

When Ian and Rachel pulled up in front of the house, Anna didn't have to look for a ring to know he had proposed. The radiance on her stepdaughter's face told her the happy news. "Do you two have something to tell us?" she asked as he lifted Rachel from the buggy.

"We're engaged!" They said in unison, then laughed.

"I'm so happy for you." Anna hugged Rachel, keeping her conflicting emotions hidden. She stepped back, looking at Ian. "And for you. I know you'll make her a wonderful husband." She hugged him, too, smiling as he whispered that he'd do his best to make Rachel happy.

Rachel held out her hand, showing her the ring. "Isn't it beautiful?"

"My goodness!" Anna grinned at Ian. "Couldn't you find a bigger one?"

He grinned back. "No, ma'am. Though they did have one with several diamonds, but it seemed gaudy." He looked at Rachel, his eyes shining with love. "This one reminded me of my Rachel, perfection alone."

Rachel blushed prettily and kissed him on the cheek. "You're so sweet."

"Mushy," muttered Davy, glancing at Trent as he and Duncan walked up. "Do you and Mama do that mushy stuff?"

Trent ruffled Davy's hair. "I'm not as good with words as Ian."

Anna met Trent's gaze with a tender smile. "I'm not complaining."

"Neither am I."

Duncan hugged his sister, whispering something that made her laugh and blush. Then he shook hands with Ian. "I don't know anyone I'd rather have for a brother-in-law."

"Nor do I," said Ian with a grin.

Trent shook hands with Ian. "Congratulations. She's a wonderful woman."

"I know."

Trent grinned at Rachel. "I'm happy for you, honey, but I'm sure gonna miss your cooking."

"Anna can cook just as well as me."

"But I'm out of practice." Anna smiled ruefully. "Have you decided on a date for the wedding?"

Rachel took a deep breath and glanced at Ian. His happy grin vanished as he reached for her hand. "Two weeks from today," he said in a firm voice.

Anna barely contained her gasp. "Two weeks?" she said weakly. Trent slipped his arm around her shoulders, giving her strength. She cleared her throat and managed a smile. "Well, we'd better plan on a trip to town Monday. Can you make your wedding gown so quickly?" A wicked little imp in the back of her mind tried frantically to think of a way to break the sewing machine.

Rachel laughed softly. "I'm too excited to sleep, so I could probably make it in two days. Since Reverend Hargrove isn't riding his full circuit yet, he'll be coming back through that weekend. By his next round, he'll probably take longer to get to us, and we don't want to wait that long."

Anna noted her stepdaughter's blush and decided a quick marriage was probably wise.

"I'm supposed to go to Washington in six weeks on business for the cattlemen," said Ian. "We could spend a week or so in Fort Worth, then see a bit of the country and the Capitol before I have to go back to work."

"What a wonderful honeymoon."

"I think it will be." Ian put his arm around Rachel, hugging her to his side. "We'll have to live in town because of my law practice, but I've purchased a ranch about an hour's ride away from here. We'll start on the house as soon as we return from Washington and hopefully have it finished before winter. We can stay there on weekends, at least, so you can visit more easily.''

"Isn't he wonderful?" asked Rachel, sighing contentedly.

"Yes, he is." Anna was happy they would be close by, at least part of the time, but the thought of losing daily contact with her dear stepdaughter saddened her. "Well, let's go inside and make some plans." When Trent moved his arm from around her shoulders, she caught his hand. She looked up at him, silently asking him not to leave her side. He nodded in understanding.

Anna was relieved and pleased when Ian seemed to enjoy their simple supper of corn bread crumbled in milk. Though he had eaten with them several times, they usually had more of a variety dishes. They spent the evening discussing the wedding, making a list of people to invite, and what to have at the wedding breakfast. Then they spent another five minutes trying to explain to Mitch and Davy why it was called a breakfast even though it would be served after the morning wedding and likely would be around midday. Laughing, they finally gave up.

Not long after dark, Trent left to take up his position in the pasture. Duncan would go down at bedtime, catching a few hours' rest before he kept watch from one to four, when Anna took her turn. Though they each slept part of the night, they were growing weary from the routine. Shane had offered to send men over to relieve them, so she asked Ian to tell him they could use help on Monday night.

After Ian left, Duncan went down to the pasture. Anna put the boys to bed, then peeped in on Rachel. The day had caught up with her; she was already asleep. Anna slipped quietly out the door and walked to the corrals.

Going through a gate into the pasture, she stopped to check on the three saddled horses that were tied to the corral fence. She hated having the horses stand there all night, but they had to be able to ride immediately if trouble came. They rotated horses each time, using the six that seemed to see better at night.

She moved quietly to where Duncan and Trent had spread out their bedrolls. Duncan was lying down, but he sat up when she approached them. "You all right, Anna?"

"Everyone else is asleep, but I'm too restless to go to bed." She shrugged and surveyed the darkened prairie, making out the shape of a horse here and there in the pale moonlight. "I didn't feel like being by myself."

"Do you want to lie down here?" asked Duncan.

"No, thanks. I don't think I could sleep."

"Wake me up when it's my turn." Duncan laid down, turning so he faced the other way.

Anna sat next to Trent as he leaned against a big rock, curling up against him when he put his arm around her.

"Feelin' down?" he asked softly.

"Uh-huh. I'm happy and terribly sad at the same time."

"That's understandable." He rested his chin against her forehead. "I'd volunteer to kiss it and make it better, but Duncan would tan my hide if he caught me kissin' you in the vicinity of your heart."

Anna giggled, burying her face against his chest to muffle the sound. "I love you."

"I love you, too, sugar." He nudged her face up for a long, tender kiss. "This will have to do for tonight," he whispered. "A good horse thief won't disturb the horses nearly as much as the coyotes did. He'll hit some ranch tonight."

"Why?"

"Half-moon. Not completely dark, not too bright. If he's

careful, he can see where he's going, but won't be easily seen. I took Williams' horses on a night like this. So keep your ears peeled.''

"Isn't that supposed to be keep your eyes peeled?"

"At night, they're about one and the same.''

"All I can hear is the beat of your heart.'' She yawned and snuggled closer. "It's strong and steady and makes me feel safe.'' He tightened his arms, and Anna drifted off to sleep.

A few hours later, she awoke when Trent shifted her. He leaned down, whispering in her ear, "He's here.''

Chapter Twenty-One

"Where?" whispered Anna.

"At the far edge of the pasture," said Trent. "I expect he'll make his way around the herd and take a couple out by the road."

Anna moved away from him, reaching for her rifle. Trent leaned over and nudged Duncan. "We've got company."

Duncan scrambled to his knees and picked up his Winchester. A soft nicker came from the other side of the pasture, as if one of the horses had greeted the intruder. "That's odd," he whispered.

"Yes, it is. Sounds like they know him." Trent frowned thoughtfully as he picked up his gun.

Crouching low, they made their way to the horses, slipped the guns in their sheaths and mounted. From the saddle, Trent had a clearer view. The thief slowly drove four or five horses across the valley—away from the road. "What the devil?" He watched him for a few seconds, then looked at Anna in amazement. "He's taking them toward the breaks."

"He must have already cut the fence on that end of the pasture," said Duncan.

''Could the sheriff be right? Is there a safe trail through there?'' Trent tried to think of some place he had missed.

''Not on our land. But there might be one on Kingsley's. Do you think it's Bender?'' asked Anna.

''I doubt it. He doesn't have enough sense to handle animals that well.'' Trent grimaced as the man picked up several more horses. ''He's gettin' greedy.''

Afraid of spooking the herd and driving them into the barbed wire fence at a hard run, they rode at a fast walk. Angling across the pasture, they hoped to get ahead of them, but the thief took the herd through an opening in the fence sooner than they expected. He had collected at least twenty horses.

Trent, Anna and Duncan changed directions, picking up speed, and headed for the downed section of fence. The thief spotted them and pushed the horses to a run down the valley. There was no fence crossing this portion of the ranch. It was wide-open into the breaks.

By the time they cleared the fence, their mounts had warmed up enough to let them run full-out. The thief looked back and saw they were gaining on him. Spurring his horse viciously, he dashed around the frightened, speeding herd until he was in front of them.

Anna and Duncan rode around the south side of the herd. Trent went around on the north. He quickly lost sight of them in the swirling dust and darkness and had to shift farther out to see where he was going. He bent low over his horse, and they gradually moved toward the front of the herd. As the dust lessened, he sat up, looking for Anna. He spotted her chasing the thief as the man veered off to the right. Duncan was closing in on the lead horses.

Trent slowed Polecat enough to let the other animals pass, figuring he'd go after Anna while Duncan turned the herd. Having two handling the horses would have been better, but the valley was wide. He thought the boy could get them moving in a circle before they reached the breaks. Then they would eventually slow down. The last horse raced by, and Trent urgently searched landscape for Anna.

A searing pain exploded across his forehead, toppling him from the galloping horse. He crashed to the ground, jarring every bone in his body. His last thought before he lost consciousness was that he must have broken half of them.

Anna knew right where the fool was headed—a long narrow ravine that intersected with dozens of others. If he reached it, she'd lose him. Her only consolation was that if she did, he'd probably break his neck trying to get away from her.

The man knew her land well, but she knew it better. She turned Ginger, riding around a grove of scrub oak, over a rise, across a flat stretch and over a hill. Reining in her horse, Anna checked to make certain she was far enough down the hill not to be silhouetted against the sky. Heart pounding, she pulled the rifle from the scabbard, cocked it and waited.

He should be coming around that boulder right about now. She lifted the Winchester to her shoulder, sighting the gun at rider height above the trail. Seconds later, the thief came into view, slowing his horse through the rocky terrain. Anna took a deep breath and held it, focusing through the sight at her prey, and squeezed the trigger.

The bullet hit him in the right shoulder, knocking him from the horse. The dun shied, then spun around and raced back up the trail, disappearing around the large rocks. Anna thought the animal looked familiar, but she'd only gotten a glimpse of it in the darkness. She cocked the gun again, pointing it at thief, and rode cautiously toward him, guiding her horse with her knees. "Throw your weapons out here where I can see them."

The man sat up with a groan and tossed a pistol out in the open. "That's all I've got. Rifle is on the horse. Dang it, Anna, why'd you have to shoot me?"

Recognizing his voice, she stared at him in shock. "Sully?"

"Yeah." He moaned again. "Lord, that hurts. You gonna let me bleed to death?"

"I just might for all the heartache you've caused us." She knew he always carried a large hunting knife. "Throw your knife out here, too." Muttering, he obeyed. "Stuff a handkerchief against the wound and stand up. It's a long walk back to the ranch house."

"I can't walk. Call Cactus. He'll probably come right to you." Fumbling, he untied the handkerchief from around his neck with one hand and stuffed it beneath his shirt against the wound.

"That's low, even for a thief. Riding one of my horses while you steal the rest." Anna moved closer, watching him carefully. "Put your hands up where I can see them."

He held his left hand up in the air, resting the right against his chest. "I can't lift this one with a bullet in my shoulder. I was only gonna take three or four," he said gruffly, remaining seated. "The others came along because they wanted to."

"Because you rode Cactus. You knew the other horses wouldn't put up a fuss." Anna whistled, and Cactus came running up the trail. He stopped beside her, close enough for her to reach the reins without taking her gaze off Sully for more than a second. "Good boy." Wrapping the reins around her saddle horn, she watched the horse trader. "Did you buy horses from the other ranchers you robbed?"

"Uh-huh. Then I'd ride that particular horse when I went

back after another one. Worked every time. Downright clever of me.''

Anna silently admitted that it was, but she wasn't going to tell him that. She drew her pistol and slid the rifle in the sheath hanging from the saddle horn. ''Mount up, Sully.'' She unwound the reins and guided Cactus over to the horse trader, keeping the gun on him as he struggled into the saddle. ''Don't try to get away from me.''

''I ain't in no shape to ride fast. You are going to tend to my wound when we get to the house, aren't you?''

''As long as you cooperate, I won't let you bleed to death. Why did you do it, Sully?''

''Got me a new lady friend. She likes purty things and likes for me to be around. I'd make more money if I raised horses instead of tradin' them. Even if I couldn't brag about the line, folks could tell they were good animals.''

He chuckled, then winced and shifted his arm. ''I hid 'em on Kingsley's place. There's a perfect box canyon on the other edge of the breaks. Got water and plenty of grass. He has that land fenced off. He only uses it when the grazing gets low on the rest of the ranch. I doubt he's had a man over there in three months, so he doesn't have any idea I cut the fence to go through. I've been careful to keep out of sight during the day. Since I came through here awhile back, I figured no one would even suspect me. Especially when they'd be so quick to blame Malloy.''

''Some folks thought he did it, but not the sheriff.''

Sully looked at her in surprise. ''Why not?''

''He's smart enough to see that Trent isn't the criminal type. I expect eventually Sheriff Taylor would have figured out it was you. Now, head back up the valley. Believe me, Sully, if you try to get away, I won't think twice about shooting you again. You've wronged the man I love, and I'll prove he's innocent whether you're dead or alive.''

* * *

Trent roused slowly, opening his eyes and struggling to focus on the stars above him. A few extra, odd-shaped ones seemed to dance right in front of him. He closed his eyes briefly. When he opened them again, he was relieved to see that the waltzing lights had disappeared.

He gingerly moved his arms and legs and wiggled his fingers. Everything still worked. Everything also hurt, but his head most of all. A narrow stream of blood ran across his forehead and down his temple. He reached up with a trembling hand, half expecting to find a hole in his head or maybe a bullet smashed against his skull. Instead, he felt a two-inch or so streak without any skin, lots of blood but no real damage. If the shooter's aim had only been a fraction better, he'd be a dead man.

The ground began to vibrate, the sound growing stronger by the second. Afraid Duncan had turned the herd and was unknowingly driving them right toward him, Trent raised up on his elbows to take a look. Polecat stood a few feet away. His vision blurred again, but he thought he made out the shape of several approaching horses.

"There he is!" shouted a voice he didn't recognize.

He lay back down, figuring that if they saw him, they wouldn't trample him. The riders stopped in a circle around him. Three or four men dismounted. Two of them grabbed Trent beneath the arms and hauled him to his feet. Pain roared through his head at the quick change of position.

"We got you now, Malloy. Your horse thievin' days are over."

Squinting, Trent tried to focus on the face spinning in front of him. His throbbing head felt like a bull had stomped on it. "Bender?"

"That's right. And this time, you'll get your just punishment. Pete, throw me your rope. We're going to send a message that we don't tolerate horse thieves around here.''

A young cowboy tossed Bender a rope. ''String him up,'' he cried, his voice breaking in his excitement.

''Wait a minute,'' shouted Trent. ''We were chasing the thief. Anna and Duncan were on the other side of the herd. Duncan is trying to stop them. Anna rode off to the south after the horse thief.''

''I don't believe you,'' snarled Bender. ''Tie him up.''

Another man swung down from his horse, carrying a short piece of rope, the kind used to hold a calf's feet together when they were branding. He tried to pull Trent's hands around behind his back. Trent fought, but couldn't break loose from the men holding him. ''Anna might be in trouble. At least send somebody to help her.''

''Maybe he's telling the truth,'' said one of the men holding him.

The man behind him grabbed one hand and wrapped the rope around first one wrist, then the other. Wincing as he cinched the rope tight, Trent tried again. ''We only saw one man, but there might be others waiting.'' With his hands tied, the men released him, but stayed where they were.

''I'll go see if I can find her,'' said another young man. ''I don't want no part in a hangin'.''

''There's a trail on the other side of those two hills that leads into the breaks,'' said Trent. ''They were both headed for it.''

''He's lying,'' said Bender.

''What if he isn't?'' asked the young cowboy. ''Mrs. Caldwell might get hurt, and you'll be hanging an innocent man.'' He spun his horse and rode across the prairie, following Trent's directions.

''The boy's right. We should take him back to the ranch

and let the boss send for the sheriff,'' said the man standing next to Trent.

"I sent for the boss when we first spotted Malloy," said Bender. "I figure he'll want in on this."

"We can't just lynch him," said another man. "That'd be murder."

"It's justice," cried Bender. "For what he done to Rosie, and for stealing from the woman who saved his no-good hide."

"Not everyone agrees with you, Bender," said Trent. "Are you going to kill them, too?"

An argument broke out between the ones who wanted to string him up and those who didn't. It seemed they were equally divided on the issue. As the disagreement grew louder and more heated, Trent weighed his chances of getting away and hiding in the darkness. He decided against it. If he ran, Bender would shoot him in the back and say that his trying to get away only added to the proof of guilt. Even while he argued, Bender was tying one end of the rope into a noose.

Trent noticed other riders coming toward them from Kingsley's ranch. He looked at one of the men next to him. "What did you do, cut a hole in the fence?"

"Kingsley had us put in a gate earlier in the week." He shook his head. "This is sorry business."

"Then help me get away," Trent said softly.

"Can't. That's the boss comin', now." Suddenly, the man grinned and leaned toward him. "But I just thought of something. There ain't a tree anywhere close that's big enough to hang a midget."

That didn't encourage Trent too much. Bender was dumb enough not to think about it, but Kingsley wasn't. If the rancher wanted him dead, he'd find a way.

* * *

When Anna spotted the rider galloping toward them, she put away her revolver and took out the rifle, cocking it. "Hold up, Sully. Friend of yours?"

"Not that I know of. I ain't got nobody helpin' me."

The cowboy slowed as he approached. "That you, Mrs. Caldwell?" he called.

"Yes." She didn't raise the Winchester to her shoulder, but kept the barrel pointed at the man. "Who are you?"

"Mike Rhodes, from the Kingsley Ranch. Malloy said you were over this way. Is that the horse thief?" he asked as he came near enough for normal conversation.

"Yes." Anna paused, listening to faint shouts in the distance. Fear sent a shiver down her back. "Why didn't Trent come with you?"

"Bender and some of the men are talkin' about hangin' him. Not everybody is agreeable to it. You'd better get over there, ma'am, and stop them."

"Bring him." Anna nodded as the cowboy drew his gun, aiming it at Sully. She put away the rifle and lightly spurred her horse. The mare responded instantly, quickly working up to a run. They covered the distance in minutes, but it seemed like forever.

Nearing the group of men, she slowed Ginger and slipped another cartridge into the rifle so it would be fully loaded. Until she shot Sully, Anna had never fired directly at another person. She hoped she never had to again, but she would do anything to protect Trent, even if it meant killing someone.

They were arguing so loudly, no one noticed her approach. Unable to see exactly who was where, she stopped within hearing distance. Judging from the conversation, Kingsley had just arrived.

"You can't hang him," said one of the men.

"Yes, we can."

Anna recognized Bender's voice.

"There ain't a tree around here big enough," said the other man. A few others laughed nervously.

"Then we'll use the ranch gate," declared Bender. "That big ol' beam would hold ten men."

"No." Kingsley's tone dared anyone to defy him. "Let the law handle it. We'll take him to town in the morning."

"No!" Bender drew his pistol, pointing it at Trent.

Anna raised her rifle and took aim, but she faced Bender's side, and he wore a dark shirt. If he moved at the wrong time, she might hit the man standing beyond him. She eased silently to the ground and tiptoed across the soft grass.

The other men, including Kingsley backed away from Bender and Trent.

Anna moved closer, where she had a clear shot, with no chance of accidentally hitting Trent or anyone else.

"Bender, drop the gun," ordered Kingsley.

Bender shifted the pistol toward his boss. "You may not have the guts to kill him, but I do. If you try to stop me, you'll die with him."

"The only one going to die is you," said Anna.

Bender froze.

"There's a Winchester pointed at the middle of your back. Throw down the gun." When he hesitated, Anna feared he might shoot Kingsley or Trent anyway or try for her. "If your hand even twitches, you're a dead man." She hoped he didn't realize it was too dark to see such a tiny movement.

"She's a crack shot," said Kingsley. "She won't miss."

"Let go of the past, Ned." Trent spoke quietly. "Don't hold on to the hurt. It'll eat you up. I know. Start living again."

"I can't. I ain't nothin' without Rosie."

"Then find a woman who'll make you feel like something. You have a lot of years left. Do you want to live with a memory or with a flesh-and-blood woman who'll love only you? Rosie never could be true to any man. It's just not in her nature."

Bender hesitated, then slowly lowered the gun, letting it fall from his fingertips, and drew a ragged breath. "Hating you is easier than admitting she didn't love me."

"Hurt has a way of hiding the truth. It was easier for me to hate the old man than accept my transgression in kissing his wife."

Anna lowered the rifle and walked toward them. Halfway there, reaction set in, and she started to tremble.

"You figure all that out in prison?" asked Bender.

"Partly. Most of it I learned through the love of a very special woman. Maybe you can find someone who'll wipe away the past like Anna has done for me."

Bender glanced back at Anna, then stepped aside. Another man picked up his gun and stuffed it in the waistband of his pants.

"Cut him loose," ordered Kingsley. The cowboy closest to Trent pulled out a pocketknife and cut through the rope binding his hands.

When Anna reached Kingsley, she stopped. "Sully Smith is the horse thief."

"Sully! You caught him?"

"Driving half my herd down the valley. Rhodes is bringing him up here. I shot Sully in the shoulder. I'd appreciate it if you'd tend to it, then take him to the sheriff in the morning."

"You and Malloy will need to go with us to tell the sheriff what happened."

"We'll be ready."

"I think I see them over there," Kingsley said, pointing

at two riders coming toward them. He turned, gazing up the valley. "Looks like Duncan is bringing in the horses. Do you need help getting them back in the pasture?"

"No, thanks. They can stay out here tonight."

"Hand me your carbine, Anna, and I'll put it away for you," Kingsley offered. "It's hard to hug a man with a rifle in your hand."

Anna handed it to him, then turned, finding that Trent had walked up right behind her. She threw her arms around him, and he held her close. "Thank God you're safe."

He tipped his head to kiss her, and Anna saw a cut on his forehead and dried blood on his face.

"You're hurt! What did they do to you?"

"It's just a graze."

"They shot you?" She spun around, glaring at the men who had been watching them. "Who shot him?"

Every one of them started easing away. "We're not real sure, ma'am."

"It happened so fast. The horses stampeded, then we saw a rider behind them," said a man climbing on his horse.

"We thought it was the horse thief," said another, grabbing the reins of his horse.

"We were just tryin' to stop him."

"Didn't want him to make off with your herd."

They mounted their horses faster than a whirlwind could snuff out a match and headed out to meet Rhodes and Sully. Kingsley brought over her horse, leaving it beside Polecat. "I owe you both an apology. I've learned not to judge a man by his past."

"Or let jealousy cloud your judgment?" asked Anna.

"That, too. I've also learned not to wish for what I can't have. If I want a wife and family, I'd better mend a few broken fences between me and the schoolteacher."

"I wish you well," said Anna.

He nodded his thanks and rode off after his men.

Trent chuckled softly. "Well, sugar, you got rid of them pronto."

"Are you hurt anywhere else?"

"All over. And my head feels like I've been shot."

"You have," she said dryly, putting her arm around his waist and propelling him toward his horse. "You'll feel better when we get you home to bed."

"I like the sound of that. Your bed or mine?"

"Yours. Tonight. But if you cooperate, things might be different tomorrow night."

"Oh, yeah?"

"As I recall, you said you couldn't marry me until the thief was caught."

"Yep, I think I remember saying something like that."

"He's caught." Anna kissed him tenderly. "And so are you."

Chapter Twenty-Two

When they arrived in town the next morning, word quickly spread that the horse thief had been captured. The ministers of the Baptist and Methodist churches—the only two in town—dismissed services early, and folks poured out into the streets for an impromptu celebration. Cowboys wandered out of the wagon yard, saloons and hotel to join in. Even the saloon gals donned proper dresses and came to see what all the fuss was about.

Upon learning Sully Smith was the culprit, reactions ranged from shocked disbelief to those who swore they'd been wary of him for years, trusting him like a rabbit did a coyote.

Kingsley had removed the bullet from Sully's shoulder and patched him up the best he could. The doctor tidied things up, then relinquished his patient to Sheriff Taylor who escorted him down the alley to the jail.

Trent, Anna, Duncan and Kingsley explained what happened to the sheriff, including how Trent had been shot. They asked the lawman not to investigate that part of the incident since it happened in the excitement of the moment and wasn't likely to occur again. By earlier agreement, none of them mentioned how Trent had almost been hung.

When they left the sheriff's office, they were instantly surrounded by the crowd, everyone talking at once and anxious to hear the story. Kingsley finally quieted them down and briefly told what happened. Anna expected him to take some of the credit, but he didn't. He was also open about how his men had mistaken Trent for the thief and shot him.

"Three cheers for Mrs. Caldwell, Malloy and Duncan," hollered Tim O'Brien. "Hip, hip…"

"Hurrah!" shouted the enthusiastic audience as the men waved their hats in the air.

"Hip, hip…"

"Hurrah!"

"Hip, hip…"

"Hurrah!"

Then it seemed as if every person in town wanted to commend Anna on her bravery and marksmanship. They all had a kind word for Trent, too. Some even apologized for misjudging him. The men shook his hand, and several of the women, both married and single, took the opportunity to kiss him on the cheek—to his embarrassment and Anna's annoyance.

Anna made a tiny sound of disgust. "Here comes Othelia Upton. If she kisses you, I'll kick her shin."

He laughed softly. "I almost hope she does, just to see you do it."

Davy and Mitch raced by with Lizzie's sons. "We're going over to the Spencers', Mama," called Davy.

"We'll be over in a little while." Anna smiled at him, her heart swelling at the proud look in his eyes.

"Well, Mr. Malloy, you proved us wrong." Mrs. Upton stepped up in front of him and held out her hand, palm down, as if she expected him to kiss the back of it.

He shook it instead. "Yes, ma'am."

"Of course, I realized some time ago that you were a man of integrity."

"Oh? When?"

"That day in Haley's."

Trent couldn't resist. "Because I asked for your help?"

To his surprise, Mrs. Upton's expression softened into a sweet smile. "No. Because of the way you talked to the little girl and the anguish I saw in your eyes at her mother's fear. Their feelings and what they thought of you mattered a great deal to you."

"Yes, they did. I appreciate you speaking to her on my behalf."

"You're quite welcome." Again, her smile was genuine and friendly.

"You should do that more often."

"What?" she asked with a tiny frown.

Trent leaned forward, speaking softly near her ear. "Stop puttin' on airs. When you're being your sweet self, Othelia, you're a very attractive woman."

"Oh, my!" she exclaimed softly, her cheeks turning pink. Trent winked, and she blushed even more. Laughing, Mrs. Upton turned to Anna. "My dear, I still say you shouldn't have such a handsome rascal working for you."

"I agree. In fact, I was going to remedy that problem today, but we forgot the courthouse was closed on Sunday. We can't get a marriage license until tomorrow."

"Nonsense. I'll go find the county clerk and tell him to open his office right now. Meet us over at the courthouse," she called over her shoulder as she bustled off.

"What did you say to her?" Anna looked up at Trent with a grin.

"Told her to quit puttin' on airs."

She raised an eyebrow but before she could ask what else he said, the blacksmith's wife grabbed her hand, pumping it up and down. The woman gushed about how Anna had shown up the men, proving a woman was better than them anytime.

A few minutes later, Trent tucked Anna's arm around his, and they slipped away to the courthouse. Sure enough, Mrs. Upton and the county clerk were waiting for them. In a matter of minutes, they had the marriage license.

An hour later, they stood in the Baptist church with their family and close friends—Shane, Ian, Hank, Sheriff Taylor and the Spencers. Even Dig was included. The Uptons were there, too, though Anna and Trent didn't have the chance to invite them. Othelia simply informed them they were attending the ceremony.

The minister asked if Trent had a ring. He shook his head. "No, sir. Haley's isn't open today, and we kinda came to town unexpectedly." Glancing at Anna, he shrugged. "I'll get one tomorrow if the boss will let me draw my pay a week early."

Anna and the others laughed. "I think that can be arranged," she said softly.

Holding hands and gazing at each other, they quietly took their vows, pledging themselves to each other before God and man.

"Mr. Malloy, you may kiss your bride," said the preacher with an indulgent smile.

Trent framed her face with his hands, kissing her reverently. When he felt a tug on his pant leg, he ended the kiss and looked down at Mitch's solemn face.

"Does this mean you're my new daddy?"

"Yes, it does, son."

"Whoopee!" Mitch danced a jig, then threw his arms around Trent.

He picked him up and hugged him. Then handed him to Anna so she could give him a sloppy mother's kiss and a squeeze. Davy and Dig wanted a hug, too, as well as Rachel and Duncan. Then their friends crowded around wishing them well.

"I don't know about anybody else, but it's past my dinnertime," said Shane. "I reserved tables at Ivy's. You're all invited. Dinner's on me."

At the restaurant, they ate Ivy's special chicken-fried steak and laughed as Shane and Ian sang silly songs, trying to outdo each other. Trent's knee rested against Anna's beneath the table all during the meal. She touched his hand and arm often, and even leaned over and kissed him a couple of times. Though he knew this wonderful woman loved him, he had to keep reminding himself that no one would be scandalized if he so much as touched her hand in public.

He noticed Ian and Rachel slip out of the restaurant after the meal but figured they wanted to be by themselves for a while. They returned half an hour later, about when the little boys decided it was time to end the party and go do something more interesting. The adults took the hint and bid the newly married couple farewell.

Duncan was staying with Tim. Both had solemnly promised to behave—no drinking or womanizing. Rachel and the other boys were staying with the Spencers. Trent and Anna planned to go to the hotel, though he worried a bit about the thin walls.

Rachel and Ian waited with them until everyone else had left. He draped his arm around Trent's shoulders and handed him a house key. "I want you and Anna to stay at my place as long as you're in town. It will give you more privacy than you'll have at the hotel. I took your room there. Rachel and I have already moved your things over to the house and hauled my stuff to the hotel."

"That's mighty kind of you, but I don't want to boot you out of your own house."

"I'll be fine, unless you decide to stay here more than a week. Then I'll have to bother you for more clothes."

"We'd only planned to be here a couple of nights. Even with Shane's men taking care of the stock, we don't want to be away from the ranch too long."

"Enjoy your time alone. There's a little food in the larder, maybe enough to last a couple of days. Help yourself. I usually eat here anyway."

"Thanks. I appreciate it." Trent glanced at Rachel as she hugged Anna. He looked back at Ian with a grin. "Mind your manners around my daughter."

Ian laughed. "Yes, sir."

Trent unlocked the door to Ian's house, tucked the key in his pocket and swung Anna up in his arms. Smiling as she giggled, he carried her through the doorway and shoved the door closed with his heel. Slowly lowering her feet to the floor, he turned her to face him. "Hello, Mrs. Malloy."

She caressed the back of his neck with her fingers. "Hello, Mr. Malloy."

His smile faded. "I still can't quite believe it's true. I've wished for this moment so long. I'm afraid I'll wake up and find this is just another dream."

"Did you ever dream you'd spend your wedding night in Ian's house?" she asked, her eyes twinkling.

"No, can't say that I have."

Anna smoothed her hands down his chest and around to the small of his back. Her eyes dancing with mischief, she slid them lower, moving her fingers in slow circles on his backside.

His breath came out in a rush. "This has to be real. It feels too good not to be."

Her silver eyes darkened with desire. "I'm not shy about

making love in the daytime. As long as there isn't anyone else around.''

His smile was slow and easy. "Then we'd better not waste a minute. We won't have many chances like this.''

Curling his hand around hers, he led her into the bedroom. It was definitely a man's room—not a frill in sight. Trent hadn't paid any attention to the parlor furniture, but the matching marble-topped walnut dresser, washstand and bed were of the highest quality. The lines were rectangular and fairly plain, the kind he would like if he were a rich man.

The fresh, clean sheets had been turned back, and a small bouquet of wildflowers placed between the pillows. "Looks like Rachel and Ian did a little more than bring our things over here," Anna said with a smile.

"Thoughtful of them, but I prefer the way your sheets smell. Just like you. Even if I'd ridden away as soon as I was well, I'd never smell lavender again without thinking of you.''

He reached up and slowly pulled the pins from her hair, setting them on the dresser. When it fell loosely down her back, he ran his fingers through the silken strands, carefully combing out any snarls. "I love your hair. The second night of the blizzard, I sat on the sofa for a couple of hours watching you sleep. Your hair was spread out across the quilts like a waterfall, and I wanted to touch it in the worst way.

"Then the cover slipped off your shoulder." He smiled ruefully. "There you were in that high-necked, prim nightgown, and I wanted you more than I'd ever wanted any other woman." He leaned down, kissing her gently, teasing her lips as he unbuttoned her blouse. Easing it off her shoulders and down her arms, he met her gaze. "And it wasn't because I hadn't been with a woman in five years, either. I wanted to wrap your goodness around me, fill my soul with your sweetness, my senses with your beauty.''

"Don't expect so much from me." When she was free of the blouse, she pressed her palm against his cheek. "You'll only be disappointed."

"Not a chance." He laid the blouse on a nearby chair and settled his hands at her waist. "When I was younger, I used to dream of finding a woman like you—someone kind and gentle, but strong, too, who could stand with me against hardship and sorrow. When I walked into Huntsville prison and those iron doors clanged shut behind me, my dreams died. The only thing that kept me sane was that someday I'd walk out a free man." He closed his eyes and drew her against him.

"Only I wasn't free. I was a prisoner of the wrong I'd done. Williams had tried his best to ruin me, but I finished the job for him. I was the one who destroyed my honor and integrity, and I wasn't doing so great getting it back. The last thing I remember before passing out in the blizzard was asking God for another chance. I needed to redeem myself, to prove I was trustworthy."

Trent tightened his arms around her. "He gave me so much more. He gave me you. You're my salvation, Anna." He held her for a few minutes, his heart overflowing with love, his soul rejoicing with thanksgiving.

But soon, the sensation of her softness pressed against him reminded him where they were, and that this was their wedding day. He had won the right to love her, not only with his heart but with his body as well. Dipping his head, he kissed her on the neck, smoothing his hands up and down her back.

"I'm sure glad you didn't wear a corset," he said, straightening and bringing his hands around her ribs and up to her breasts.

She gasped softly, then smiled. "I never do, not even on special days. They get in the way."

"Of some things." He chuckled, delighting in his freedom to touch her the way he longed to.

"Of everything. They're a bother. I'll never have a fashionably tiny waist, but I don't care."

"Your waist suits me fine." He kissed the swell of her bosom. "And so does everything else. I want you, Anna."

They undressed each other quickly, then tossed the wildflowers and covers clear off the bed. Anna lay down, holding her hand out to him. Trent curled his fingers around hers and lay down beside her, his gaze traveling slowly over her. "I never knew a woman could be so beautiful."

She pulled his head down for a fiery kiss.

Trent had intended to take his time and prolong the pleasure, but in moments he trembled with need. Anna had no more patience than he did. Their union was swift and sure, melding not only their bodies but their hearts and souls into one. Time and again during the evening and night, they loved and laughed, slept now and then, and loved some more.

As dawn's light filtered through the curtains, Trent lay on his side, resting his head on his arm, watching Anna sleep. Never in his wildest dreams had he imagined a woman or a love like this. She wiggled a little, then licked her lips and yawned. A minute later, she slowly opened her eyes and looked at him with a contented smile. Scooting closer, she yawned again and turned to face him, sliding her hand around his waist. "Good mornin', love," she said softly, her eyelids drifting closed.

Soft and cuddly. "Good mornin', sugar."

"Been awake long?"

"Just a few minutes. But I've come to an understanding about something."

She tipped her head back and looked up at him. "What?"

"Now I know why men dream of marrying a pretty widow," he said with a mischievous grin.

Anna laughed—then confirmed it all over again.

They wound up having Ian and Rachel's wedding in town after all. Rachel finished the wedding gown a few days before the ceremony. Made in white embroidered silk, the skirt draped lightly across the front and hung with gathered fullness at the back in a waterfall-drapery over a long, slender bustle. The matching blouse, which tucked into the skirt, had a standing collar. The long sleeves were fashionably full above the elbows and gathered into a puff at the shoulders. They tapered to a tight fit around the lower arms. A wide silk ribbon trimmed her waist, drawn to a point at the center of the front and tied in a long, loose bow at the back.

Lizzie gave her two new dresses for the trip to Fort Worth. Anna bought her another, as well as a beautiful cambric-and-lace bridal set consisting of nightgown, chemise and drawers to match.

When they were alone, Trent teased Anna about the fancy nightgown. "Seems silly to call it a bridal set when she probably won't even put it on the first night."

Anna bawled. The cry did her good, even if it made Trent feel like a heel.

By the time of the wedding, she was reasonably composed. The church was packed, and she wished they'd had the wedding in the morning when it was cooler. Trent muttered that he'd never seen so many rich ranchers in one place outside of a fancy saloon in Fort Worth noted for high-stakes gambling. Anna had never been in a saloon, fancy or not, but she'd never seen so many wealthy men together, either. Their presence was a good indication of Ian's standing.

Rachel honored Trent by asking him to give her away. Anna's eyes misted when she saw them coming down the aisle. Rachel was the most beautiful bride Antelope Springs had ever seen, and Trent was so proud she thought sure he would bust the buttons right off his suit vest.

The circuit rider preacher and Baptist minister shared the service. After prayer and a short opening, Reverend Hargrove asked, "Who gives this woman in marriage?"

"Her mother and I," said Trent, his voice firm and strong. Then he laid his hand on Rachel's shoulder and said quietly, "And the love of her father."

Crying silently, Anna caught his hand when he sat down beside her. Leaning toward him, she whispered in his ear, "Bless you."

He put his arm around her, resting it on the pew, curving his hand around her shoulder. "I already am," he whispered back.

Anna watched the ceremony as if in a dream. She had the strangest feeling that, somehow, Edwin shared the time with them, and that he approved of his daughter's choice.

They held the wedding supper at Ivy's, filling the restaurant to capacity and then some. Ian insisted on paying for the meal, for which Anna was grateful. Otherwise, she might have had to take out a small loan from the bank. Knowing they had made it through the hard times without a loan, Rachel would have been horrified if she'd ever learned of it.

Rachel and Ian left the party in the early evening, going to their house in town for the night. Anna and Trent went to the hotel a few minutes later, leaving the remaining guests, all ranchers, to their discussion of grass, cows and government bureaucracy. With the younger boys at the

Spencers' and Duncan at Tim's, they found themselves alone again.

"I think we'll have to come to town more often," said Trent as he helped her undress. "I love the kids, but I like having you all to myself behind a locked door, knowing some sleepy little boy won't come wandering in at the wrong time."

"It is nice," she said tiredly, wondering if she'd adequately prepared Rachel for her wedding night. Even though the girl knew what to expect, Anna feared it might not be the wonderful experience she hoped for.

Trent slid his arms around her, resting his chest against her back. He kissed her on the cheek. "Worried about her?"

She nodded. "A woman's first time isn't always easy."

"Ian will be gentle and patient. Not like I was on our wedding night."

Anna turned in his arms, smiling as she kissed his chin. "I liked our wedding night."

"Good." He winked at her. "Want to repeat it?"

They picked Ian and Rachel up the next morning to take them to the train station. As she waited for Rachel to throw a few last-minute things into her suitcase, Anna surreptitiously studied her face, breathing a sigh of relief when she saw only joy and the radiance of love. They chatted for a few minutes until the men carried the baggage out to the buckboard.

When she was sure they were alone, Rachel hugged Anna. "Thank you for being so honest with me."

Anna smiled as Rachel stepped back. "Judging by the glow on your face, I assume things went well."

A twinkle lit Rachel's dreamy eyes as she nodded.

Anna laughed and slid her arm around Rachel's waist as

they started for the door. They stopped on the porch, watching Trent tease Ian as they tried to fit the bags in the buckboard. "We've been blessed with two wonderful men."

"Yes, we have."

Successful in loading the luggage, Trent and Ian laughed and looked toward the house, their smiles brightening when they saw their wives standing there.

"We're cherished," Rachel said softly.

"Yes, we are." As they walked to the buckboard, Anna met Trent's gaze, his expression filled with tenderness and love. Her prayer was not lengthy, nor was it eloquent, but it came straight from her heart.

Thank you, God, for giving us both another chance.

* * * * *

Harlequin® Historical

Love,
Americana Style

JOE'S WIFE
by Cheryl St.John
Available in February 1999
(29051-9)

THE TENDER STRANGER
by Carolyn Davidson
Available in March 1999
(29056-X)

Available wherever
Harlequin books are sold.

HARLEQUIN®
Makes any time special ™

Anglophile

('an-glə-fil)
One who greatly admires or favors England
and things English.

+

Dreamer

('drē-mər)
One who lives in a world of fancy and
imagination.

=

MY LORD PROTECTOR
by Deborah Hale
England, 1748 (29052-7)

THE BRIDE OF WINDERMERE
by Margo Maguire
England, 1421 (29053-5)

ROBBER BRIDE
by Deborah Simmons
England, 1274 (29055-1)

Harlequin Historicals
the way the past *should* have been.

Coming to bookstores in February 1999
and March 1999.
Available at your favorite retail outlet.

HARLEQUIN®
Makes any time special ™

Look us up on-line at: http://www.romance.net

HHMED3

COMING NEXT MONTH FROM

HARLEQUIN HISTORICALS